TO SEE A STRANGER

Margaret Lynn

First published 1961
by
Hodder and Stoughton Limited
This edition 1990 by Chivers Press
published by arrangement with
Hodder and Stoughton Limited

ISBN 0 86220 787 8

Copyright © 1961 by Margaret Lynn
Foreword copyright © Gwendoline Butler, 1990

British Library Cataloguing in Publication Data available

*The characters and situations in this book are
entirely imaginary and bear no relation to any real
person or actual happening*

Printed and bound in Great Britain by
Redwood Press Limited, Melksham, Wiltshire

FOREWORD

In her cleverly named *To See a Stranger*, first published in 1961, Margaret Lynn has created a brilliant variation on the gothic suspense novel. In the classic gothic tale the heroine is imprisoned in a house or castle, surrounded by friends she cannot trust, wooed by a lover she fears. But in *To See a Stranger* the heroine Dorcas is imprisoned in her own mind. She awakes from a dream to find herself the stranger, her own impulses the ones not to be trusted. She seems to have a loving husband, a charming daughter, and a beautiful home, but when she looks in the mirror she sees a face she does not know and cannot like. Even her name is different. Dorcas or Lisa, which is she?

The plot is cunningly worked out in a deceptively simple way, the style of writing being straightforward and easy with no straining for effects or artificial humour. The narrative unwinds itself naturally, holding our attention all the time because the story is so strongly dramatic and we do passionately desire to know what happened and how.

The characters who play out this drama are sympathetic and warmly portrayed: the daughter Joanna, Dr Hugh Broderick, Russell Winslow, whom Dorcas, whoever she was, once loved are all people we can like even if they puzzle us. But to go too deeply into the mystery of identity and love would be to give away too much of the plot.

The setting for the story is a delightful country house in the south of England. But this house itself, so beautiful and calm, frightens and mystifies the heroine. As the story begins, it is a warm summer's day, this warmth is in itself a cause for alarm to the bemused heroine when we first meet her, and it begins with a wedding, but not the wedding she expects when she awakes. From that moment the reader is gripped and must read on. The story of Lisa-Dorcas is one to read straight through at a gulp.

GWENDOLINE BUTLER

Gwendoline Butler has won the CWA Silver Dagger, the Romantic Novelists Association Award, and the Ellery Queen Short Story Award. She is a former Chairman of the CWA Gold Dagger Fiction awards Committee.

THE BLACK DAGGER CRIME SERIES

The Black Dagger Crime series is a result of a joint effort between Chivers Press and a sub-committee of the Crime Writers' Association, consisting of Marian Babson, Peter Chambers and chaired by John Kennedy Melling. It is designed to select outstanding examples of every type of detective story, so that enthusiasts will have the opportunity to read once more classics that have been scarce for years, while at the same time introducing them to a new generation who have not previously had the chance to enjoy them.

TO SEE
A STRANGER

1

I KNEW the moment I awoke that it was a lovely day, and not only because of my certainty that this day was bound to be perfect. I could feel the heat and the brightness of the sun through my closed eyelids and I lay like that, as I always do on waking, conscious of the world around me but not yet part of it.

When I was a child Henrietta used to say, 'Now it's no use pretending to be asleep, Miss Dorcas, because I know you're not. You can't deceive *me*.' Although I had not really meant it to be a deception. It was a childish habit and I had never grown out of it. Sometimes – if I had been especially naughty and knew that a just retribution awaited me, or nervous over a forthcoming exam, or broken-hearted because poor old, blind Scrappy (who should have been a pure bred boxer but wasn't, owing to his mother's loose morals) was going to be destroyed that morning; or later, that agonising time when Russ's letters had been so long overdue and the fear and suspense had been almost unbearable – sometimes on occasions such as those it had seemed easier to face up to the morning.

But today there was no need to; there was only happiness bathing me like the golden warmth of the sun. A delirious happiness that told me how wonderful it was to be alive – to be twenty and deeply in love, on my wedding day. Especially when the man I loved was Russ.

I could possibly be a little prejudiced where Russ is concerned, but I, don't think so. My father, mutual friends, people whom we knew at home, Russ's fellow officers; when Russ smiled, everyone responded to it. There was something very special in Russ's smile.

For that matter, there was something very special altogether about Russ...

In ten, in twenty, in fifty years' time, I was positive that it would still be just as wonderful to be loved by him. There would be as much fun in sharing our old age as there would be in sharing our youth.

Dear Russ – dear, kind, sweet Russ.

I said it softly, shyly, almost unbelievingly to myself... Dorcas Winslow... Lt.-Commander and Mrs. Russell Winslow... and shivered with happiness.

I hadn't known there could be such wonder and contentment, until I loved Russ – or such fear and anxiety, either.

But I wasn't going to think about the war today, the suffocating dread which seized me whenever I thought about a telegram arriving...

I wasn't going to think of anything but the perfection of this day which nothing could mar – least of all the fact that instead of the white wedding in our own church in Aldersford there would be a quick service in a London registry office, in a blue suit, with no bridesmaids, and only Father and strangers as witnesses, and no reception other than a brief toast from Father before we left, not for Italy and France and Spain, but for our week's honeymoon in a little cottage near Aylesbury.

I wouldn't change any of it.

I didn't need the honeymoon abroad, the guests, the bridesmaids. I didn't need anyone else at my wedding except Russ.

And as for the dark blue suit – well, I knew that Russ would love it. It was just the exact colour that he always said matched my eyes; and the ridiculous, frivolous bit of white nonsense was all that he said a hat should be. They hadn't really been intended for my wedding clothes even though we'd planned to marry on Russ's next leave. We just hadn't been able to resist the opportunity when the leave had occurred earlier than we expected.

I would never forget answering the phone the night before last, when I thought him to be thousands of miles away, and hearing his voice, vibrant with an excitement that all his casualness couldn't conceal, asking me if I could be in London to marry him the day after tomorrow.

I hadn't been able to do anything but stammer helplessly, 'Russ – oh, darling...'

'I can't get away until late tomorrow,' he went on, 'but if you came to London we could be married the following morning. It would save an awful lot of time travelling. I haven't told you this, sweet, but if you'd like it we can have the loan of old Holly's cottage in Bucks. It's pretty rural but I've seen a photograph of it and it looks ideally out of this world for a honeymoon. What do you think, Cassy – am I rushing you too much ... ?'

I'd no idea who old Holly was and I still hadn't been able to answer him coherently, but it hadn't mattered. There had never been a need for words between Russ and me. And as I lay in bed in London, I thought how it had always been like that with us, right from the very beginning.

I could hear Father splashing around in the bathroom which divided our two rooms and knew there was no point in getting up until he had finished. In any case, I wanted to lie there a little longer, aware that the sun was shining because of the brightness against my eyelids, but not caring if it had rained.

When I opened my eyes the first thing I would see would be the blue suit, hanging outside the wardrobe where I had left it the previous night. I had been afraid that it might have creased from being packed in the suitcase, but it hadn't.

I had laid everything ready – the new white undies, the white hat and gloves, the blue shoes which I had had such trouble obtaining to match the suit, the pair of borrowed nylons, my battered old prayer book which I insisted upon carrying. I'd put everything ready before we had gone to meet Russ at the station and I hadn't laughed at myself over the 'something old and something new' business. If it was crazy to be superstitious, all right, I was the prize village idiot. But I was just not taking any chance!

Dorcas Winslow. Mrs. Russell Winslow.

I kept saying the words over and over again to myself.

It was warm in bed – warmer than I had remembered from the previous night, and I could tell that I had thrown off most of the bedclothes. It had been cold last night standing on the platform; although when the train had finally screeched to a halt and I had caught a glimpse of Russ in the throng of other servicemen, I couldn't have told anyone a single thing about the weather. Not with Russ shouldering an impetuous way across the crowded platform and catching me close in his arms, and then the bliss of his rough, stubbly chin against my cheek.

The world had stood still, as it always does when I see

Russ, when he puts his hands on my shoulders and looks down at me.

Oh, Russ – dear, darling Russ...

And now, suddenly, I was eager and impatient for the day to start.

I opened my eyes.

The blue suit wasn't where I knew it should be.

That was the first thing I noticed.

I was lying on my left side, so that I should have been facing the wardrobe, with the blue suit hanging from the front of it.

But the blue suit wasn't there and as I lifted myself on one elbow to look for it I realised with a distinct sense of shock that the room was completely strange to me.

It was a spacious room and very pleasant, with the sun streaming in through the two windows on my right – and with expensive furniture, I imagine, but the light grained wood was unfamiliar and the lines of it seemed severe and rather bare. The off-white carpet looked ankle-thick, but there was a coldness about all that expanse which not even the heavily brocaded curtains and cushions of a rich, deep pink could offset. But what intrigued me most was the ceiling. It was done in blue, a lovely muted shade of blue like the velvety denseness of a sky at dusk.

I'd never seen a dark ceiling like that before and didn't think I would have liked it in my own bedroom. There was something rather oppressive about it.

Everything looked very opulent and very modern – straight out of the glossy pages of a fashion magazine. But there wasn't a single object in the room which was familiar to me – not even the pair of green slippers discarded carelessly by the side of the bed in which I lay, or the dressing-gown thrown over the arm of the nearest chair.

I sat up in bed and looked around in bewilderment.

This certainly wasn't the hotel bedroom in which I had expected to wake. And where were the old slippers I'd packed? And the warm, serviceable dressing-gown because the weather had been cold when we left home yesterday morning, not warm and close like this? The new flimsy dressing-gown and fluffy mules for my honeymoon were still in the suitcase.

But there was no sign of my suitcases. Or of my toilet requisites. Not a jar or bottle of the costly array which graced the long, low dressing-table belonged to me.

I could even detect a perfume clinging to myself which was as unfamiliar as everything else. It was a delightful fragrance but I couldn't remember ever having used it before, and decided finally that it wasn't really my type. It suggested a subtle sophistication. On an older woman I could imagine it being quite devastating.

It was all rather silly and mysterious but I wasn't really disturbed. Any minute now the solution would come to me.

In the blissful confusion of last night anything could have happened and I would hardly have been aware of it. It didn't matter as long as I wasn't late for my wedding, and Father would make sure of that.

There was a clock ticking on the bedside table and the hands pointed to seven-thirty. Plenty of time, although judging from the warmth of the sun I thought it should have been later than that. But perhaps we were in for an April heatwave.

My eye was caught by the large coloured photograph in a frame next to the clock.

It was of two women – or rather, of a woman and a girl, although at first I scarcely noticed the girl. It was the woman who held my attention because there was something familiar about her. It wasn't the feeling that I had seen her somewhere before – I was sure I hadn't – but she reminded me vaguely of someone.

I thought she was definitely good-looking. Not pretty, and not beautiful. More than pretty, I mused, which was quite the wrong word to use of her; and yet I wouldn't have called her beautiful. She had a very calm face – remote, detached, aloof – any of those words seemed to fit her; even disdainful, and I thought that if her expression had been more animated she would have been quite lovely in a way. But her mouth spoilt her. Her features were good – dark, clear-cut brows, finely curved cheek bones, a nicely modelled nose – but her mouth spoilt all the rest. It might have been well shaped but you didn't notice whether it was or not. All you noticed was the discontent that marred it. And more than discontent – perhaps disillusion, unhappiness. But the discontent predominated.

Yet when I stared at the photograph for a few minutes I changed my mind. It was her eyes really that I didn't like. They were well spaced and blue, quite a deep, clear blue, but there was a coolness in them which suggested a satirical amusement – a lack of all warmth and kindness which I found distasteful. Perhaps if her hair had been framed more softly about her face . . . But the red-gold, almost chestnut hair was drawn rather severely back and coiled somewhere round the back of her head.

Although she stirred a memory in me, I didn't like her.

The girl was quite pretty, in a significant sort of a way. She had small, dark features, and eyes which were practically as black as the short, curling hair. She was smiling very faintly and although I couldn't see her teeth I was sure that they would be small and even and dazzlingly white against the dusky skin. Her mouth was the only bright splash of colour.

I thought she seemed by far the nicer of the two, but for all that the older woman drew my attention back and held it.

I wondered how she would look without that expression of cool disdain. I studied her dispassionately, trying to penetrate that pose of detachment; and came to the conclusion that it wasn't a pose at all. The woman was probably as completely disinterested in everything and everybody as she looked.

It was only then that I noticed for the first time the other bed.

I must have been blind not to see it before, because it was separated from mine by no more than about five feet, the width of the bedside table which held the photograph and the clock. Both beds shared the same bedhead – a large panel of quilted brocade of the same blue as the ceiling, and were furnished identically with pale blue sheets and pillow-cases and rich pink spreads.

And from the tumbled state of the other bed it had obviously been occupied.

I sat and stared at it and despite the warmth of the morning a little cold shiver ran down my back.

How could I possibly wake in a strange room and have no recollection of how I came to be there?

And then the only possible explanation – the obvious one

– came to me. I'd fallen off to sleep again, of course.

I lay back on the pillows and reflected how very realistic some dreams can be, right down to the last detail of that room which was so clearly impressed on my mind – even to the perfume on my own body...

I put my hands on myself and ran them down over my breasts and waist, down the length of my hips and legs.

And I made a surprising discovery.

I had always been very slender, too much so, perhaps. But the body my hands explored was different. Still slender, but the breasts and hips were fuller, more – mature?

I ran my hands down again and the flesh was firm and real beneath my fingers, but there was no mistaking the fact that the almost boyish lines had filled out. Quite nicely, too, I thought, because I had always felt that I could do with an extra pound or two in the right places.

But although those extra inches felt so real to me, they would probably disappear when I awoke. I pinched my arm and watched the whitened flesh slowly regain its colour. And it was then I noticed how sunburnt I was.

It was only April; there hadn't been much chance so far this year to acquire any tan and I needed a lot of sun before I changed colour. But the arm I held out before me was a rich, golden brown which spoke of many hours' sunbathing.

I slapped it suddenly with the other hand – almost viciously, because I was tired of this dream. I wanted to awake to reality, to my life – to my wedding day with Russ.

I stared disbelievingly at the wedding ring on my left hand.

It wasn't the one that Russ and I had chosen on his last leave. That was a plain solid gold ring which symbolised everything that was between us – not this fragile-looking, intricately figured one.

I got hold of it, with anger beginning in me, but the ring wouldn't come off. I couldn't get it over the first knuckle no matter how I tried, and I made my finger sore in the effort. Suddenly, inexplicably, I hated that ring. I hated the feel of it on my finger, even in my dream – the tightness, the possessiveness of it. And most of all I hated the thin white groove that was revealed when I moved it – a strip of flesh which proclaimed long intimacy with that fancy gold band.

I think it was that strip of flesh which put the first doubt in my mind.

It looked white and somehow obscene against the brownness of my hand and I pushed the ring back into place with a savage little movement of childish rage, and thrust the hand under the bedclothes out of sight.

I hated everything to do with this room, the tumbled bed next to mine, the cold, aloof woman in the photograph which I petulantly pushed round so that I need no longer see her; the crushed cigarettes in the ashtray on the table between the two beds, which had no right to be there because I didn't smoke. But most of all I hated that wretched, fancy ring because that was more real than everything else.

If this wasn't a dream, then what was it? How else could I explain waking in a room which I knew I had never seen before? A different perfume on a changed body? A ring which was so familiar with the flesh of my finger?

It was too fantastic to be anything other than a dream, and when I finally awoke I would have a good laugh over it. Yet even as the thought crossed my mind, I knew, with certainty, that I wouldn't laugh.

I think, even then, that a sense of loneliness was creeping over me. That I had begun to realise that this was no dream, no chimera of either a sleeping or a wakening mind. I couldn't begin to guess how or why. But neither, any longer, could I doubt its reality.

Yet when I saw a door open in the far wall I was totally unprepared for the shock of seeing a man – a complete stranger – come striding into the room.

It was beyond that doorway that I had heard the splashing water, and despite the unfamiliarity of my surroundings I had not doubted for a moment that it was my father who was bathing in there.

But this man, wrapped in a white bathrobe – dark, greying hair still damp and tousled from his bath – this was no one that I knew; and yet he came walking into my bedroom as casually as if it were something he did every day of his life.

He didn't even glance at my bed and I was too astounded to move or speak as he went to the dressing-table and began brushing his hair. I couldn't even feel indignant, but

I suddenly became aware that the sheets weren't covering me very well and I reached down and pulled them up to my chin. As I did so I was thinking that Russ wouldn't be any too pleased about this.

I must have made a slight noise with the sheets or else he sensed my eyes fixed stupidly upon his back, for he glanced round over his shoulder, the hair-brushes suspended momentarily in mid-air.

'Sorry, did I waken you?' he asked, but I scarcely heard him because now I had the feeling that I knew him. There was a resemblance but it took me quite a few minutes to place it, because this man was older than I remembered. He was Father's stepbrother, a good deal younger than Father, as I remembered him – about forty, I should think, and his hair had been only slightly sprinkled with grey and there had been no bald patch such as I could see now. He had shown no signs of the slight paunch which now bulged the front of the bathrobe, and the face was older, too, with deep lines engraving his cheeks - the face of a man in his middle fifties. But I was positive it was the same man.

I'd never met him until recently. I've forgotten where he'd spent most of his time – Canada, or somewhere like that, I believe – but I remember that Father had never approved of him and I hadn't liked him because of the way he looked at me. He'd been to the house only two or three times but I knew it was uninvited and Father was barely civil to him. And then he'd rung Father up at the hotel yesterday evening and although Father had tried to put him off he'd come round and had dinner with us, and hardly taken his eyes off me throughout the meal.

I hadn't liked him then and I didn't like him now.

I didn't answer him. I was too dazed by his possessive presence in my bedroom.

This was mad – completely mad! I just didn't believe it!

It was bad enough to wake up in a strange room when I had no recollection of how I got there, but for Charles Landry to be occupying it too...

I glanced incredulously at the empty, tumbled bed next to mine.

He couldn't possibly have slept there! Could he?

Could he?

I looked helplessly at his back as he finished brushing his

hair. Of all the questions which were seething through my mind there was only that one which I could frame sensibly, and I didn't dare ask it.

If he hadn't looked at me, hadn't spoken to me, I could perhaps have convinced myself that somehow I had strayed into this bedroom by mistake. But he had accepted me here so naturally . . .

He wasn't really any relation to me. Even if I hadn't been only an adopted daughter, my father and Charles Landry were the result of previous marriages on the part of Father's father and Charles's mother before they married each other.

I had thought him about fifteen years younger than Father, but the Charles Landry that I saw now looked fully as old as my father. He hadn't seemed young to me last night – someone of forty doesn't seem young to you when you're only twenty yourself – but I felt certain that he hadn't been so obviously middle-aged.

Yet I was equally certain that it was the same man.

And the sight of him aroused the same distaste in me – an antipathy which I don't think was altogether to do with the way he eyed my body, although that hadn't helped. I couldn't even call it a mutual aversion, as he very obviously didn't share it.

But of one thing I was quite certain. He was the last person I wanted to find in my room.

My room? It was a bit difficult to make an indignant protest when I hadn't any idea which one of us was the interloper. I didn't know how to begin.

It was hot and uncomfortable with the bedclothes tucked around my neck and I was beginning to be worried about the time. When I'd pushed the photograph round it had moved the clock and I could no longer see its face; but I knew it must be hours since I awoke at seven-thirty. I hadn't wanted to rush this morning. I'd wanted to have a leisurely toilet to make myself look really nice for Russ. . . .

If only Father would come. Wherever I was, I couldn't believe that he would be far away. If he would only come in and explain all this to me. Or not even that. It would be enough if he would just come and tell me to hurry up and not keep Russ waiting. Just so that I could start the day from here, now.

When the knock came on the door I was so positive that

it was Father that I called out impetuously, 'Oh, come in,' and I never gave a thought to what construction he would put upon the sight of Charles Landry brushing his hair in front of my dressing-table.

But it was a slim, elderly woman clad very neatly from the prim, high neck of her dress to her feet in a dull grey, an exact replica of the colour of her hair. As I looked at her face I had the feeling that her nature would be as colourless and as grey as her clothing.

When I heard Charles Landry say carelessly, 'Morning, Miss Rose,' I had to smother a little exclamation. I couldn't think of anyone more incongruously named.

She was carrying a teatray which she set down on the table by my side. I was watching her anxiously. Her face must surely betray some emotion – surprise, disgust, derision – when she saw me. She couldn't just take my presence for granted.

But she did.

She said calmly, 'Good morning, Mr. Landry. Good morning, Mrs. Landry.' Her voice was cool and brisk.

She was pouring out the tea as she spoke and I looked at her horrified.

'Mrs. Landry' she had said. '*Mrs*. Landry.'

I heard her continuing, 'I brought the tea myself, Mrs. Landry. As you can imagine, we're very busy in the kitchen this morning. Cook would like a few final instructions from you as soon as you can spare the time.'

She passed me a cup of tea as she spoke – sugarless, milkless. I looked at it in distaste. I wanted a drink of tea at that moment, almost desperately. But I wanted milk and sugar in it.

When she left the bedside to take another cup to Charles Landry I reached out and helped myself generously to both. I glanced up to see her looking disapprovingly at me.

'You don't *take* milk and sugar in your tea, Mrs. Landry.' Her voice held an injured note.

Well, I thought indignantly, *I* ought to know how I like my tea. This is the craziest household . . .

But I couldn't drink it. I took one eager sip and made a wry grimace as the sweet, sickly liquid hit my palate. She had been watching me, for when I put the cup down, if her colourless face could have expressed much emotion, it would have registered deep satisfaction.

Charles Landry was saying, 'I shan't be down to breakfast, Miss Rose. I'm in a hurry to get off. I'll get a quick sandwich in town. By the way, I wouldn't disturb Miss Joanna just yet.'

'Miss Joanna is already up, Mr. Landry. I told her she would have done better to have rested in bed a while longer. There's nothing she can do, and this will be a long tiring day for her.'

He grunted. 'Oh, well, the young ones are all alike. They have to be always on the go. See my things are laid out for when I get back, Miss Rose. I shan't have much time to spare and Joanna would never forgive me if I made her late.'

I thought helplessly – Are they all mad?

He had gone out through another doorway as he spoke, throwing the last words over his shoulder. I caught a glimpse of a smaller room before the door slammed behind him.

He wasn't away many minutes and I was still wondering how to question Miss Rose, who was quietly tidying the bedroom, when he returned fully dressed.

The woman was already leaving the room and he followed her to the door, pausing only briefly as he reached it to give me a quick, questioning scrutiny.

'Are you all right, Lisa? You look rather pale.' And then, as he turned away, 'it's all these preparations, I suppose, but you'll be able to take it easy after today. I'll be back as soon as I can.'

Lisa!

He was out of the room almost before he finished speaking, with that brisk impatience which seemed to mark all his movements, and I gazed after him with the beginnings of despair.

Lisa! Mrs. Landry!

Were they all mad – to accept my presence here so naturally, to address me as Lisa, Mrs. Landry? Or were they mistaking me for someone else? But how could anyone look so like me that, close as they had been to me, they could fail to detect the difference? And in any case, how had I, Dorcas Mallory, got into the position where I could be mistaken for someone else? For Lisa Landry?

But however the mistake had come about, of one thing I

was certain. I wasn't staying any longer. Whoever they mistook me for, *I* knew who I was, and I knew where I was going.

I was going to find my father and Russ.

The clock said ten minutes to eight, but it must have stopped. It couldn't possibly be only twenty minutes since I had first opened my eyes in this room.

But it was ticking merrily away, and the hands moved slightly as I watched. Well, so much the better. I had no idea where I was but I was determined I wasn't going to be late for my wedding.

My bare feet sank into the off-white carpet at every step. I didn't like to use the green slippers and my own were nowhere in sight, but that carpet was cosier and softer than any slippers.

The windows were open but the air that flowed in was warm and balmy. I had never known an April day so mild before.

The view from the windows was as unfamiliar as everything else, but it was a very lovely one. The grounds must have been fairly extensive; in the distance only pastures and woodland were in sight. The gardens were very beautiful and ablaze with colour, and away to the right I caught a glimpse of an open-air swimming pool, vividly blue beneath the cloudless sky; but I didn't stop to linger over the view. I wanted to be on my way, but first I was going to have a bath in case I hadn't time when I got back to the hotel.

The bathroom was a shambles. I stood in the doorway and looked at it in distaste. Everything in it was dead white – floor, walls, ceiling, bath, washbowl, towels, Nowhere in the whole room was there a patch of colour. Just that dead white and chromium.

It looked soulless.

The floor was swimming in water and littered with sodden towels and before I could fill the bath I had to wash it out; but there were plenty more towels on the rail and an abundance of hot water.

I was glad to soak off that strange perfume, but disturbed once more by that slight difference in my body. It was hard to define – was it because it didn't seem quite so supple, was it *really* fuller in places? Could I possibly be imagining it?

But I wasn't imagining the ring on my finger; although I soaped the finger well, I couldn't remove it.

I went back into the bedroom with one of the huge white towels draped round me, but couldn't find my suitcases or my clothes.

The sliding doors which almost covered the wall at the far end of the room rolled back to disclose a long row of garments; but though I went through them all and, stifling my reluctance, through all the drawers, there was not one article that was mine.

I rang the bell in a little flare of temper. I didn't care how crazy the household was, nor that I had no right to be in it. I wanted my clothes.

I had expected Miss Rose, but it was a girl who came. She looked young, and not too bright.

I said sharply, 'Will you bring my clothes, please?'

The request did nothing to add to her brightness. She stood there just inside the doorway and over her shoulder I caught a glimpse of a pale green carpeted upper hall and a low table containing the biggest bowl of roses I had ever seen. I found myself thinking, quite irrelevantly, what a price someone must have paid for those, at this time of year.

The girl asked, 'Which clothes, madam?'

'My own,' I said, with as much patience as I could muster. 'The ones I was wearing last night when I came here.'

She gave me a little mute gesture towards the sliding doors, and I shook my head.

'They're not in there. They're not anywhere in this room,' I said, but evidently failed to convince her because she began lethargically sliding the hangers backwards and forwards across the rail. I watched her with an irritation which didn't decrease when after a moment she pulled out a soft, primrose yellow dress in some sort of material which I couldn't place, and held it triumphantly.

'This is it, madam,' she said. 'This is what you wore last night.'

I looked at her in disgust and threw the yellow dress across the nearest chair.

'Would you mind asking Miss Rose to come here?' I requested, very politely.

At least, if forbidding, Miss Rose had seemed intelligent, I thought.

It was a long time before she knocked and came in. She looked as grey and colourless as before.

'I'm sorry to keep you waiting, Mrs. Landry,' she said, 'I was on the phone with the caterers. As you know, they'd promised that some of their people would be here at eight o'clock and it is now a quarter past the hour.'

I checked the impulse to tell her that I *didn't* have any idea what she was talking about, and that I *wasn't* Mrs. Landry. The sooner I was out of this madhouse, the happier I should be.

'I want my clothes, Miss Rose,' I said, quietly.

'Yes, Mrs. Landry. Which ones in particular would you be requiring?'

'The things I was wearing last night.' I gave an impatient exclamation as she started looking through the racks of clothes. 'They're not in there,' I said, and as she turned she caught sight of the yellow dress on the chair.

'Oh, the dress is there,' she said.

'That isn't mine,' I said, as calmly as I could.

'That's what you wore last night.'

'I've never worn that dress in my life,' I cried indignantly. 'It isn't mine.'

She gave me a very strange look and then she asked, very quietly, 'What did you think you were wearing, Mrs. Landry?'

'A tweed suit,' I said, 'and a matching overcoat.'

She echoed my words. '*Tweed*? And a matching overcoat?'

She made it sound unclean.

'Well, why not?' I demanded. 'It was a very cold evening.'

I could see her eyeing me again in that strange, speculative way.

I'd been wondering before she came in whether I should ask her how I had come to this place – even where it was. But I decided against it. It was obvious that they weren't going to produce my tweed suit, and all I wanted was to get rid of her.

'I think,' she said, slowly, 'you would perhaps be wiser to lie down for a little while longer, Mrs. Landry. These last few weeks have been very hectic ones for you. You *must* be feeling the strain.'

The strange looks she had been giving me could not compare with the one I gave her then. But I agreed pleasantly.

'Yes, perhaps I'll do that, Miss Rose.'

I thought she looked relieved. She took the yellow dress and hung it back in its place.

'If I've time when I've finished with Miss Joanna, I'll help you to dress, Mrs. Landry.'

I gave her my sweetest smile.

'That's very kind of you.'

Neither the smile nor the words must have rung quite true. She gave me a very suspicious glance. As she moved to the door she asked, 'Is there anything else, Mrs. Landry?'

'No,' I said, but I couldn't resist adding, 'Except – don't keep on calling me "Mrs. Landry".'

Quietly she said, 'Very well, madam,' as she went out.

I looked at the long row of clothes and had no compunction in choosing something to wear.

There was a very plain cream linen suit which looked ideal for a warm morning and I laid it across the bed and rummaged through the drawers for the necessary underclothes.

Whoever owns all these, I thought, must have had stacks of coupons, and not all honestly acquired. They couldn't possibly have been.

The funny thing was that everything fitted perfectly – as if it had been made for me; even the beautifully expensive high-heeled cream shoes. And although I hadn't time to care much whether it did or not, I could feel the linen suit clinging to me snugly without a wrinkle.

I hated borrowing someone else's make-up but I had to have something. As I approached the dressing-table I could smell the perfume that had clung to me in bed. I opened the top drawer and sorted through the array of cosmetics until I found a lipstick and powder which looked suitable.

No one can apply lipstick successfully without a mirror. And that was the first time I looked in one.

And I went on looking and looking, and the lipstick dropped from my fingers and fell with a little clatter on to the dressing-table.

Because the face that stared back at me from the mirror was the face of the cool, disdainful woman in the photograph.

2

I FELT cold and dizzy and the image of that woman wavered and swam before me, and I was grateful that it did. I didn't want to look at her. I didn't want to look in the mirror and see that face.

I wanted to see my own reflection – the face that I knew so well. The face of a girl of twenty, with dark gold hair curling nearly on to her shoulders, and blue eyes which were alight and bright with the love of living, and a mouth that laughed.

Not a woman in the middle thirties with almost straight chestnut hair and cool, disinterested eyes, and a discontented mouth.

But the dizziness passed and the woman was there in the mirror before me and although her eyes were no longer coldly disinterested but wide with horrified disbelief, it was still the woman of the photograph.

I put up a quivering hand and touched my face and saw the mirrored woman do the same. I smoothed the red-gold hair with faltering fingers and the woman in the mirror uncovered a few grey hairs as I did so.

I knew, sickeningly, that that was not Dorcas Mallory I was gazing at. That Dorcas Mallory had nothing in common with this almost middle-aged, disillusioned woman.

But I *was* Dorcas Mallory. I was young and alive and happy – or I had been until I saw that wretched woman gazing back at me from the mirror, and I would be again when this senseless but suddenly frightening mystery had been explained.

I sank back limply on to the seat and that hateful woman sank down with me.

Was this *her* room – *her* clothes, *her* perfume? Was she Lisa Landry; and if she was, what had happened to give her mouth that discontented droop and wipe all warmth from her eyes?

I bent closer to the mirror, but somehow she was changed and it took me a little while to realise that it was because the interest in my eyes was reflected in hers, displacing their indifference.

And suddenly I smiled – a gay, spontaneous smile because just for a moment it amused me to know that I could manipulate that face in the mirror as easily as a puppet on strings.

The woman was really quite lovely. With that smile transfiguring her face she had all the beauty which I had sensed lay dormant beneath the mask of discontent.

But I didn't really feel like smiling, and I didn't care that the woman's face slipped back into its habitual expression. If she wanted to look bored and cynical, let her. Perhaps she had cause to be.

My concern was in getting Dorcas Mallory to the registry office in time for her wedding.

I patted powder hastily on my face, ran a comb through my hair and used the lipstick. I noticed then that unconsciously, without even looking, I had arranged her hair in exactly the same way as it was in the photograph. It didn't make me any happier to realise how naturally and easily I had done it, because it was one of those very simple looking hair-styles which can be extremely difficult to fix. Unless you're used to it.

I felt furiously angry with myself. I'd never fixed a hairstyle like that in my life. The fashion was for long hair curling on to the shoulders and that's how I wore mine.

I ran the comb through it again, disarranging it wildly with a childish satisfaction, and I shut my eyes whilst I smoothed it back in order. When I looked, I found that I had automatically arranged it in exactly the same way again.

I slammed the comb down so viciously that it bounced from the dressing-table on to the floor and I kicked it pettishly out of sight beneath the furniture.

There was a lost, lonely feeling rising in me, and I wanted Russ and my father, and the sane homeliness of my own bedroom – or even the impersonal comfort of the hotel room. Anywhere that was familiar and had nothing to do with these oppressively luxurious surroundings and would allow me to recapture the wonderful, intense happiness of knowing that in a very short time I should be married to Russ.

But I didn't even know where I was, and everyone in this incredible household seemed utterly mad. Even if in some fantastic way I looked like the woman in the photograph, they must know that I came here only last night, and they must have my clothes somewhere. And my handbag containing a considerable amount of money.

I'd probably need some of that, too, to get back to London.

It was then that I noticed the telephone. It was on the bedside table and I sat down on the bed I had so recently occupied and looked at it thoughtfully.

The little circular card in the centre said Chadwell St. John 26, and conveyed nothing to me. I'd never heard of Chadwell St. John.

But I could at least get in touch with my father and find out what had happened.

It took me a few minutes to get the number of the hotel from Enquiries. I sat drumming my fingers impatiently on the instrument for a little while before the operator put me through and a voice at the other end answered politely, 'Darlton Hotel. Good morning.'

For a moment I felt so happy to be once more in contact with the world I knew, that I couldn't speak. It was wonderful to realise that in just a few seconds I would be talking to my father and he would arrange everything for me. I was so light-headed with relief that I put out my tongue at the woman in the photograph.

I said happily, 'Could I speak to Mr. Mallory, please?' I added quickly, to save her the trouble of looking, 'It's room number 57.'

I hummed lightly under my breath as I waited. I even stretched out my feet and admired the expensive, obviously hand-made, cream shoes.

I heard the receiver being picked up at the other end and I said, excitedly, 'Hello, Daddy – for Heaven's sake what's happ – '

The voice that had answered me before cut in.

'I'm sorry, madam – we have no Mr. Mallory registered here.'

I said indignatly, 'But of course you have! He's in room 57.'

'Not in room 57 or any other room I'm afraid, madam.

We have no Mr. Mallory staying with us.'

I could feel myself spluttering as I spoke. 'But you have! We booked in yesterday afternoon – I was with him. I'm Miss Dorcas Mallory – we had rooms 55 and 57.'

'Madam, I'm sorry, but we have no one here by that name at all – neither a Mr. Mallory nor a Miss Dorcas Mallory. Have you perhaps got the wrong hotel?'

'Not if that's the Darlton? No, I'm *not* mistaken. If you look in the register – we both signed in only yesterday afternoon. Please look again, you *must* have missed it.'

I could plainly hear the sigh of resignation at the other end and then after another long wait the very polite, 'I'm sorry, madam – '

'But you *must* have. I know he's there. Are you sure you're looking for the right name? It's spelt M-a-l-l-o-r-y . . .'

It didn't do any good and I was muttering angrily to myself about gross incompetence as I slammed the receiver down.

For a moment I realised how desperately I had needed to hear my father's voice, and no longer felt like putting out my tongue at the woman in the photograph. Then I found myself hoping that she had some money lying around somewhere.

I found quite a large amount in a drawer, but I didn't count it. I didn't like taking it at all, so I removed only five notes from the roll and hoped they would be sufficient.

I shut the door of that bedroom behind me with a little sigh of thankfulness. The perfume from the huge bowl of roses was wafted towards me as I crossed to the head of the stairs and looked down.

I saw a large, pleasant hall with a wide expanse of glass doors thrown open to the warm morning air. There were flowers everywhere – roses, carnations, sweet peas – masses of them; and as I watched, the young maid who had answered my ring a short while ago brought yet another bowlful and placed it on a low table.

I waited until she had disappeared through a door at the end of the hall before I went down, treading softly on the thick green carpet. Most of the doors leading from that large hall were open and I could see what looked like a very modern cocktail bar, with high scarlet leather stools and bar, and mirrored walls ... I caught a glimpse through another open doorway of a low, sunny room with a pale grey carpet and chairs in startling colours of bright red and blue, and bowls and vases of flowers everywhere.

Moving cautiously, with the guilty feeling of a trespasser, I had almost reached the open glass doorway when I heard someone say, from close behind me, 'Mrs. Landry?'

I nearly jumped out of my skin. On the soft carpet I hadn't heard the woman's approach. Her grey, colourless eyes were watching me curiously.

'I thought you were going to rest a while longer, Mrs. Landry?'

The sense of intruding where I didn't belong made me falter. That and Miss Rose's watchful eyes.

'Yes – no. I didn't feel like resting,' I stammered.

'You have a long day ahead of you, you know. I'll tell Cook you're ready for breakfast.'

'No – ' I stopped her. 'No – I don't want any ...'

'Now, Mrs. Landry ...' Somehow she was shepherding me back across the hall. How, I didn't know, because she didn't touch me; but I had a feeling that it would have been useless to resist.

I said feebly, 'I don't really want any breakfast – '

'You should have something, if it's only your usual toast,' she said firmly, and I found myself going with her into a dining-room of bright yellow walls, with a peacock blue carpet, and chairs and curtains of deep burnt orange.

I was dazzled by all those vivid colours. I'd never seen anything like them before and I couldn't possibly imagine ever growing to like them. I could better appreciate the beautiful delicate china and the silverware on the table.

From her position near the doorway Miss Rose guided me to the table and I sat down facing her, resentful and rebellious. She rang a bell and stood there impassively until a maid – a different one this time – brought the fresh tea and toast she had ordered and set them down in front of me.

I didn't want anything to eat, although if Miss Rose thought that slices of thin toast were my usual breakfast, she was vastly mistaken. I like bacon and eggs, and a good helping of them. Normally.

But today wasn't a normal day and I crumbled the toast uselessly on my plate. Uncomfortable under her penetrating eyes, I poured out a cup of tea and it wasn't until I was drinking and really enjoying it that I realised I had put neither milk nor sugar in it. I stared at the strong, horrible-looking stuff and I tried it again.

And I still liked it.

I gave Miss Rose a look of unadulterated loathing.

I wished she'd go. She looked too much like a jailer standing there, even her eyes unmoving; and I went on rolling little pellets of toast and pushing them aimlessly round my plate.

She didn't move until I'd finished the tea and then she said, 'If you feel like seeing Cook now, Mrs. Landry . . . ?'

'No, I don't – and I'm not Mrs. Landry,' I said. I pushed back my chair and added rudely, 'Thank you for my breakfast but I didn't want it, and now I'm going.'

She looked startled and put out a hand as though to stop me, and I thought grimly to myself, Just you try to; you interfering old woman.

I could have pushed her back through the window with pleasure, and I probably would have done, because I felt certain she meant to try to stop me from going and I was just as determined I was going. But we were interrupted.

It was the young girl of the photograph who came in, her arms and legs bare and very brown against the briefness of the white shorts she was wearing. She looked exactly as she looked in the photograph and I guessed it must be a fairly recent one, but she was smaller than I would have thought. Her teeth were as dazzling white as I'd expected them to be.

And she was as mad as the rest of the household.

She said carelessly, 'Hi, Lisa,' and helped herself to a large rosy apple from the bowl of fruit on the table. She bit into it and added, 'I thought Rosie said you weren't getting up just yet – didn't feel so good or something?'

I'd opened my mouth to say something – I don't know what – but before I could speak Miss Rose said, 'I don't think your mother *is* feeling too well this morning, Miss Joanna. She's eaten no breakfast and I'm sure – '

I'd been standing staring at her, outraged, and then the words came gasping out in bewildered fury. 'You're mad,' I said. 'All of you – you're completely mad . . . '

I was aware vaguely of the consternation on both their

faces but I was still choking out the word 'Mad – mad' as I flung past them and fled out through the open windows.

I heard Miss Rose calling in agitation, 'Mrs. Landry – Mrs. Landry . . . ' and I know the girl tried to stop me; but I was off, running across the lawns to where I could see the curve of the drive. I was aware as I ran that I had left the money behind in the handbag I had borrowed but I didn't care about it. I didn't care about anything except getting away from that dreadful house and its insane occupants.

I didn't even know where Chadwell St. John was or how far from London or how I was going to get there, but I think I could have run all the way if necessary. And that's what I would have done.

Except for one thing.

To gain the drive I had to skirt round some flower beds, gay and colourful with massed blooms. I had actually passed them and reached the drive, when I stopped dead and turned and stared unbelievingly at them.

I went back slowly, but I hadn't been mistaken.

There's nothing else you could possibly mistake for those tall dahlias with blooms as big as footballs. I'd always disliked them for their garishness, but I'd never hated them as passionately as I hated them at that moment. That was when I began to feel really sick.

As I went back into the house I think both Miss Rose and Joanna made a move towards me but something stopped them – perhaps something in my face. I don't know.

There had been a pile of morning papers lying untouched on a sideboard. I'd noticed them as I sat drinking my tea but hadn't opened one of them. Now I did so. It was only necessary to pick up one. I'd already known the answer when I saw those dahlias in full bloom.

You don't have dahlias blooming in a garden in April.

The date was in August, as I'd guessed it would be.

But what I hadn't guessed was that the date would be in August – 1959.

From a long way off I could hear someone saying, 'Mrs. Landry – Mrs. Landry . . . ' but it didn't mean anything to me.

I hadn't known it was possible to feel so sick and cold.

I could see Miss Rose and the girl Joanna hovering around

me and I knew who they were – only too well I recognised them. But I seemed to be looking at them through the wrong end of a telescope – as though divided from them by a long, narrow tunnel; and they were trying to crawl up the tunnel towards me. Enclosed in the same tunnel I struggled desperately to back away from them, but for every painful inch I retreated they seemed to gain two.

I heard someone saying weakly, 'Leave me alone ... Leave me alone ... ' and after a while I realised that it was my own voice I could hear.

If they would only go away and I could crawl out of my tunnel and run – run ... But where should I run to? Where *could* I run to? To Father and Russ waiting for me in London on my wedding day? But they wouldn't be waiting for me now.

I was too late. I was more than fifteen years too late. Fifteen years ... nearly as much as the whole span of the lifetime I remembered.

I heard someone saying, childishly, plaintively, 'I'm going to be sick,' and felt the nausea rising overwhelmingly in me. I hoped I wouldn't be. It would be a shame to throw up over Lisa Landry's expensive linen suit and thick pile carpet. The feeling gradually subsided and then I became aware that one of those two – Miss Rose, I think – had crawled right up the tunnel to me while I was fighting back the nausea and was trying to force the contents of a glass down my throat.

I was indignant the way she had sneaked up on me. I wished I had been sick all over their precious carpet.

There was a strong smell of brandy under my nose. If Miss Rose thought she was going to make me drink brandy she was much mistaken. I hate intensely, even the smell of the stuff.

Miss Rose won. I opened my mouth to tell her that she was wasting her time, and she meanly tipped in some of the brandy. I wished I'd been ill bred enough to spit the stuff right back in her face.

I was mad enough to do just that, too, but surprisingly I found that I liked the taste of that brandy in my mouth. So I swallowed it, and even meekly accepted the rest.

I wished I hadn't though. After a few minutes it helped to dispel some of the coldness but it also helped to thaw the merciful numbness which had been protecting me.

I felt it going, exposing me to the fantastic reality of a nightmare from which there was no awakening, which defied reason. I could only flounder hopelessly in a panic of terrified confusion.

I heard Miss Rose saying. 'Your mother's ill, Miss Joanna. I think we ought to get a doctor – '

I shook my head frantically, 'No!' I said. 'No! I – '

'It would be better, Mrs. Landry. I'm sure that if Mr. Landry – '

She'd misunderstood my denial. I knew she had.

I said passionately, 'I mean that I'm not her mother. How could I be – she's nearly as old as I am myself . . . '

The girl looked at the woman in startled dismay.

'I think you're right, Rosie – we *should* get a doctor. I'll phone – '

'No,' I said. 'No – just let me go . . .'

But go where? Even as I said the words, the uselessness of it all sickened me. I had never felt more alone.

'I want to go home,' I said piteously. 'Please let me go home.'

'You must lie down for a little while first, Mrs. Landry,' Miss Rose said, adding, as I made another motion of protest, 'and then you can go home.'

I knew she was lying, that she had no intention of letting me leave the house. The quickly added promise had been only to pacify me. But if she could use strategy, so could I.

'I'll lie down,' I said, 'If you'll promise not to send for a doctor. Please! I'm not ill . . . '

I don't think she trusted me any more than I trusted her but she gave in, if reluctantly. She went upstairs with me and drew the curtains to shut out the strong sunlight, and stood at the foot of the bed while I kicked off my shoes and lay down, not caring whether I crumpled the linen suit or not.

After she had gone I waited a full ten minutes before I got up and tiptoed to the door and silently opened it. She was outside, exactly as I had known she would be, and her pale colourless eyes met mine inquiringly, suspiciously.

'Were you wanting anything, Mrs. Landry?' she asked, and I shut the door and went back to lie down miserably on the bed.

She was acting as a jailer, but for the time being at least it didn't really matter. I would have got away if I could, but the urgency was gone. After fifteeen years, a few hours more or less couldn't possibly matter, and I felt so unutterably weary that I was glad of the soft comfort of the bed beneath me.

There were so many questions and so many answers – and none of the answers fitted the questions and even a lot of the questions didn't make sense.

If I could only have spoken to Russ, or my father – to anyone whom I had known...

I had the idea, then, to ring my father up at our home. He, surely, would be able to explain so many things.

I asked for the number and waited in a rising fever of excitement. I should have thought of this earlier, of course. To speak to my father – perhaps even Russ might be there ... If they could only tell me how the last fifteen years had been spent – but of course they would know, because although I couldn't remember them, those years *must* have been spent with them. Could it even be possible that Russ and I were married...

The operator's voice cut across my thoughts.

'I'm sorry, caller, but Long Distance say there is no such number as the one you asked for.'

I had a long and vehement argument with her, hating her more intensely every moment. I had not hated so many people in all my life as I did that morning. I felt that everyone was conspiring against me.

Eventually she put me through to Enquiries, who only confirmed what she had already told me. There wasn't even an Adrian Robert Mallory listed among the Alderford subscribers.

I couldn't go on arguing with them. I put the receiver down and lay back against the pillows, utterly exhausted. And I was still lying there when the door opened and Charles Landry came in.

I had forgotten all about him, and was too listless to feel indignant about his abrupt entry. Perhaps he had the right to enter without knocking. This was probably his own room, for all I knew.

I believe I was even conscious of a faint feeling of relief. He was the only contact I had with the world I remembered.

I raised myself on one elbow as he swung the door shut behind him and strode across to the windows. As he swept the curtains impatiently back the sunlight came in, flooding the room in brightness.

'Mr. Landry – ' I said, and he came back towards the bed and stood looking down at me, a heavy frown knitting his brow.

'What's all this about?' he demanded. 'Miss Rose tells me that you're not well?'

'I shook my head. 'I'm not ill. I – '

'I didn't see how you could be. You were all right first thing this morning – a bit pale, but that's all.' He sounded brusque and yet I thought I could detect a kindness beneath the bluntness.

I said, 'Mr. Landry, please – '

'No look, Lisa – ' The kindness was definitely there now, mingling with the impatience. ' – let's have no more of this nonsense. Just because you don't happen to like Michael is no excuse for making this fuss, today of all days. He's what Joanna wants and I've given my permission, and that's all there is to it.'

'You don't understand,' I said. 'Michael? I don't know Michael – I don't know what you're talking about. Please – '

'Oh, yes, you do know what I'm talking about. And if you don't know Michael it's because of the stupid prejudice you've developed against him. There's nothing wrong with the boy – d'you really think I would risk Joanna's happiness without making full inquiries about him and his background?'

'Please listen to me,' I begged. I swung my legs off the bed and looked beseechingly up at him. 'This is all a most dreadful mistake. You're wrong in thinking that I – '

'You're the one who's wrong, Lisa. And the only mistake is yours, in thinking that I would let you get away with this. I'll not stand by and see you spoil that child's wedding day with this ridiculous display of tantrums. You've already upset her more than enough this morning. I didn't think you'd be quite so petty-minded as all that, Lisa. Now let's have no more nonsense, and no matter what you feel about this, I expect you to put on a good face in front of all those guests. I'll not have Joanna further distressed by you making your disapproval of the marriage obvious to everyone.'

There was no kindness in his voice now, only a grimness. He was already turning away as I made a final plea. 'You *must* listen to me,' I cried.

He paused only to say briefly over his shoulder, 'I haven't time to discuss this further with you. Hurry up and get dressed or you'll be late.'

He went through into the dressing-room, leaving the communicating door open, but it seemed impossible to say anything more.

I felt embarrassed and uncomfortable. Whoever these people thought I was, they all accepted me without question, and seemed quite sincere in their attitude towards me. I must be very like the woman they knew as Lisa Landry; but where was *she?* And how had I come to be in her place?

My head was beginning to ache with the whirl of confusing thoughts. The sun was too bright and I wanted to draw the curtains again.

Then suddenly I felt his hand on my shoulder. I hadn't heard him cross the thick carpet and my jangled nerves made me gasp at his touch. He was very smartly dressed in a morning suit but his face looked dark with displeasure.

'Lisa!' he said, and gave my shoulder a little peremptory shake.

I felt tears of impotence springing to my eyes. I didn't want anger, not even from Charles Landry. I wanted sympathy and understanding. I wanted familiar voices and faces. I wanted Russ. My whole being ached for Russ.

He probably couldn't have known the cause of my tears, but they softened his attitude.

'Come on, old girl,' he said, a little awkwardly, as though unused to having to appeal to anyone, 'for Joanna's sake, be a good sport.'

I stared helplessly through my tears as the door closed behind him. Be a good sport, he had said – don't spoil Joanna's wedding day. Didn't he know – but he couldn't know – that I had woken up this morning to what should have been the happiest day of *my* life.

Be a good sport...

I had been dimly aware for some time of the sounds of activity outside. When I looked through the window there seemed to be dozens of people hurrying around. Immediately beneath the windows was a large paved terrace, its low enclosing walls ablaze with rambling roses. The french windows of the rooms below were thrown wide, and at either end of the terrace long buffet tables had been set up.

I watched the scene morosely, angry with myself because of the tears I could still feel burning under my eyelids. Did Charles Landry *really* expect me to go down there and mingle with the guests when they arrived?

No matter whom he mistook me for or how furious he might be, that was one thing that no power on earth could make me do. This should have been *my* wedding day. And the long years stretching between couldn't count because I had no memory of them – only of the happiness which had flooded through me on waking this morning.

I turned, startled, as the door opened behind me, and then stood looking, my heart a heavy ache of wistful yearning and passionate rejection.

It was the girl, Joanna, looking quite breathtakingly lovely in a rich, full dress of oyster satin, the delicate, fragile veil that framed her face held in place on her dark head by a head-dress of pearls.

She was really beautiful. In white, she would have looked sallow and insignificant, but in the rich warmth of that oyster satin she took on the bloom of a sun-ripened peach.

She stood for a few moments on the threshold, her hesitation caused, I think, by the conflicting expressions which I knew showed in my face.

She asked, and there was a little inflexion of anxious doubt in her voice, 'How do I look?'

I let my breath go out in the softest of sighs as I pushed the envy resolutely from me.

'You look lovely,' I said, with deep sincerity, and her face cleared miraculously.

She came into the room and twirled herself round childishly, looking with satisfaction at the full frothing skirts.

'Do you really think so? I'm glad now you wouldn't let me have white, Lisa.' She stopped suddenly, facing me. 'Oh, you're not dressed. You'll never be ready in time. *Are* you ill? Daddy said you were much better when I passed him just now.'

I said weakly, 'Just a headache...'

'Are you sure that's all? You were acting pretty queer, you know, a while ago.' She sounded dismayed and her face was clouded with anxiety.

I wanted to talk to her, to explain to her, to beg for some understanding and help in my bewilderment; but she stood there looking at me, her whole presence touched with that magic charm that enhances all brides, and I couldn't say anything that might trouble the bright surface of her happiness.

I had intended to slip away as soon as I got the opportunity – perhaps when they all left for the church; but I knew, as I looked at this radiant girl on her wedding day, that I could do nothing to mar its perfection for her. I knew what it was, how it felt to be ...

Be a good sport, Lisa ...

And although I wasn't Lisa, this girl and everyone else here thought that I was and it wouldn't hurt me to delay disillusioning them for a few hours. If it would help Joanna, then I would be Lisa for just a while longer.

I said, 'I'll get dressed. I won't be long – '

'I'll get Rosie to help you – if you're sure you're all right . . . ?'

When I nodded and even managed a reassuring smile she ran across to the door, her full skirts rustling behind her, calling, 'Rosie – *Rosie* ...'

'I'm here, Miss Joanna.' Miss Rose's voice reached us clearly. She couldn't have been far away. 'I'm just coming to give your mother a hand. I promised her that – oh, Mrs. Landry, you haven't even *started* to get dressed.'

'No,' I said, and I actually felt guilty, as though I had let them all down. 'No – I must have fallen asleep ...'

'Well, you run along, Miss Joanna. We'll be quicker without you, and I can hear your father calling you.'

From the landing I could hear Joanna calling out, in anguished tones, 'Oh, *no,* Daddy – it can't possibly be that time. We *can't* go until Lisa has left and she'll be *ages* yet ...'

She ran back into the room, almost falling over her full skirts in her frantic haste.

'Lisa, Daddy says we simply *must* leave now if we're to be at church on time – '

'For Heaven's sake, Miss Joanna, mind what you're doing. You'll ruin that dress.'

'But I *can't* go yet,' the girl wailed. 'Lisa can't come walking into church in the middle of the ceremony . . . '

'Then Lisa will have to miss the ceremony,' Charles Landry said from the doorway. He looked grim and angry and I stopped unbuttoning the linen suit as he put in an appearance. He added heavily, 'But I shall expect you to be downstairs to receive the guests when we get back, Lisa.'

'Yes,' I said. 'Yes – I'm sorry.' I spoke jerkily. I was beginning to suspect that I was a little bit afraid of him. 'I promise I'll be down.'

'Then we'd better go, Joanna. I'm determined you're not going to be late.'

The girl still looked indecisively in my direction.

'It's a bride's privilege,' she suggested.

'Not this bride,' Charles said. As he went out he called back over his shoulder, 'Don't forget, Lisa. . . . '

I didn't answer him. I resented his tone and found myself feeling a fleeting sympathy for Lisa Landry; but Miss Rose was waiting to take the linen suit from me so I went on undoing the buttons.

I saw her give me a curious glance as I passed her and went into the white bathroom, and after a moment she followed me and began picking up the towels from the littered floor.

'I'm sorry the rooms are in this state,' she said quietly, as she went about her task, 'but I wouldn't allow the girls to disturb you. But why don't you use your own bathroom, Mrs. Landry?'

I mumbled something as I dried my face. I hadn't known there was another bathroom but supposed now that that was where the other door in the bedroom led to.

I was beginning to realise that Miss Rose could be justified in thinking that Lisa Landry was acting very strangely.

I wondered if she were a person I could talk to – if she could help me to any understanding, but I decided I'd better not risk it just then. I'd no idea how soon Joanna and the others would be back and I'd promised to be down in time for their return.

I went back into the bedroom and hurriedly, and with distaste, made-up the strange face that confronted me in the mirror. Fifteen years could have changed me from a young girl of twenty into a woman of thirty-five, but the difference the mirror showed me was more than just a question of years.

Miss Rose had put out a dress of heavy, slate-grey silk and I shrugged my way into it and smoothed it down over my hips. It was pencil slim and fitted me perfectly, and looked as unobtrusively expensive as only a very costly dress can do. I liked the pink hat that went with it. It suited Lisa Landry's hair-style. I wasn't even surprised to find that the pink gloves were exactly my size. By that time I should have been amazed if they hadn't been.

When I had finished and stood back to survey myself, Miss Rose said, 'You look beautiful, Mrs. Landry. Miss Joanna will have her work cut out not to be put in the shade.'

She surprised me with the compliment but I repudiated it swiftly.

'Oh no! Joanna looked lovely.' I added, diffidently, 'Will they be long before they're back, do you think?'

She consulted the plain, leather-strapped watch on her wrist. 'Another fifteen or twenty minutes, perhaps. You've just time for a cigarette before they come. But aren't you wearing any jewellery, Mrs. Landry? I thought you'd planned to wear your pearls?'

I said in some confusion, 'Yes – will you get them for me?'

When she lifted them out of the box they were gleaming and lustrous, and smoothly cold against my skin. I'd never had real pearls before. Father had always said I was too young for them, but he'd promised I should have some for my twenty-first birthday...

I put those thoughts resolutely from me for the time being. Miss Rose was handing me a perfectly matched pair of pearl ear-rings and in the act of taking them I said suddenly, 'Oh – these are for pierced ears.'

She gave me a startled glance and even before she spoke I knew what to expect.

'Yes,' she said quietly. 'Can I help you with them?'

I fitted them in with a little cold shiver running down my back. I ought not to have been surprised. I was beginning to realise that I knew practically nothing about this body of mine.

Without a word I put on the huge diamond ring she passed to me. I didn't like it, although it must have cost a small fortune.

Miss Rose said, 'Your perfume, Mrs. Landry?' but I shook my head. I didn't want to use Lisa Landry's perfume, delightful though it was. I looked far too much like Lisa Landry for my own peace of mind – I didn't want to smell like her, too.

I went downstairs slowly, Miss Rose following in my wake.

I knew now the reason for all those masses of flowers and their heavy scent did nothing to ease the persistent throbbing in my head. As we went through the hall Miss Rose picked up a box from a table and opened it. When I saw what she was offering me I shook my head again.

'I don't smoke,' I said, and knew immediately, by the uneasy look she gave me, that I had given the wrong answer.

But all she said was, 'Now, Mrs. Landry...'

I took one because it seemed the easiest thing to do; but it wasn't until I had drawn the smoke deep down into my lungs, with the delicious, almost sensual langour of the confirmed smoker, that I realised suddenly that I was gratifying a previously inexplicable craving of my body.

Miss Rose said, 'Perhaps you'd like to have a quick glance round to see that everything is to your liking, Mrs. Landry? I gave Cook what instructions I thought best, and the catering people seem very efficient, but there may be one or two little things you would like altered.'

'I'm sure there won't be anything, if you've seen to it, Miss Rose,' I said, quite sincerely. For all her grey colourlessness she was efficient to her fingertips. In any case, she was far more likely to know how Lisa Landry would have liked things than I was.

Through the open windows I could see an enormous wedding cake, rising like a giant iceberg. It was a colossal thing, the biggest I had ever seen, and I felt a twinge of pain at the memory of my own wedding cake – the simplicity of all my own arrangements, the memory of Russ. Most of all, at the memory of Russ.

Dear Russ – I must find him soon. I must know where

he is, what he is doing, how much of this last fifteen years we have shared.

I could feel panic welling up in me again; a feeling of claustrophobia caused by this luxurious house and these smart, well-fitting clothes I was wearing. They were all part of something I knew nothing about, something I didn't want to know about. Something I was frightened of knowing about.

I crushed the cigarette out in an ashtray so fiercely that it burst open, spilling the tobacco. I couldn't go through with this. Not any longer.

I turned as the panic took full hold of me; and as I did so the first car swept up the drive, the white ribbons flowing from the bonnet, and Joanna got out.

She came into the hall, her dress whispering around her, laughing up into the face of her new husband.

A glowing, vital bride who might, perhaps, if she had been luckier on this blessed day, have been Dorcas Mallory.

3

MICHAEL reminded me of Russ. So strongly that at first glance I caught my breath with a curious little ache in my heart. Afterwards when I had time to observe him more closely, I could see that the resemblance was not so much in features as in expression.

He had the same open air of kindness and tolerance which was so large a part of Russ's charm, the same boyishly candid smile.

And I couldn't possibly imagine what there was about him to have antagonised Lisa Landry.

Joanna brought him forward. I was sure I could detect an air of anxious appeal in her manner, a slight indecision on the boy's part. As she brought her face forward for my kiss I said gently, in answer to that silent supplication, 'This is the most wonderful day of your life, Joanna. Always be as happy as you are right now.'

I looked at Michael and as I took his hand I held my face up to him in an obvious invitation. I saw the faint look of surprise which crossed his open countenance, and the tremulous gratitude in Joanna's eyes, and I knew that neither of them had expected Lisa Landry to make that concession.

I said, 'Take care of her – Michael.'

'I will, Mrs. Landry – always. I promise,' he said, earnestly, and in his voice there was the same deep sincerity so familiar to me in Russ's.

I closed my eyes for a moment as the yearning for Russ swept through me. When I opened them again the hall seemed suddenly, miraculously, filled with people – all chattering, laughing, kissing, handshaking.

I saw Charles Landry as he came in; and he glanced keenly at me, then at Joanna's radiant face, and some of the sternness relaxed from the heavy lines of his mouth. I stood by his side, in line with Joanna and Michael, and was greeted familiarly and sometimes formally by a host of people; and anxiously though I scrutinised each face there was not one that I knew.

Some of them kissed me, but not many, I noticed. I had the feeling that Lisa Landry was not a person who easily tolerated intimacy. After a time I began to realise that neither was she a person who was very well liked.

I'm not quite sure where I got the impression from – a shade too much casualness in a greeting, a degree of uncertainty in another, as though Lisa Landry was known as an unpredictable woman, a shadow of constraint on any gathering.

But I was also quite sure, with only several exceptions, that I was supposed to know them all. There were very few introductions and when there were, the people were introduced to Charles Landry, too, so I guessed that they were probably friends of Michael's who were unknown to the Landrys.

Eventually, when we went out on to the terrace, someone tried to put a glass into my hand. 'Here, Lisa, take this while there's still some left.'

I smiled politely. 'No, thank you. I don't drink.'

The man – he was big, fat, red-faced – looked at me in amazement and then broke into guffaws of laughter.

'Oh, that's rich. Hear that, Charles – Lisa tells me that she doesn't drink.'

I saw Charles's faint disapproving frown and heard someone near at hand say, in a quiet sardonic voice, 'Since when, eh?'

I took the glass rather than provoke further comment. I hadn't meant to drink it, only to hold it in my hand as an excuse for not accepting another. I was deeply perturbed a little later when I realised that I had drained it to the last drop. It was neat whisky, and I liked it!

What was worse, I could detect the same gratifying of a craving as the cigarette had provided.

But I wasn't given much time to dwell on any deplorable habits which Dorcas Mallory might have acquired during the last fifteen years. Nor was I unduly concerned when presently I found myself with another drink in my hand, and realised that I was practically chain-smoking. It all helped to have a steadying influence that got me through the day.

I caught snatches of conversation thrown at me as people drifted by...

' . . . never seen Joanna looking so lovely. You must be very proud of her, Lisa . . . '

'Yes . . . ' I nodded, smiling politely.

' . . . heard Charles is having a house built for them . . . '

A non-committal nod, a polite smile.

' . . . looking wonderful, Lisa . . . outshining the bride . . . '

'I hope not.' A shake of the head, a polite smile.

' . . . spending the honeymoon . . . ?'

'You'll have to ask Joanna . . . ' A polite smile to hide the sudden aversion.

' . . . did. Somewhere in Italy . . . '

' . . . seen much of you lately, Lisa. Must fix up something with you and Charles . . . '

'Thank you . . . be very nice . . . '

' . . . make a wonderful couple . . . '

'Don't they . . . ?'

'Thank you . . . ' For another proffered glass of whisky, that. How much can you hold, Dorcas Mallory?

' . . . can't tell you how pleased we are that Michael . . . his father and I were only saying, Mrs. Landry, how . . . ' The bridegroom's mother, obviously.

' . . . just as pleased. Excuse me, must see to . . . ' The

strategic withdrawal, a polite smile.

It wasn't all so easy.

I caught more than a few curious or astonished glances, an occasional raised eyebrow, a strained silence that made me realise that Dorcas Mallory had said something which sounded peculiar coming from Lisa Landry.

Once Charles said to me in a furious aside. 'What the devil did you mean by saying that to that old bitch . . . ?'

But as I had no idea which old bitch he meant, I turned the polite smile on him too and walked away. I knew that he puckered his brow thoughtfully as he watched me go.

A while later – or it might have been before that incident, I was too confused to remember clearly – someone said, '. . . must make a foursome up. How about tomorrow morning, Charles?'

'That'd do fine,' Charles said. 'How about it, Lisa – does it fit in with your plans?'

I said, quite without thinking, 'I'm sorry – I don't play golf.'

There was a little astonished silence.

'That's a damned silly thing to say,' Charles said, with a note of anger underlying the exasperation.

'Yes – I'm sorry.' I spoke quickly. 'It was a poor joke. Of course, tomorrow morning will do nicely.'

Joanna came up, fresh and unruffled, still radiant.

'Oh, Lisa – Daddy – there you are. We're just going to cut the cake. I want you to be there.'

She whispered ecstatically to me as we went with her towards the white iceberg, 'Isn't everything just wonderful, Lisa? Just as perfect as I've always hoped my wedding day would be.'

The knife turned over in my heart and for a moment I was lost again in a world of bewildered loneliness.

I heard her say 'Lisa?' on a little note of interrogation and I smiled at her – not the polite smile, but one of sympathetic understanding.

There was the usual spate of toasts and speeches, and I found a glass of champagne in my hand. I hoped it would mix with the whisky, because it was succeeded by two or three more – I lost count. The only thing that amazed me was that it didn't go to my head or have any effect upon me whatever. By that I concluded that Dorcas Mallory had become used to holding her liquor well.

It wasn't a very pleasant thought.

I was thankful when at last Joanna disappeared upstairs to change, with her giggling bridesmaids in tow. When she came down again she drew me on one side, her face suddenly serious.

'I couldn't go without thanking you for being so nice about everything, Lisa.'

I asked, very gravely, 'Did you think I would spoil your wedding day for you, Joanna?'

She hesitated a moment. 'Well – this morning when you were – oh, you know, acting rather – strangely . . . Well, I thought for a while that it *was* only an act – that it was your way of showing . . . '

'I had a bad headache – and perhaps things have been rather hectic lately?' I suggested.

'Oh, I know. I realise that now – since you've been so absolutely wonderful. With Michael, I mean. I wanted to tell you how sorry I am that that's what I thought . . . I know you've been against me marrying Michael. You wouldn't ever say why you didn't like him, but – '

'I think you're a very lucky girl to have got him for a husband,' I broke in gently. 'You were very wise to marry him before someone else snapped him up.'

Her smile was brilliant and her eyes shone with gratitude.

'Oh, that's just what I've always felt about him. With someone as wonderful as Michael . . . '

I said, 'Run along, Joanna – Michael's waiting for you.'

'I've never known you be as nice, Lisa,' she said. 'Somehow – you're quite different . . . '

I had hoped that when they finally got off, the rest of the crowd would gradually dwindle away. I was tired of acting a part, of being Lisa Landry. And once Joanna had gone I wasn't particular how well I played the part. I had done it for her, and had had my reward, if I needed one, in her gratitude. But although the majority went, quite a few lingered and I had to carry on the farce.

By the time the last one went I was so tired I wanted to cry, and my head ached intolerably. The people from the caterers were busily engaged in clearing away, helped by what I presumed were members of the household staff. Miss Rose was hovering around and as I passed her she asked, with a slight anxiety, 'I hope everything went all right, Mrs. Landry?'

'I'm sure everything went perfectly,' I assured her mechanically.

Charles Landry had disappeared into the house and I followed him through the open french windows, grateful for the coolness of the room after the heat of the sun. It was the room with the pale grey carpet and the bright chairs, and Charles Landry was sprawled out in one of them, idly fanning himself with a paper.

'Well, thank God that's over,' he said. 'This heat ... '

'Mr. Landry,' I said, 'I must talk to you.'

'O.K., Mrs. Landry, go ahead,' he said lazily. He added, 'I think everything went off all right, didn't it? Joanna seemed happy enough about – '

I broke in. 'Mr. Landry, please I – '

'What *is* all this Mr. Landry business, Lisa?' He sounded vaguely irritated. 'You said it once – you had your little joke – perhaps it was amusing. But no joke is funny when it's repeated too often.' He added, not unkindly, 'Why don't you sit down? You look tired, Lisa – '

'I'm not Lisa,' I said, bluntly.

The paper he was fanning himself with faltered only for a moment before the movement was resumed.

'What do you mean by that?'

The tiredness was taking control of me – of my mind and my body. I had never known such unutterable weariness. I tried to be patient and only succeded in being agitated.

'I've just told you ... Please listen to me – I'm not Lisa. I'm not – '

He said, 'Sit down, old girl. Sorry – you don't like me to call you that, do you? Anyway, sit down. You've had a tiring day and in all this heat, too. Think I'll go up and have a cool bath and get out of these damnable clothes. Why don't you – '

'You'll listen to me first,' I interrupted, in a sudden burst of fury which spent itself almost as soon as it began. 'I'm tired of play-acting in someone else's house, in someone else's clothes, in someone else's life. I want to be myself I want to go home ... ' I trailed off miserably into silence. After a moment I added, quite without conviction because I despaired of making him understand, 'I'm not who you think I am. You must believe me. I'm not Lisa Landry.'

The quietness must have been more convincing than my agitation. He gave me a very curious look. 'If you're not Lisa Landry,' he said, 'who do you think you are?'

I sat down wearily in one of the red chairs and pulled the hat from my head.

'I'm Dorcas Mallory,' I said, dully.

He had stopped fanning himself, the paper arrested in mid-air.

'Who?' he asked, very quietly.

'Dorcas Mallory. You must remember me. My father – or at least, my father by adoption – is your stepbrother Adrian. You *must* remember me.'

'I don't know what the hell you're talking about,' he said.

'I never had a stepbrother. Or any other sort of a brother,'
'But you *must*. Your stepbrother –'
he said bluntly.

I looked at him aghast.

'But I remember you,' I cried. 'You came to see my father – we saw you in London only last ni – We saw you in London. You had dinner with us – you *must* remember us?'

He grinned suddenly. 'I remember you, old girl. I ought to after being married to you for over twenty years.'

'Oh, please – this isn't a joke,' I pleaded despairingly. 'Please...'

'What makes you think you're – who was it – Dorcas Mallory?'

'Because I *am*!'

'You're not, you know. You're Lisa Landry.'

'But I don't know anything about Lisa Landry – only that you all mistake me for her. I don't know what I'm doing in this house – how I came here – how long I've been here.'

'You're not feeling too good, are you? All this heat, I shouldn't wonder, and the wedding on top of –'

'I'm not ill. Please try to understand. It's nothing to do with the heat or the wedding ... ' I trailed miserably into silence again.

'Tell me what makes you so sure you're this other person?'

'How are *you* sure who you are?' I asked him. 'It's because – I just know I am,' I ended helplessly.

'You've been under a good bit of strain lately,' he suggested, and I raised my hands in a little hopeless gesture.

'I can't remember – I don't know where I've been or what I've done – not for this last fifteen years. The last thing I remember was that I was going to be married in the morning – Father had brought me up to London – and that was in April, 1944. I don't remember anything after that until I woke up this morning and I thought it was my wedding day. I didn't know then that what seemed like last night to me was more than fifteen years ago – I just can't remember anything of those years between. But I woke up in this house with no recollection of how I came to be here – and all of you mistaking me for someone else. I don't know how long I've been here – but *you* must know, Mr. Landry.'

He said, very slowly, 'Yes, I know. You've been in this house ever since I had it built, ten years ago – as we all have. Before that, we had various houses and flats – nowhere for very long, because we didn't seem able to find anything really suitable.'

'But how do I come to be with you? Why aren't I with my father – or Russ?'

'Russ?'

'Yes – ' I explained diffidently. 'He was the man I was going to marry.'

'I see.' He was tapping the chair arm thoughtfully with his fingers. 'Before the war,' he went on after a moment, 'we lived in Canada.'

I repeated after him stupidly, 'Before the war . . . ?'

'Yes – we were married in Canada. You were born there and lived there all your life until we came to England in 1943.'

'But that's ridiculous!' I exclaimed. 'I've never been to Canada in my life. And I can remember everything perfectly well until 1944 – it's the fifteen years after that which are blank. As to saying that you and I are married . . . '

'We were married in 1939,' he said imperturbably. 'Joanna was born two years later'

'In 1939, I was only fifteen years old.' I could even laugh at such a preposterous idea.

'You were twenty at the time. Would you like me to show you your birth certificate?'

I said suddenly, sharply, 'No! You know none of this is true. I'm not –'

'You were born Elise Fournier in Ottawa, and you were Elise Fournier until you became Elise Landry, twenty years ago. You're tired and overwrought, Lisa – this wedding has been a strain to you. You're suffering from a slight loss of memory but probably a good night's rest –'

'It's not just loss of memory,' I cried. 'You're telling me all these things, but you're not talking about *me*. You're telling me about things that happened during the years that I *can* remember – and none of those things happened to me. I can remember every detail of my life up to that night in London – not just the big things, but all the little details... I'm Dorcas Mallory –'

'You never were Dorcas Mallory, Lisa,' he said gently, and I could only gaze at him stupefied with horror. 'You're suffering from some delusion. But you were never Dorcas Mallory. Do you think I don't know my own wife when I've lived with her for twenty years – or Joanna, her own mother?'

'But it's not true,' I moaned. 'It can't be...'

'It is, though. You've had a vivid dream, perhaps – with Joanna's wedding in your mind, you dreamed and when you woke, just becuse you temporarily couldn't remember who you were, you associated yourself with a character in your dream.'

'No –' I said. 'No...'

'Can't you remember anything about yourself – about your earlier life in Canada? Or anything of these last few years?'

'Nothing – how could I?'

'Well, it'll come back to you in time. The thing to do is not to worry about it. I believe that temporary loss of memory is quite a common occurrence.'

'But I can remember my life – not the one you're telling me is mine – but *my* life, up to fifteen years ago. I *know* that I'm Dorcas Mallory –'

'You knew that I had a brother – a stepbrother. But I haven't – nor ever had one. That was as much a fabrication of your mind as the rest is, Lisa.'

'No.' I looked at him piteously. 'No – you must be mistaken.'

'How could I be mistaken about something like this?

Or Joanna – or Miss Rose – or any of the people who have been here today? They all know you –'

'But I don't know them – not any of them.'

'You don't know your own child?'

'You mean Joanna? But how could she be . . . how could I not remember a thing like that – like having a child?'

'Would you like to see her birth certificate, too?' he asked, rather dryly. 'And our marriage certificate? I have them all.'

'But how can I remember everything so well about myself – about Dorcas Mallory – everything of that life, of my father, of Russ . . . ?'

'These people never existed except in your own mind, Lisa. Not any of them.'

I bowed my head in my hands in anguish. I think I could have borne anything but that – to be told that there was no such person as Russ, that he had no existence except in my own imagination.

I felt Charles's hand on my shoulder, in a clumsy gesture of comfort, and for the first time I realised the full implications of what he had told me.

This man was my husband. According to him, for twenty years I had lived side by side with him, had borne his child – perhaps loved him, for all I could remember. Certainly I must have lived in the closest intimacy with him all these years.

The thought filled me with horror, for all his rough attempt at kindness. He seemed so many years older than myself – I couldn't stop thinking of myself as a girl of twenty. I hadn't had time yet to adjust myself to the thirty-five years I realised Dorcas Mallory had lived. But if I were truly Lisa Landry, I was forty years old.

To have doubled my remembered age in a span of less than twelve hours, to be married to this man who filled me with repugnance, to know that the only life I remembered was nothing but the delusion of a disordered mind – all these things were fantastically horrible. But to realise that nowhere on this earth – no matter where I went, no matter what I did, no matter how I prayed – nowhere would I ever see Russ again, that was a sadness which was not to be borne.

I would have wept if this had been a sorrow which tears

could ease. I *could* have wept for my lost love, with scalding tears which would have eased the anguish.

But for a love that had never been – for that loneliness, for that desolation, there could be nothing.

I tried to accept it.

To say that I failed was a complete understatement.

Reason told me that everyone else could not be wrong and I the only right one. But reason had no chance at all against the desperate longings of a heart.

I didn't want to be Lisa Landry. How could I be her, with her cold aloofness, when there was so much warmth in me? How could I be forty years of age when I had the vital eagerness in me of a girl of twenty? How could I be Charles Landry's wife when in my heart I knew I was Russell Winslow's love?

I think, in his way, Charles tried to help me. But there was an impatience underlying his well-meant kindnesses, an irritability which he couldn't quite conceal. Perhaps it wasn't easy for him. It couldn't have been. No man could relish the knowledge that his wife had no recollection of him, his child, their twenty years together – that she repudiated all thought of them with horror, as I had done. As he must have known I still did.

It may have been that he realised the desolation which enveloped me – or was discerning enough to perceive that no matter what I did I couldn't fully overcome the aversion I felt towards him. If that aversion sprang only from the remembrance of how he had looked at Dorcas Mallory's legs and from Adrian Mallory's disapproval, then it was ridiculous and futile to harbour a resentment against him for those reasons because Adrian and Dorcas Mallory had never existed.

But no matter what the cause, I couldn't rid myself of my prejudice against him. Perhaps some of it had roots in the fact that whatever he said or did only served to impress deeper into my mind that I was Lisa Landry.

There were so many things to prove my identity beyond shadow of doubt, but I didn't want proof that I was Lisa Landry. All I wanted was proof that I wasn't.

Charles had insisted upon showing me the certificates he had talked about. I hadn't wanted to look at them but I couldn't very well refuse. If these were mine – and they must be mine – then I had been born Elise Constance Fournier, child of Elizabeth and Dominique Fournier of Ottawa, Canada, on the 14th March, 1919. The marriage certificate told me that Elise Constance Fournier and Charles Landry had been married in Montreal, on the 20th of June, 1939.

I'd asked Charles where they were now, these parents that I couldn't remember.

'They're both dead,' he said. 'I never knew them so I can tell you nothing about them. They died before I met you.'

'Had I brothers – or sisters?'

'No – you were an only child. When we were married – '

But I didn't want to talk about that and I'd changed the subject abruptly.

Charles had insisted upon my going with him to play golf on the morning after Joanna's wedding.

'We promised,' he insisted, when I protested.

'But I don't know those people – and I can't play golf.'

'Nonsense!' He spoke briskly, with that hint of impatience underlying the word. 'You play quite passably – and you've known them for seven or eight years now.'

I said hopelessly, 'But I can't remember them. They'll talk about things that I know nothing about. I won't know how to answer them.'

'Oh, that won't matter. Say anything. They'll only think you're being stand-offish again. I don't think they really like you very much or you them, dear Lisa, so what do you care?'

I looked at him helplessly. 'Then it seems – '

'Oh, for God's sake, Lisa,' he said irritably, 'You can't shut yourself away in the house all the time. You'll have to make an attempt to carry on normally.'

I was still rebelling against it all that morning. It was only later that I really made an attempt to accept the truth of what he said.

That morning my head ached from a sleepless night of tormenting doubts. I had had to fight a desperate battle with myself before I succeded in forcing my mind to accept the presence of this man in the bed next to mine. The prospect of it had horrified me as the night approached. I couldn't share his room, or live in any kind of intimacy with him, however slight. He was almost a stranger to me. I couldn't accept him as my husband. I couldn't, I couldn't!

I had a wild instinct for flight, but I had nowhere to go. And I don't think I would have been allowed to go. I was certain that, unobtrusive though they were about it, both Charles and Miss Rose were watching my movements.

And in the end I had had nothing to fear.

I had tried to put what I was feeling into words. I had tried to be tactful – after all, this man thought he was my husband – but I was so wretchedly apprehensive that all I succeeded in doing was to jerk out halting, incoherent sentences.

I stumbled on miserably and I wasn't helped by the sardonic twist of his mouth. When I finally faltered to a halt he seemed to sit there for an interminable time looking speculatively at me before he said, with a jeering note in his voice, 'What are you afraid of? Not me, surely? But of course you won't remember, will you, that for some years now you've kept your very chaste couch to yourself? You'll have forgotten that I seek my amusement elsewhere these days.'

I felt so much sick relief that I was ashamed, because under the cynical jeering I was sure I could detect a bitterness of hurt pride.

But it was still bad enough having to share the same room, even though the two bathrooms and the dressing-room made for a certain amount of privacy, and having to listen through the long hours of the night to the heavy breathing from the next bed.

I was still feeling resentful about that when he told me I would have to carry on normally.

'It's not normal to me,' I said bitterly, and was sorry when I'd said it because he had been trying to help me.

When we went out, a huge car, all chromium and cream with red upholstery, was standing at the front door. It looked colossal, unlike any car I could ever remember. I guessed it must be some American make.

Charles slung the golf clubs into the back and slid into the passenger's seat.

I looked at him aghast. 'I can't drive,' I said.

'Of course you can! You're a very good driver, as a matter of fact.'

'But not this – this monster. It's so big – '

'You've driven this monster, as you call it, most of eight thousand miles since we got it. Stop thinking about these things, my dear Lisa – what you can and what you can't do. You'll find it all comes perfectly naturally to you. In any case, you know you hate me to drive – well, perhaps you can't remember, but you do.'

'Have I a licence?'

'Of course you have, and have had for this last ten or twelve years, maybe more – ever since you got fed up with my driving. Isn't it in your handbag? Never mind if it isn't. No one's going to stop us – certainly old Benton in the village knows you well enough not to ask you to produce a licence.'

I got in reluctantly. Frankly, I was terrified. As far as I knew I'd never driven in my life and certainly I had never even *seen* a car of this size before. It looked a mass of gleaming buttons and gadgets, and the radiator loomed remotely in the distance.

But I found that Charles was right. I made my mind as blank as I could and although if I had thought about it I wouldn't have been able to tell which was the starter from the cigarette lighter or any other of those buttons, after a moment I realised that the engine was purring quietly under the expanse of cream and chromium. I touched the accelerator and a deep rush of sound startled me, and then somehow we were off.

I knew, even as we went down the drive, that my mind and body were automatically attuned to that car. In some forgotten way, it was as natural for me to drive it as it was for me to eat. I knew just one moment of panic as we swung through the gates into what seemed an incredibly sharp turn and narrow road for our length, but I needn't have worried. I negotiated it with ease, with a fine judgment which couldn't help but convince me that I had made that turn many times previously.

I didn't know the way but Charles directed me, and we went down through a pretty little village. It had a well-tended green bounded by stately trees, and many of the smaller cottages were thatched. I wondered if this was

Chadwell St. John, and then we were through it and over a sharp, hump-backed bridge. I caught a glimpse of a river, fringed by willows which were weeping right down into the water, before we climbed a narrow, thickly wooded hill.

I didn't know the road but I seemed to know instinctively the danger spots, and it was a weird feeling to realise how ignorant the mind could be of the body's capabilities.

It was the same with the golf. If I thought about it, I had no idea which iron to use, but when I blanked out my mind I found that I reached involuntarily for the right one.

We played eighteen holes and I didn't do too badly. It was pleasant out there on the course and I was glad to be away from the house. Back at the clubhouse Charles called for a round of drinks. He ordered whisky for me without consulting me and for a moment I had a defiant wish to refuse it. When it came I was glad I hadn't, but felt that sooner or later I would have to do something about this habit.

But it wasn't a problem I felt like tackling. If I had accustomed my body, during these last few years, to heavy smoking and drinking, just now, when I needed the solace of both, wasn't the time to take myself in hand.

I asked Charles later, when we were having lunch, how long I had been drinking.

He looked amused. 'Oh, a lot of years now. Why?'

'I just don't like the habit,' I said.

'I've never seen you the worse for it, if that's what is bothering you. No matter how many you've knocked back.'

I didn't think that made it any better.

I was beginning to realise that I didn't like myself.

I wandered disconsolately over the house, searching hopelessly for anything that was familiar to me. In a bureau drawer I found several snapshots, mainly of Joanna – in various stages of her life, from infancy to the present day. I studied them closely, almost despairingly. Surely if this were my child I should remember something about her – there must be *some* incident of her childhood that I hadn't forgotten . . . She seemed to have been a serious, dark-eyed baby who had developed into a solemn-faced, dark-eyed little schoolgirl, and finally into a grave dark-eyed young woman.

There were a few of Charles, quite recent ones, I think, as were the only ones I found of myself. There were two or three of us taken together, with a background of palm trees or terraces or sunlit bays – obviously at some Continental holiday resort. There was one of me in ski clothes – could I really ski? – with the sun casting black shadows against the whiteness of the snow. Another of me in a bright blue swimsuit which was no bluer than the water of the terraced swimming pool by which I sat. One of Charles in a gondola and another of him at the helm of a slim, white-sailed yacht.

Some of the snaps had a date and the location on the back – written in my handwriting – 1957, 1958, June, 1959. I supposed that was how I had acquired this deep suntan, but I noticed that in every one of them Lisa Landry had that same disdainful indifference written plainly on her face. The photographs saddened me. None of them – whether taken at St. Mortiz, or Capri, or Cannes, or Naples, or Venice, or Lugano – meant anything to me.

But how many times had Russ and I planned – 'Someday when the war is over' – to visit all those places together. We had looked through old travel catalogues, we had planned our route, we had been ideally happy just thinking about the holidays we would have.

'Someday when the war is over....'

The war was over now – over by how many years? – and I had visited all these places. But not with Russ.

Always my mind came back to him. The sense of loss, the emptiness ...

I went out into the gardens. I knew my way around well by that time. All too often I'd wandered round in the forlorn hope that somewhere there would be something I could point to and say – *that* I remember.

In the stables at the back of the house I had found a chestnut mare who had whinnied with delight at my approach. Riding was something that had always given me great pleasure – or so the Dorcas Mallory of my mind remembered – and on several mornings I had had the chestnut out. She was swift and sure-footed, with a mouth as soft as silk, and she had given me the only few carefree moments I had known since the morning of Joanna's wedding. But I had no previous recollection of her.

It was the same with Candy – the golden spaniel bitch

who was confined mainly to the stables because Charles didn't like dogs around the house. The first time I went round there she had come bounding out in whimpering adoring ecstasy.

She knew me, too. I could have no doubt about that, or about the fact that this was where I belonged. And still I could not accept it.

I took the big American car out and searched vainly for some landmark that I knew. But although I drove miles around the lovely countryside it was as strange to me as if I had never seen it before.

I think at first Charles seemed rather anxious about letting me go off alone but gradually his vigilance relaxed. If he had feared at first that I would run away from here, perhaps he had realised – as I had – that there was nowhere I could run to. Or perhaps I had settled into a routine to which he was accustomed. For all I knew, I may have been in the habit of spending many hours alone away from the house. I had no means of knowing how Lisa Landry had passed her time.

Occasionally someone or other would drop in for a drink, but these were mostly men – friends of Charles. Again, I got the impression that Lisa Landry had not been very popular, with the women at any rate. Nor did the men seem to have much time for me. Or was it because I avoided everyone as much as I could? Was I perhaps being as aloof and disdainful as the Lisa Landry of the photographs?

I had no real means of knowing. I was as much a stranger to myself as they were to me.

I went out with Charles on the odd occasions when he asked me to, but I don't think Lisa and Charles Landry had been in the habit of spending much time together.

I mentioned to him once that it might be better to tell people that I had lost my memory, but he shrugged the suggestion away.

'What do *you* care?' he said. 'You're not answerable to them for your behaviour. Let them think what they like.'

And I didn't really care. I was still playing a part but some day, I was certain, the curtain would come down and I could be myself again. It *had* to happen like that. I couldn't go on being Lisa Landry all my life. I couldn't.

For one thing, in less than three weeks I was beginning

to realise what a lonely life she had led.

Although in the beginning Charles had been around the house most of the time, as the days went by he spent more and more hours away from it. Sometimes I knew where he went, when he slung his golf clubs into the back of the car – not the cream and chromium one, which seemed to be my exclusive property, but a pale blue one of the same powerful propensities – and with a harsh grating of gears would hurl the unleashed fury erratically down the drive. Whenever I saw him manhandling the car in that fashion I was always extremely grateful, and not in the least surprised that Lisa Landry had learned to drive.

At other times he seemed to go off up to town for the whole day but I never questioned whether it was business or pleasure which took him there.

I knew he spent a good deal of time on the river which I had discovered bounded the grounds to the south. He had a small yacht, or sailing dinghy – anything on the water is just a plain boat to me, I don't understand the niceties of difference between one type and another. Lisa Landry may have done, but I doubted it. Although once or twice he asked me to go golfing with him I had the impression that it was a tacitly understood thing that I wouldn't wish to go sailing.

I thought that under happier circumstances I might quite have enjoyed it. Once or twice I wandered down to the river and watched the boats. I was amazed how many there were until I learned that the local yacht club had its headquarters about a mile downstream. I believe Charles was its president, or something like that.

One evening I accompanied him to the yacht club dance and spent practically the entire evening in the bar. I was well pleased to leave the dance floor strictly alone after one duty dance with Charles – who danced surprisingly well, I discovered. Dancing was something I could remember Dorcas Mallory had loved. How many times had Russ and I ...

There were too many nostalgic memories of the divinely happy hours I had spent dancing with Russ. If they were dream hours only, then they were poignant, exquisite dream hours, and tenderly precious to me.

I felt, too, that Lisa Landry was living up to her reputation by clinging to a bar stool. No one seemed to expect her to do much else. Certainly not Charles, who very thoughtfully, if rather mechanically, saw to it that there was always a full glass beside me.

He didn't drink much himself, I noticed. I wondered what, at heart, he really thought about the amount of drinking that the woman next to him was doing.

It wasn't easy to read his mind or to know what went on in it, although I studied him a lot, covertly.

Was there ever a time when he and Lisa Landry had been close to each other? The idea seemed wholly preposterous to me; and yet there must have been a mutual attraction that had brought them to marriage, to parenthood – and now to indiffernce. How many years had the attraction lasted before it gave way to the antipathy which existed now? Was it possible that the Lisa Landry of twenty had ever been in love with him?

It was futile to speculate, because if I didn't like him, neither, in all honesty, did I like Lisa Landry. Looking at the matter fairly I found it just as difficult to believe he could ever have found anything to love in her.

Was it possible that anything Lisa Landry did could have the power to hurt him? Or was he happy in some world of his own making?

It was impossible to see through that enigmatical veneer of cool composure. The only impression I got about him – and I would have been hard put to it to define my reasons for it – was of a secret amusement in him, as though he were constantly jeering at himself.

I was so convinced about this that whenever I looked up suddenly I always expected to surprise a cynical twist on his mouth. The expression was never there but nothing could shake my belief in its existence, somewhere in the hidden depths of his mind.

Was he perhaps as lonely in his way as Lisa Landry had been, as I was?

I don't think I had ever realised before how friendless and lonely a person could be until I assumed Lisa Landry's identity.

Sometimes I walked down into Chadwell St. John and wandered idly along the main street, looking in the shop windows. Once or twice I went into the shops, but not very often. I suppose everyone in the village knew who I was, but by the barely concealed surprise on the shopkeepers' faces I assumed that Lisa Landry had not been in the habit of patronising them. On those few occasions I bought purchases I didn't really require, and not even to myself would I fully admit that my only reason was my need for contact with people – with anyone. That the loneliness in me was a canker which could in time destroy.

I wouldn't fully face this fact. Probably because I was afraid to face up to something that I didn't know how to rectify.

I went occasionally into the little tea shop for the same reason, and had a cup of tea I didn't need, for the pleasure of addressing a few inane remarks to the waitress. And sometimes into the Royal Oak, the low timbered, typical village pub which faced out across the green. For a drink I was honest enough to know I *did* need, even though that wasn't the reason for my visit. But in there, as in the café and the shops, I was eyed rather askance and I knew that as soon as I left, speculation was rife about the unusualness of my visits.

But the evenings were the worst, when the darkness fell and the walls of that beautiful house closed around me as surely as any prison walls.

Once I sat down at the piano and idly touched the keys, wondering whether I would find myself able to play or not.

Dorcas Mallory could – quite well, and had always enjoyed doing so, but I had no idea whether Lisa Landry knew one note from another.

I touched the keys tentatively at first and then, as I gained confidence, with a feeling of pleasure. There had been so many things Lisa Landry could do of which Dorcas Mallory had been ignorant or incapable, and I was delighted to discover that this was something in which the latter could excel.

There was a great pile of music but I played from memory, tunes that Dorcas Mallory had played many times, and for a while I was happier than I had been since that fateful morning of Joanna's wedding. I let my fingers wander over the keys, recalling melodies at will, even exercises learnt painstakingly as a child. Tunes of which my father had been fond and would ask me for – 'Play this one, Dorcas' – sitting in silent enjoyment, gently beating time with one finger on the arm of his chair. I ranged from Brahms to Rossini, Beethoven to musical comedy, Mendelssohn to current tunes of the times I was recalling. But it wasn't until I drifted into one of the Chopin studies that I realised where memory had taken me. As 'So deep is the night' it had been very popular at that time, and it had been 'our tune' – Russ's and mine.

It was one of those silly, very precious little things which can only be between two people deeply in love. We had had our first dance together to this tune and ever after, whenever we had heard it played, our eyes would meet with a soft smile of reminiscence.

I went on playing it, and when the last note died away in the silence, the stillness remained haunted by memory. It was all around me. I sat there in despair, aching with longing. And after a time I crept away in the darkness, up to the bedroom with the deep blue ceiling that threatened to crush me, and I couldn't accept anything about the present, no matter how hard I tried, because to accept it was to deny Russ. And that would have meant losing faith with life itself.

4

A FEW days later Charles asked me to go to London with him and I agreed gladly.

Anything – even London with Charles – was preferable to being confined to the house as I had been for the last two days. The lovely weather had broken at last and the gardens lay sodden outside the streaming windows. The heavy rain had battered the petals from the dahlias and the late roses, and the leaves from the trees dropped wetly before the driving wind.

We set off in the pouring rain and I drove fast, as I invariably did; Charles had automatically occupied the passenger seat. The windscreen wipers worked furiously to cope with the streaming downpour and visibility wasn't any too good. But the roads were exceptionally quiet and in any case I had an almost uncanny confidence in my own abilities as a driver.

It can be a very peculiar sensation to sit back and criticise or approve one's own accomplishments with the impartiality of an onlooker. For I took no credit or blame for what Lisa Landry could or could not do; her actions had been entirely out of my control. I could only follow blindly in her footsteps.

I didn't know London. All I remembered of it was from that brief visit of Dorcas Mallory's on the eve of her wedding . . . and that girl had been too starry-eyed to notice much about a war-scarred city.

But I noticed that even if I didn't know my route, I was in no way disconcerted by the amount of traffic we encountered. Lisa Landry had probably come here often and this was soon confirmed – by the clerk behind the hotel reception desk who addressed me by name on sight, by the head waiter of the restaurant where we dined, by the attendant at the doorway of a night-club we went to.

If Charles had asked me to come with him out of kindness, I'm afraid I probably gave him cause to regret his charitable action. I wasn't a good companion. I found that I could be just as miserably depressed in London as back at the house, and I wasn't surprised when Charles suggested one morning that I should go home. I didn't know whether to be relieved or not. It didn't matter very much either way to me.

He gave me hurried and rather impatient instructions about my route through London, rather as though he felt I ought to remember the way well enough from past journeys. I was a bit hazy about some of it but I didn't bother to ask him to go over it again.

And of course I got lost. But for that, I suppose, I should not have found myself waiting to turn at the traffic lights opposite a building I knew. Behind me was a line of vehicles, and that's exactly where they stayed when the lights finally changed – all hooting and shouting in an absolute frenzy of frustration which I hardly heard, even less cared about. For I was still staring at the name above the entrance with unbelieving eyes.

The Darlton!

The hotel I had phoned on the morning of Joanna's wedding because Dorcas Mallory had stayed there. And the fact that I had recognised it instantly, even before I read the name, was surely proof that she *had* stayed there, that the only life I remembered was not just an hallucination.

Still heedless in my excitement of the clamour behind me, I drove farther on until I found a vacant parking space and manoeuvred into it with a recklessness which would have horrified the owners of the cars I squeezed between.

I was trembling as I walked back down the street. Had I been mistaken? Had I only *imagined* I remembered the Darlton?

I went in through the revolving doors, and the roar of the traffic outside was hushed to a gentle murmur behind me.

And I recognised it – newer furnishings, different decorations, strange faces behind the big reception desk at the far end – but I recognised it. I sank on to the circular red plush seat in the centre of that entrance lounge in dazed and fearful wonderment.

I sat exactly where Dorcas Mallory had sat all those years ago as she waited for her father to make inquiries about train arrival times. I could see it all so vividly that my only wonder now was that he was not coming striding across to me, talking to me in that quick, rather nervous way that he had; taking my arm and leading me through those blacked out revolving doors – to the station. To Russ.

The hotel was busy with people constantly coming and going, and no one took any notice of the woman who sat, lost in memory. I don't know how long I sat there. I was only aware of the blessed peace which was in me at last, of the comfort which sprang from that sense of belonging.

I think it was a long time before the idea came to me to go upstairs, to see if I could remember correctly how to find the bedrooms that Dorcas Mallory and her father had occupied.

The lift was busy and I had to squeeze my way out on the second floor, but it was exactly as I knew it would be – the first turn to the left – and there were the two doors next to each other, numbers fifty-five and fifty-seven.

All I had to do, I thought, was to open those doors and there would be the blue suit and the ridiculous white hat, and the suitcases still unpacked for their journey to that cottage near Aylesbury, and my father waiting to take me to Russ. The feeling was so strong in me that I had my hand on the door before I remembered the fifteen years that had gone.

But I wanted to go into those rooms, I wanted to cling on to the peace I had found in this place.

When I went downstairs the young man at the reception desk was pleasant, but not to be hurried, and I waited fretfully while he checked the register. He looked up at me, his face expressing just the right degree of regret.

'No, I'm sorry, madam. Rooms fifty-five and fifty-seven are already let. We have – '

'How long for?' I asked. 'When will they be vacant?'

He checked again and told me that they wouldn't be vacant for two or three weeks yet. He couldn't know of the disappointment that was in me.

'We have other rooms,' he assured me, still with an earnest desire to please; but I shook my head as I turned away.

'It doesn't matter...'

But it did. I had wanted so very much to go into those rooms – to spend the night in one of them.

What had I really wanted, I wondered? What had I really expected? To wake up in the morning and find the clock miraculously put back fifteen years? To recapture time that was irredeemably lost?

Or had I perhaps just wanted, in the familiar comfort of those rooms, tangible proof of a life which didn't, which couldn't, have existed?

I sat down again on the seat but some of the peace had given way now to bewilderment.

How could Lisa Landry remember this place? Fifteen years ago she had been – where? Certainly not here. Fifteen years ago she had been married to Charles, had a child three years old, a life of her own that had nothing to do with Dorcas Mallory.

The girl who had stayed here all those years ago had never lived – it was only some desperate longing in me that made me insist upon giving her a reality she had never had.

I think it was at that point that I went slowly up to the desk again and asked to speak to the manager.

He was an older man, but pleasant, too. He said, 'Sit down, Mrs. Landry,' and waited expectantly.

He looked a little startled when I explained what I wanted. He probably thought I was a bit of a crank, but he was evidently very used to dealing with cranks because he couldn't have been nicer.

I must finally have impressed him with the importance of what I wanted, or else he was just plain obliging. He picked up the telephone and spoke to someone on it, and while we were waiting he offered me a cigarette and had one himself; and we talked about the weather until a young woman came in carrying a bedraggled looking ledger of the type that hotels keep on their reception desks to mark the comings and goings of their guests.

She put it down rather distastefully on the desk before the manager and he looked at it with the same distaste.

'It doesn't look very hygienic,' he remarked.

'I think this would be the one that was damaged during the war, sir,' she explained. 'It looks as though it has been wet at some time, and dried out.'

'Ah, yes . . . ' He nodded thoughtfully as he thumbed through the pages. 'Thank you . . . '

She went out and I watched impatiently as he went on turning the pages in an absent-minded way. I could barely restrain myself from taking the book from him as he asked, 'Now, what date was it, Mrs. Landry?'

I told him again and he found time to look up and give me his pleasant smile; and at that I couldn't sit still any longer. I got up and went round the desk to him and although he looked a little startled he got to his feet, too, and we stood there together looking through that grimy, smeared ledger. It must have been soaked with water at some time and the pages had dried in that hard, unresponsive way that paper does. Some of them were stuck together and some entries were quite illegible, but I went on turning the leaves over and over, and my throat felt funny and constricted so that I had difficulty in swallowing.

The book smelt old and musty but I hardly noticed. I fumbled the last few pages hopelessly as I approached the date I wanted, and the manager very kindly gave me his assistance.

He was an age, an eternity – would he never get the page over?

Two of them were stuck together and the ink had run, making some of the signatures indecipherable. I ran my finger down the list, and the finger was trembling so much that I could hardly control its movement. And then the names were there, at the tip of that trembling finger – blurred and indistinct. But there!

Ardrian R. Mallory....
And underneath it – *Miss Dorcas Mallory*!

I don't remember very much about the drive up to Alderford. Most of the time I was in a complete daze of excitement which put me into a fury of impatience at the least delay. I remember beginning to despair that I would ever leave London behind. It was all so unfamiliar to me and I got hopelessly lost.

I would have done better to have sat down quietly and studied a road map, and that's what I forced myself to do later on; but at the start I couldn't think of anything except that the road north led to Alderford, and that in Alderford I would find Russ.

I didn't know how, or where, or when – but I was going to find Russ. Somewhere at the end of the journey I must find him. For if Dorcas and Adrian Mallory had lived – then so had Russell Winslow.

There was so much humble gratitude in my heart – so much joyous, blessed relief.

I put my foot down flat on the accelerator and the car devoured that endless road. I swept through the smaller towns and villages, fuming at every traffic light that was against me, every crossing that held me up, every turning of which I was uncertain. Later, when I bought the map, I compelled myself to study the best route. I sat and smoked a cigarette, and realised that I had had nothing to eat or drink since breakfast, but I couldn't waste any time on such mundane things. I had waited fifteen and a half years for what I was going to find at the end of this journey. I couldn't wait any longer. Not a single unnecessary minute.

Afterwards I couldn't remember any detail of that road or the scenery. I could recall that sometime in the early evening I ran into a slight shower of rain but I was nearing my destination by then and – most wonderful of all – I was on roads that were familiar to me.

My excitement mounted when I first realised that I no longer needed to look at the map or the signposts, that I knew each turning. Some of the roads had been widened or had a bad bend cut out – but mostly they were the same roads which I had known all those years ago.

But the town itself had changed. And suddenly I knew a moment of fear. But I wouldn't allow it to linger.

The town seemed much bigger than I remembered. The houses extended much farther out, there was a big new bus station, and the one way streets confused me. I had to turn off and come out again by the Black Swan – and that too had been altered and modernised until only the name remained the same.

Even the tenor of the town had changed. It had always been a sleepy little place, with none of the brisk air of expectancy, the aura of prosperity that pervaded it now.

And yet, changed as it was, it was Alderford. I knew that.

I went past innumerable coffee bars that had not been there before, past the Odeon, round a new roundabout and up the slight rise past the park. This at least was the same as it had always been – and the tree-lined avenue beyond, with its detached houses and spacious gardens, was the road that led to High Towers. To my home and my father, who would know where to find Russ.

In another moment, as I rounded the bend at the top and left the other houses behind, High Towers would come into view. I would only be able to see its red tiled roof and gables amongst the trees, its chimneys outlined against the sky; but it would be there – comfortable and warm and safe.

It hadn't the opulent splendour of Lisa Landry's house; it might be old-fashioned and over-furnished, and cold in winter because Father didn't believe very much in new fangled ideas like central heating. He liked good roaring log fires which burned your shins and left icy shivers still running down your back. But it was home, in a way that that luxurious other house could never be.

I would turn in at the gates and drive up to the front door, past the bank of rhododendrons which was always covered in blood-red bloom in spring, round the curve of the not very well kept lawn with the oak tree in the centre where we used to have meals when it was very warm . . . and would old Henrietta still be there? She had been with us so many years and had already seemed old on that morning, so long ago now, when she had kissed me before I left to go to my wedding in London. Dear old Henrietta, always in her white starched apron which had smelt faintly of lavender when I buried my face in it as a frightened or hurt child.

And Mrs. Bakewell, the cook, who Father always declared had only married her husband because of the appropriateness of his name . . . Was she still making her melting, floury scones and those chocolate cakes . . . ?

But I was at the brow of the hill now and rounding the bend – and I could feel my face freezing slowly into horrified disbelief.

Confronting me was a corporation housing estate.

The car was already gathering speed down the hill and I slammed the brakes on hard and scrambled out from behind the wheel.

It couldn't be! It just didn't make sense! Father would never have sold that fine old house, it had been in his family for nearly a hundred and fifty years. He would never have allowed it to be razed to the ground – built over. There *must* be some mistake. I had taken the wrong road – the house was farther on, after all these years I had forgotten . . .

But I knew I hadn't. I wasn't on the wrong road and the house should have been there – exactly in the centre of that estate.

I got back in the car and drove all over the estate, but nowhere could I find a trace of High Towers. It had disappeared as completely as though it had never been.

And that was something I refused to admit.

I asked many people on the estate, but no one could help me. No one could remember what had been there before the estate was built.

Then I was luckier with an elderly couple walking arm in arm. They could both remember that there used to be a house somewhere around here.

The woman was terrible worried because she couldn't recall the name.

'Now then, what was it? Can you think of it, Dad, I can't.'

'No, I can't, Mother. It was a nice house though – '

'Yes, but it's the name – it's on the tip of my tongue.'

I didn't remind her that I had just told her the name. It seemed a point of honour with her that she should remember it herself. I asked her husband if he could remember the name of the man who owned it. Was it Mallory? But he didn't know that. He only remembered the house because he and Mother used to walk past it sometimes on a fine evening. But at least they had confirmed something which I had been certain of in my mind. The house had been there. I hadn't dreamed it.

I put Mother out of her misery before I left them.

'The name was High Towers,' I said gently.

'There,' she said triumphantly, 'there – that's it. I told you it was on the tip of my tongue. High Towers – yes, that's it.'

I drove back towards the town, depressed and miserable. I didn't know where to go or what to do.

I was facing too, for the first time, the possibility that my father could be dead. I hadn't realised until then that fifteen years can turn a man approaching sixty into a man well into the seventies.

I didn't know how to find out – I think I was afraid to. I couldn't remember the name of his solicitors. I knew their offices had been in the main street – but I wasn't sure where, and at that time of evening the place would be closed anyway.

He was a man who had not had many friends, or ever gone far from home. I didn't know how to start to find him, whom to seek for information about him. If he were dead...

The red phone box reminded me that if he still lived in Alderford and had a telephone, his address would be in the directory. I realised as I got out of the car how profoundly tired I was. If I could only have gone home...

I hadn't really expected to find his name in the book. I think I knew beyond doubt that he was dead. He would never have lived to see that corporation estate cluttering the ground where his beloved house and garden had been.

As I took my hands away from the directory the pages flopped over, and I flicked them dispiritedly with my finger. To have come so far – to have been so certain of success ..

The booth smelt stuffy but I didn't know where to go when I left it. It seemed easier just to stand in there instead of going back to the car and having to make decisions, looking at the fine print without really seeing it . . . Williams, Willis, Wills, Wilson – there were a lot of Wilsons – Windle, Windley . . .

I was suddenly afraid to look farther. It couldn't be – the possibility was too remote – Alderford wasn't Russ's home town – there was no earthly reason why he should be living here now –

I had to drag my eyes down the rest of that page.

Windley, Winifred's, Winn, Winnard, Winnett, Winship – *Winslow* . . .

Winslow, R. Greenways, Cedar Avenue.

I stumbled out of the booth and went back to the car. I knew Cedar Avenue – it was one of the lanes leading from the main road I had just come down.

I sat in the car and lit a cigarette with trembling fingers. If this was true – if this was *my* Russell – and it must be, it must, dear God, it *must* – then we were no more than half a mile from each other.

And I was too terrified to do anything about it. I could only sit there in the car and feel sick with fear of yet another disappointment.

The last rays of the setting sun slanted across my lap and I could feel the warmth on my hands. The smoke from a bonfire in someone's garden drifted in the air – I could smell it, sharp and acrid, a smell that had always reminded me rather wistfully that the long summer days were over, that autumn was here with winter close at hand.

I noticed the people walking past, the man with his dog, a young girl alone, a courting couple . . .

Russ and I had walked down this road together. The last time had been in winter – during the leave before the one in which we were to be married. There had been snow on the ground and a cold wind blowing, and we had walked instead of taking the car because of the state of the roads. We had walked hand in hand, as that couple walked now, unashamedly in love. It had still been snowing a little and the flakes had settled on the fur coat which I huddled around me, on Russ's greatcoat – I had always been so proud to be with him in his uniform – on our hair, on our eyelashes.

And we had been going down into the town to buy our wedding ring.

I knew, as I remembered all this, that I had to conquer my fear. Even if R. Winslow should not be Russ, I had to know or there would never be any peace for me in this life.

I reversed the car and went back up the hill, slowly, so as not to miss the turning into Cedar Avenue. But I knew exactly where it was and I turned into it, crawling slowly down its length, trying to read the names on the gates.

I saw Russ before I noticed the name of the house. He was in a long sloping garden which ran down from a cream-walled, green-tiled house – a large, pleasant garden that had only a low wall covered in climbing plants for boundary.

I just sat in the car and looked at him, and let the peace and happiness flow over me. I was rid for ever of the utter desolation of a world in which there was no Russ.

He was there before me after all these years – no longer the pitiful delusion of a sick mind, but living flesh and blood.

I observed small things about him first – the sloppy sweater, the old slacks which he wore as though they were comfortable friends of long standing, the secateurs in one hand and the pile of dead brushwood in the other as he straightened his back for a moment's respite from his work. He threw his head back a little as though to ease his neck, and I saw the fine play of muscles in his throat, the well-bronzed skin.

He had broadened slightly but it suited him; and he had taken to smoking a pipe. I liked that. Russ had exactly the type of face that looked right with a pipe clenched between his teeth.

He hadn't noticed either me or the car. He bent down once again and continued cutting out the old dead wood from the shrub, and I got out of the car and walked across the pavement to the edge of the garden.

I just stood there and I couldn't speak. All my love for him was in my eyes.

He must have sensed my presence, for he looked back casually over his shoulder. It was only a fleeting glance and he went on with his work for a moment before he looked round again.

He straightened slowly, looking at me with a diffident air. I think he was still unconvinced whether I needed him or was merely admiring his garden.

He was no more than four or five yards away from me, and I could see the steadfast serenity in his blue-grey eyes just as I had always known it, the humour and kindness in the lines of his mouth. Then I saw the streaks of grey among the fair hair at his temples and I realised with a sense of shock for which I should have been prepared that he was no longer a very young man – that he would be forty next birthday.

But it was still the same Russ, and I would have known him anywhere.

I waited for recognition to come to him, to see in his eyes what I knew to be in my own; and I don't know how long I stood there like that, my voice frozen in my throat, before I heard him ask, rather hesitantly as though he wasn't quite sure whether he should speak to me or not, 'Can I help you in any way?'

I looked at him in dumb supplication. You must know me, Russ – you must! You couldn't have forgotten me.

It came to me suddenly then, and I felt weak with the relief. How could he recognise me when I hadn't even recognised myself in the mirror? I no longer looked like the young girl he had loved so many years ago.

I asked softly, 'Do you remember a girl called Dorcas Mallory?'

Even as I framed the question I had seen the young boy come running across the lawn towards us. As he came he was calling out, 'Any more to take away, Dad?' and then when he saw me he stopped, eyeing me with a polite curiosity. He was about ten or eleven years old, fair haired, blue eyes, as yet with only a hint of the gentle strength that was to come, and a shy smile which already held the open frankness I knew so well.

The possibility had never occurred to me. It was too ridiculous even to imagine Russ married to anyone other than myself. How could he be, when we had been so irrevocably bound to each other? And this child . . . this boy that should have been ours . . .

How could you do this to me, Russ? Fifteen years is a long time, but how could you?

A woman appeared in the doorway of the house. From the distance she looked slight and dark – I couldn't tell whether she was pretty or not, and it made no difference. Either way I would have hated her just as intensely.

She was calling, 'Russ – Russ?' I saw her hesitate. Did I only imagine that there was resentment and suspicion in her attitude? She stood, obviously waiting, obviously in possession.

I saw Russ stir uneasily. He answered her with the one word, 'Coming.'

I wondered jealously how many times she had called him like that and he had run obediently to her command. I could sense his wish to go; and yet he wavered, as though something still held him, however reluctantly. He was looking at me with an expression on his face that I couldn't read.

I asked again, with a harshness born of my hurt, 'Do you remember a girl called Dorcas Mallory?'

The woman called again, a slightly querulous note in her voice. 'Russ?'

I had repeated the question in a bitter desire to hurt him in some way, to reproach him for his faithlessness.

I didn't expect his answer. He was already turning away, in answer to that possessive summons, but the words came back to me clearly.

'No,' he said. 'I'm sorry – I never knew anyone of that name.'

5

IN the cold hotel bedroom I woke late after a wretched night. Sleep had brought no escape from the bitterness of so complete a betrayal.

Anything else I think in time I could have learned to bear – but not Russ's denial of any knowledge of me. That wound went too deep.

It had been idiotic to think that time would stand still for him. Wherever I had been or whatever I had done during these last fifteen years, life had to go on for him; and although I had not for a moment expected to find him married, it was a natural outcome which I could have grown to accept.

But not this renunciation of any memory of me. Never that.

Whatever this marriage of his meant to him, the love we had had could surely have held a place in his heart without disloyalty. It had all happened years before he need own an allegiance to anyone else. How could he so easily have forgotten?

I was too unhappy even to care that I was once more Dorcas Mallory, that I need no longer be, and never had been, Lisa Landry; that I could live my own life again and would never have to go back to the opulent emptiness of Lisa Landry's house.

And I was afraid now to make any inquiries about my father for fear of the answer I would get. It was something I would have to do, even though I dreaded the confirmation of my fears. I didn't want to know. It was the only illusion I had left and I wanted to cling on to it. When that went, I had nothing left.

By the time I got downstairs the dining-room was closed, but it didn't matter. I hadn't wanted any breakfast, only a cup of tea, and I could get that at one of the snack bars in the street.

I wasn't quite sure what I intended doing. I thought I would probably wander down the main street and look at the brass office plates in the hope that I could remember the name of Father's solicitors. And if I couldn't, I would inquire at each one in turn. It would take time but time was the one thing I had plenty of. I had returned to a life that promised to be as empty as Lisa Landry's, and a door to door search for a firm of solicitors was about as exciting as any of my prospects.

The sun was shining fitfully through the clouds as I went out. It wasn't very warm and I shivered a little in the thin, dark green suit I was wearing.

I started off at one end of the street and it was a disheartening task. Eventually, emerging from yet another interior I stood, discouraged and undecided, on the pavement edge. I hadn't yet had my cup of tea – I hadn't, in fact, had a meal of any kind since the previous morning.

I was opposite one of the new coffee bars and I hadn't

realised that, by standing on the very edge of the pavement, I was preventing a large black car from moving off. The driver gave a gentle reminder on the horn.

It was only the faintest bleep but in my overwrought state it made me jump nervously. A man's voice called out, 'Oh, I'm sorry – I didn't mean to startle you . . . '

My heart lurched in my breast, just as it always had done at the sound of his voice, and I turned round and looked at Russ.

He was regarding me uncertainly. I could see that he had recognised me as the woman who had spoken to him last night. He inclined his head in acknowledgment but there was a guarded reserve behind the salutation which was so different from the way we had once greeted each other that I couldn't bear it.

The misery and the loneliness in my heart was too great to hide, and I had no thought of how I might be embarrassing him until I saw a faint flush creeping into his cheeks. He lowered his eyes uncomfortably and began fiddling with something on the dashboard.

I had to force myself to walk on down the street. I don't know where I found the strength to do so. But then I heard a car door slam sharply, a quick footstep behind me, and all my resolve was gone.

Without turning I knew it was Russ. I stood there with my eyes tight shut, telling myself that in a moment I would hear him say 'Dorcas' – with that special note in his voice which had always been only for me. But it never came. Instead I heard him say, hesitantly, 'Excuse me . . . '

When I turned to face him I saw only a kindly concern in his eyes. And I was absurdly grateful. For a moment it didn't matter that there was no love for me in his eyes. How could there have been? He was only speaking to a woman whom he had seen for the first time last night. And I was so hungry for the least crumb of comfort he could offer me now that it didn't matter if he thought me a stranger. It was enough just to be with him.

He said again, 'Excuse me . . . ' I don't think he knew how to go on and even if I could have helped him, I wouldn't have done. Every moment of hesitation was a reprieve from that other, final moment when I would have to walk away from him.

And then suddenly he smiled – that boyishly shy, irresistible smile of his which made you realise that after all the world was a wonderful place to live in.

'I wanted to beg your pardon,' he said.

I managed to stammer out something about it not mattering, that I was easily startled.

'Oh,' he said, 'I didn't mean for that – although I beg your pardon for that, too. I meant last night. I'm afraid I was rather abrupt . . . You seemed distressed . . . '

I tried to say that that hadn't mattered either, but just to remember it hurt and I faltered into silence. After a moment I managed to say quietly, 'Please don't apologise.'

I thought he would go, then. I could see in his eyes that he wanted to; it was no more than a fleeting expression but I knew him too well to mistake it. I think what held him there was simply that it was against his instinct to turn his back on anyone who seemed troubled.

He went on, still excusing himself, as though loath to leave the subject, 'I was in a hurry – my wife was needing me. I'm sorry if I seemed rude.'

'It wasn't that,' I said, 'I – '

'I wasn't even very truthful,' he broke in, and he said the words hurriedly, as though he feared that if he didn't say them now they would never be spoken. 'You asked me if I remembered Dorcas Mallory . . . It wasn't true when I said that I didn't.'

The rush of thankfulness which flowed over me was not so much for what he had said as for the way he had spoken the name; softly, with a tenderness that told of loving memory. Overwhelmed with joy, I must have swayed unsteadily, for I heard Russ ask in swift concern, 'Are you all right?'

For a moment I couldn't answer him. Then I murmured, 'When you said last night that you had forgotten . . . '

'Yes,' he said. 'I'm sorry. I was very troubled about the look on your face after you'd gone. I ought not to have denied it – it seemed rather important to you. But you see – well, my wife was calling . . . '

I knew suddenly what loyalty to his wife prevented him from saying outright. I remembered again the possessive note in her voice as she called him, and from the way in which he had spoken my name a moment ago I knew that I had once held a place in his heart of which his wife could be jealous. She couldn't be ignorant of the fact that Russ and I had once been engaged, on the point of marrying, and it assuaged my own jealous grief a little to know that she might resent my memory.

There was still no recognition of me, only this acknowledgment of memory. And I wanted to know what had happened to Dorcas Mallory before I told Russ who I was. I wanted to know what had caused us to part – what had gone wrong so many years ago.

I said impulsively, 'Please tell me about her?'

He looked startled. 'Who? My wife?'

I shook my head but I thought, Yes, tell me about her, too, Russ. I want to know what happened to you, too – how long you've been married, how much you love that wife of yours – about your son. 'No,' I said, 'Dorcas Mallory.'

He glanced uncertainly up and down the busy street, at the passers by who jostled us as we stood there.

I said impetuously, 'I was going in for a cup of coffee – will you have one with me?' I could tell he was going to refuse. 'Please,' I begged. 'It's most terribly important to me. I *must* talk to you and it's so difficult here. Please . . . '

I knew that he would find it difficult to refuse such an appeal, but I think it was something more than just kindness that made him walk with me across the pavement and into the coffee bar.

It wasn't very busy. I sat down at a table in the window, thinking that these minutes might well be all I would ever have of his time. Even when I told him who I was, nothing would be altered.

If I had once thought that I could run to him and pick up the threads where they had been laid down more than fifteen years ago, I knew different now.

We had a slight argument about who paid for the coffees which he fetched from the counter. When I pointed out that the invitation had been mine he said, with that brusque discomfiture which men display at such moments, 'Oh, nonsense!' so I let the thing drop.

The coffee was surprisingly good – or was it being with Russ again that made it seem so? I offered him my cigarette case, and then just as he was about to take one I suddenly withdrew the case.

'No,' I said, 'please smoke your pipe.'

'Well – ' he looked surprised, 'How did you know I'm a pipe smoker?'

'You were smoking one last night,' I said, shyly. I watched his hands as he filled the pipe. And with a sudden ache of longing I wanted to take one in mine and hold it comfortingly against my cheek, as I used to do.

I couldn't understand how he could fail to know me – no matter how changed my appearance. But I think that perhaps to some slight extent there had been something that he recognised, otherwise he would not have come into this place with me, nor be sitting there contentedly puffing at his pipe and regarding me with no trace of impatience.

And I was childishly happy to be with him again. For these few minutes life was perfect and I could feel a delighted smile spreading across my face.

I saw the quick, startled look which came into his eyes – a strange, conflicting mixture of disbelief, of shock, of wistfulness, and I wondered what he had seen in my face. Whether for a moment there had been, in this disillusioned, unhappy woman who sat opposite him, some slight resemblance to the eager young girl he had loved.

I held my breath, longing for his recognition. But the look faded from his face and the moment had gone.

Two young teenagers in tight jeans and sweaters went over to the contraption in the corner and after a slight argument selected a record. As the record started to play they went back to their table, their provocative little bottoms swaying to the rhythm. The whole place was filled with the heavy throbbing beat of the music.

Russ gave a little grimace of good-humoured resignation.

'This one I know,' he said. 'My children have it at home. They'd play it all day long if we'd let them.'

The knife turned in my breast.

'Your children?' I asked. I tried to sound casual. 'Have you more than one – I mean, I saw a little boy with you last night . . . '

'Oh, that was Steve. He's ten. Sandra's nine. They're both mad on this Rock and Roll or whatever it's called – even at their age.'

He spoke cheerfully; a well contented family man whose air of placid serenity only deepened my own stark sense of loneliness.

'You must be very proud of your children. Steve looked a fine boy.'

'Oh, he's a good kid – they both are, for that matter. Little devils at times, of course. They should have been back at school by this time but Sandra's had the mumps so Steve's been in isolation, too.'

He was chatting with a casual ease but I could discern the air of expectancy behind the unhurried manner. A series of heavily laden lorries lumbered past down the street, making a vibration through the floor of the building. I glanced out of the window in distaste.

'It's all so different,' I said, and a note of wistfulness I couldn't help crept into my voice. 'So noisy.'

'You mean the town? Do you live here?'

'No – I used to, a lot of years ago,' I said evasively. 'But it wasn't like this, then.'

'Alderford has expanded a lot since the war. New industries have brought more people – it's a flourishing, prosperous little town now.'

I said childishly, 'I liked it better as it was.'

'Well, you can't have progress without sacrificing something to it.'

'Do *you* like it better this way – busier and noisier . . . ?'

'I don't think I've every really noticed it until now. The changes come gradually and you're not so aware of them when you're living and growing with them.'

'It used to be a sleepy, contented little place – so happy and peaceful.'

Russ said, 'The atmosphere of a place has a lot to do with the state of one's own mind.'

I moved uncomfortably under his scrutiny. I knew that Russ would no more like the character I had become over these last years than I did myself. And I didn't want the one person in the world whose opinion I cared about to take me for the cold, cynically indifferent woman that I looked.

I said very quietly, 'Tell me about Dorcas Mallory?'

I could see the change come over his face . . . a softness and yet a guarded reserve. I had the strong, comforting feeling that the memory of Dorcas Mallory was locked deeply and ineradicably in his heart.

'What do you want to know about her?' he asked. There was a faint wariness in his voice, and almost a note of resentiment; as though his memory of her was not to be shared indiscriminately.

I lifted my shoulders in a little indefinite movement.

'Anything,' I said. 'Just tell me about her.'

He looked uncomfortable. He took the pipe out of his mouth and made an unnecessary business of tamping the tobacco down in the bowl; and he was frowning slightly as he did so, in a way that accentuated the lines in his face which were new to me.

Again I appealed to him as I had outside.

'It's terribly important to me.'

Russ said, a little helplessly, 'I don't know what you want me to tell you.'

I didn't really know myself. I only knew that I wanted to hear Russ say my name – to speak about me with that special note in his voice which would tell me how dearly he had once loved me. I wanted that comfort at least to take away with me.

'What was she like?' I asked, and the expression which came into his face caught at my heart. There was so much sadness mingled with the warmth and tenderness.

He said very gently, 'Oh, Cassy was – well, just Cassy. If you knew her, you'll understand what I mean.'

I made a small involuntary sound at his use of that name – one he had used only in our most tender moments, as a term of endearment.

Cassy ... Cassy, I repeated softly to myself ... and aloud I said, 'Do you remember how she looked? Was she pretty?'

I was vain enough, jealous enough, to need that reassurance.

'Well, *I* thought she was pretty,' Russ said. He smiled a little as he put the pipe back in his mouth. 'Although I may have been biased. Yes, I think she was. Although Dorcas had much more than mere prettiness. She was so – so *alive,* so vital ...'

'But her features,' I insisted. 'Her hair, her eyes ...'

'Oh, her eyes were blue – dark blue. Rather like yours, only darker. You know, a while ago when you smiled, for a minute I thought I could see a resemblance between you and Dorcas. But there isn't any, of course. You're not a bit like her. It was only the way you smiled ...'

I had listened breathlessly as he spoke, willing him to

recognise me. But there was a finality in his voice that told me how useless it was. There could be no possible connection in his mind between the two of us.

'And her hair?' I prompted, and even before he spoke I knew that my memory had not been at fault.

'Golden – a very deep golden. In fact, I don't think golden describes it really, but I don't know what else to call it. There was a bit of red in it, but it wasn't coppery ... '

How faithfully he had remembered ...

'It was long, wasn't it – almost to the shoulders?' I said, and he nodded.

'And curly.' He gave me an appraising look: 'Why are you asking me to describe her? You obviously knew her – '

'Yes, I knew her – many years ago. I wanted to know if I could remember her correctly.' I added softly. 'You don't seem to have forgotten any detail of her appearance.'

'No,' he agreed soberly. 'No, I haven't.'

'Do you remember,' I asked, 'the occasion when you came home unexpectedly on leave and called for her at the hairdressers. She walked straight out of the salon and you drove out to that little roadhouse by the river and had tea on the lawn, and it wasn't until you got back that either of you noticed that her hair was still up in pincurls?'

'Did Dorcas tell you that?' His face was alight with pleasure and amusement at the recollection of how we had laughed when we had finally noticed.

'Or the time,' I went on, 'when you brought home a dozen eggs from the farm where you had been billeted. You put them in the front seat of the car and forgot about them, and in the dark Dorcas sat on them – all the way to that dance you were going to at the country club?'

'We never did get to it,' Russ said, chuckling quietly. 'You should have seen Cassy's dress – I remember it was a white one and she'd spent all her remaining coupons on it. And did she tell you about the time the car stuck in the ford? There'd been some heavy rains and the water was higher than I'd expected. The engine stalled and wouldn't get going again, so I got out to carry Dorcas to save her getting wet. And I tripped over a stone and dropped her slap in the deepest part. They've covered the ford over now, but I never drive over it without remembering Cassy's face as she sat spluttering in the water.

Don't you, Russ, I thought wistfully, don't you?

I was remembering that day as plainly as if it had been yesterday. Russ's determined gallantry, when I had wanted to take off my shoes and stockings and wade to dry land. The consternation on his face and then the laughter which had rendered us both helpless. I had sat there in the water and Russ had stood looking at me, and we were still rocking feebly with mirth when another car had driven up and the occupants had looked at us as though they thought we were mad.

It had been like that all the time with Russ. We had always been able to laugh together, which is the next most important thing to loving. I wondered, with jealous hurt, whether he laughed with the woman who was his wife. And I knew that he must do.

But there was consolation as well for me in that moment – in knowing that the past could still hold him. He went on and on, relating incidents and episodes that I remembered well, and even some that I had partially forgotten. It seemed that now he had started talking about the past he wanted to go on, reliving those moments as I was – with the same mingled happiness and sadness.

What went wrong, Russ? What happened to us? What could possibly have happened to a love like ours?

I wanted to ask him but at the same time I wanted him to go on talking. I watched the play of emotions on his face – and I don't know how I prevented myself from reaching out and taking his hand in mine.

The coffee on the table went cold, my cigarette smouldered to ashes, Russ's pipe went out unnoticed. And still he talked to me, telling me things that I knew no one else had ever heard or knew about. Until this moment the memory of Dorcas had been too tightly locked in his breast – too deeply buried beneath another loyalty, another life.

I was lost in humble gratitude for this gift, for this affinity between us which still existed even though I knew that, consciously, he was unaware of it.

When he came to an end at last, when I knew that reality was intruding to push away the past, I was also aware, with absolute certainty, that he would never speak of all this again. He had purged himself of a great need to talk about Dorcas Mallory. He could no more forget her than he could forget himself, but he would find a contentment in his memories now which I think had been lacking before. And he would never know why, never know how it could have happened as he talked and laughed with a stranger, because there was no point in ever telling him now.

He gave a little half-ashamed laugh as he finally came back to the present.

'Good God,' he exclaimed, 'how I must have bored you.'

'You must have loved her very much,' I said softly.

'Yes, I did.' He said it very simply.

'And now?' I asked. 'Are you happy now?'

Quietly he said, 'That was a long time ago. Yes, I'm happy now. There was a time perhaps when I thought . . . Jean's a good wife and an excellent mother. There are not many men as lucky as I am.'

I took him back into the past again.

'What happened?' I asked gently.

He thought I was referring to his relationship with his wife and I could sense the immediate withdrawal in him.

'Between you and Dorcas Mallory,' I said. 'Do you know where she is now?'

He gave me a glance of startled astonishment. His eyes were suddenly filled with a deep, unending sadness.

'Didn't you know?' he said. He added very quietly, 'She died.'

I was stunned with the unexpectedness of it. I sat there, staring at him, while the shock of his words bore through me. All at once I wanted to laugh at the preposterousness of what he had said.

And I couldn't.

It was ridiculous, absurd. And I still couldn't laugh.

I could only keep my eyes fixed unbelievingly on his face; and its almost stern sadness made a little chill of horror run down my back.

I wanted desperately to deny the terrible finality of what he had said. Instead all I managed to choke out, in a strangled whisper, was, 'Are you sure?'

There was so much sorrow in his eyes that I cried out silently against it.

He said, 'I went to her funeral.'

I felt sick with the horror of it. I didn't believe it. I *wouldn't* believe it – but I still felt sick. The nausea rose in me and I thought I would never be able to control it. I put my handkerchief to my mouth with a nerveless hand and my face felt cold and hard, as though all the blood had drained from it. There was such a coldness and stillness in me that I could indeed have been dead.

I heard him say, 'I'm sorry – I thought you must know. I shouldn't have told you so bluntly . . . I should have been more gentle about it. I'm sorry . . .'

I wondered wildly what difference it could make how one was told that one was dead. And what could I say?

Because I couldn't disbelieve him.

I wanted to. With all my heart, I wanted to cry out that it wasn't true. That *I* was Dorcas Mallory. That I was here, alive, sitting before him. That I wanted the comfort of his arms round me to drive away the icy numbness of bereavement, the closeness of him against this cold, dead body of mine.

For how could I endure this double loss?

Briefly, his hand rested on mine as he said again, 'I'm sorry . . . I should have realised . . .'

I drew a long shuddering breath.

'How did it happen?'

He told me gently, and I could sense the hurt that was still in him. 'She was killed in an air raid.'

After a moment I asked, but I already knew the answer, 'In London?'

'Only a few hours before we were to have married. She and her father – '

'Was he killed, too?'

'Yes – they were together. They're buried together in the churchyard on the far side of the park.'

I nodded dumbly. I knew where he meant. It was the church that we – that Dorcas Mallory and her father – had attended. And Russ, too, when he had been on leave. We – *they* – had gone there together and shared the same hymn book, the same prayer book – the prayer book that Dorcas Mallory should have carried on her wedding day.

Poor Dorcas Mallory – so young, so in love, so happy . . .

And poor Russ, who had had to bury his love instead of marrying her – who could still suffer in speaking of it.

I said, 'You've been very kind. I was trying to find – Mr. Mallory. I didn't know that he was dead.'

'Can I help you in any way?' he offered, and I shook my head.

'You've been very kind,' I said again, listlessly.

The town hall clock chimed twelve, slowly and ponderously. Russ glanced at his watch in dismay.

'I had an appointment at eleven-thirty,' he said. 'The time – I'd no idea ... May I give you a lift anywhere?'

For a moment I couldn't speak. He was knocking the cold ashes from his pipe, slipping a tip under his saucer, preparing to go out of my life.

'Please ...' I begged. He glanced at his watch again.

'Yes – ?' he prompted, but in his mind he was already hurrying away.

I shook my head mutely. There was nothing more I could say. If Dorcas Mallory might have had a slight claim on his time, I had none.

He hesitated for a moment before getting to his feet and holding out his hand. But I dared not take it; I would never have let it go again.

He stood uncertainly with his hand still outstretched and seemed as though he would say something. Then perhaps he realised how inadequate any words would be.

His hand dropped to his side and he inclined his head gravely towards me and then he was walking towards the door. For a moment longer I could see him in the street. Then he was gone.

I felt the tears rushing to my eyes and tried to stop them, but I couldn't. Heedless of the people around me, of the attendant behind the counter, I buried my face in my hands and wept like a child.

I was roused at last by a touch on my shoulder. I looked up to see the attendant regarding me with mingled concern and curiosity. The place was filling up for the lunchtime rush and I was the centre of attention, but I was past caring what anyone thought.

Let them stare – most of them had probably never seen a dead woman crying before, I thought miserably. I fumbled for a handkerchief in my handbag.

'You all right, miss?' the attendant asked, and I nodded briefly.

I had to force myself to get up. It seemed absurd to be trying to move when all I wanted was to be as dead as

Dorcas Mallory. I envied her bitterly.

I asked the attendant how much I owed him.

'The gentleman paid, miss,' he said. He was collecting the empty coffee cups together and pocketing Russ's tip as he asked, diffidently, 'Wasn't that Mr. Winslow you were with?'

I didn't like the glance that went with the question. Instinct made me leap to the defence of Russ's reputation in this town.

'Was that his name? I didn't know him,' I said shortly. 'He – gave me some bad news about someone very dear to me.'

The attendant didn't know whether to look sceptical or disappointed as I left him. I don't suppose he believed me, but perhaps it wouldn't get to Jean's ears.

I went back to the hotel for the car without really thinking about what I was doing. But I wasn't surprised to find myself pulling up outside the churchyard.

The sun was shining feebly as I got out of the car and opened the heavy iron gates. They screeched noisily as they swung back, and I could remember that they had always needed oiling.

The church looked cold and austere and there was a forbidding greyness about the graveyard which chilled me. Had it always looked like this or was I seeing it differently today?

It was warmer round the back where the graves were newer and fresh with flowers, and I started searching among them before it occurred to me that it was useless to look for Adrian and Dorcas Mallory's grave among these recent ones. They had been dead and buried more than fifteen years – a few days after the last occasion I could remember worshipping in this church.

At that time, I could remember, the new graves were being dug on the far side of the church, and presently I found it. It stood out among some neglected ones by its neatness. There was a headstone of black shining marble and the same stone surrounded the neat oblong of newly cut grass. There were no flowers – had I really expected them after all these years? – but the grave was clean and well kept. By whom, I wondered? Was it Russ who paid for its upkeep? And did he ever come here?

I sank down on to the stone at the foot and looked at the inscription.

Adrian Richard Mallory died April 1944, aged 59 years.

And underneath:

Dorcas Mallory, dear daughter of above died April, 1944, aged 20 years.

I sat there sadly and looked at the words, and I read them over and over again, and still they didn't make sense.

Adrian Mallory . . . yes, perhaps, because I had been expecting it; but that didn't help the deep sorrow I felt at knowing that I would never see him or hear his familiar voice again.

But not Dorcas Mallory – never Dorcas Mallory!

How could I possibly be sitting here and reading my own epitaph, chiselled in marble more than fifteen years ago? How could I be lying down there in the dark under that mound of grass while here, above, a fitful sunlight played across my hands as they rested on my lap?

All these years . . . what had it been like to lie there in the dank cold? What did you look like down there, Dorcas Mallory? Was your flesh decomposed? Were your bones crumbled? Had that dark golden hair rotted yet from your grinning skull . . . ?

I was powerless against the gruesome horror that filled my mind. The chill, rank odour of that grave was in my nostrils and there was only a Stygian blackness before my eyes. I was dead and yet not buried. I was buried and yet still alive.

Madness was waiting for me, like a grave yawning at my feet. I shrank in shuddering terror from the hands reaching up to drag me down into that freezing darkness; I struggled frenziedly against the sudden weight on my shoulder which forced me ever deeper; I fought with an insane strength against that terrible pressure, screaming and screaming and not knowing it was my own voice I heard until the sound ceased with startling abruptness beneath the sharp, stinging slap across my cheek.

The blow cut the flesh. I could taste the blood in my mouth. When I looked up Charles was standing there before me, his hand upraised again. I made a feeble movement to ward off the blow. It was only then I realised that the weight I had felt on my shoulder was his other hand.

I mumbled, 'No – no, don't – no . . . ' and he lowered his arm uncertainly.

'Lisa,' he said, and I drew in my breath with a gasp of gratitude. I hadn't known how thankful I could be to hear myself addressed by that name.

I was trembling uncontrollably, but the world came back to me. I was no longer a mouldering corpse in a grave, an inhuman monstrosity that lived and went on breathing after death. I had life, an identity – a present, even if no past and an unenviable future.

I hadn't known, either, how pathetically pleased I could be to see this man who was Lisa Landry's husband. How reassuring could be the pressure of the hand still on my shoulder.

He looked strained and anxious. I had never seen him look as old as he looked now and I was strangely touched that he could be so concerned about me. There were beads of moisture on his face, and I realised for the first time that it was raining. Judging by the state of the ground, it must have been raining for quite a time. When I looked down at myself I saw that my suit was dark and discoloured with the wet.

I got stiffly to my feet, swaying unsteadily, but although he put out an arm to help me he didn't speak. He stood looking at me in an unnatural silence, and apart from its tautness and pallor his face was expressionless.

I moved uncomfortably beneath that blank, unflinching regard and the wetness of my clothes was cold against me. I shivered, restraining my teeth from chattering only with an effort.

Charles stood back, and as I turned to go down the path in front of him I couldn't resist one final, lingering glance at the grave. There was only a sadness left in me now. And I was glad that Charles hadn't questioned me about that hysterical madness. I didn't want to talk about it. It wasn't anything that I could expect a normal person to understand; apart from that I would have found great difficulty in talking to Charles about it.

The wet churchyard and the road were entirely deserted as the screeching gates clanged mournfully behind us. Charles's blue car was parked behind mine and when I would have gone towards my own he waved me almost imperiously towards his.

'Get in,' he said, and added tersely when I made a faint movement of protest, 'I'll arrange to have it picked up later. Get in.'

He slammed the door almost before I was seated and went round and got into the driving seat. It was the first time he had driven while I was with him but I wasn't sorry to relinquish the wheel. I was still trembling with shock and thankful to relax against the warm upholstery.

He drove off with a harsh grinding of gears, swerving violently round the cream and chromium car.

The afternoon had darkened dismally with the rain and some of the shop lights were on in the main street as we drove through. The coffee bar where I had sat with Russ was ablaze and cheerful in the gloom but I averted my eyes. I knew that I would never see it again, that I had no wish to.

I made another half-hearted protest as we passed the hotel.

'My bill...'

Charles said briefly, in a clipped, taut voice, 'I paid it.'

And then we were speeding up the long incline, and the town was behind us and Charles put his foot down on the accelerator and kept it there.

He didn't so much drive a car as fight it. He waged a constant, savage battle with the gears, with the wheel, with the brakes. At any other time I might have been nervous at the way he swung us blindly round corners at full speed or sent us hurtling through narrow lanes, but not now.

I was empty, drained.

And after a while I was cold. The wetness of my suit had penetrated to my skin. We ran out of the rain after the first hour but the clouds were lowering and grey and there was a cold dampness in the air. I didn't like to ask Charles to put the heater on, so I sat huddled in my seat. I clenched my teeth tightly together but even so they still chattered spasmodically; and in the heavy rush of sound as the big car charged into the gathering twilight I don't think Charles noticed.

I was disturbed by his silence. There was a strange quality in it which I couldn't define. He kept his eyes fixed unwaveringly on the road, and the lines of his face were set and hard and quite inscrutable.

It was a long time before I became aware that this tense rigidity contained an implacable, barely controlled anger. There was no outward sign of it but it was something I could sense, as if I vaguely remembered it. I had no concious recollection of having encountered this cold anger of his before. Yet something repellent about it was unpleasantly familiar to me.

One part of me would have liked to provoke the anger into the open but the rest of me – the greater part – was too numbed with cold and unhappiness to care.

As the darkness drew in and I could no longer see his face clearly, I began to think that perhaps the anger had already spent itself in his mind. He was driving with less violence, I thought, though that may have been due to tiredness after many hours at the wheel. He smoked almost incessantly. For what notice he took of me, he might have been alone in the car.

I think the journey would have ended that way, too, if we had not had to stop for petrol. He got out of the car while it was being filled up and walked stiffly around, and in the lights of the petrol station I saw that his face was still set and stern. There was a snack bar attached to the garage, its windows condensed with steam from the warm interior. I shivered in the cold damp air and thought longingly of hot coffee, but Charles collected his change and climbed back into the car.

I comforted myself with the reflection that we couldn't be more than forty or fifty miles from home now – and then realised with a distinct shock that that was the first time I had regarded Lisa Landry's house as home. The realisation gave me a moment of bewildered dismay, almost a feeling of betrayal.

I was suddenly aware that Charles had pulled up by the roadside. A car coming in the other direction illuminated us briefly in its headlights. I saw when it had passed that the trees were still outlined against the not quite dark sky.

Charles's voice was heavy with the suppressed anger I had sensed in him during the drive.

'Well,' he said, 'what did you find out?'

I was filled with a great weariness and had no wish to discuss it with him. Nor was there anything in his manner to invite my confidence. Yet I conceded that he had every right to question me.

I said slowly, 'I found out that Dorcas Mallory did exist – exactly as I had remembered her.'

When I didn't go on he said, with sharp impatience, 'Well?'

But it was a long time before I could say, 'Dorcas Mallory died more than fifteen years ago.'

He was so long in speaking that I thought he intended to say nothing more.

'Who told you?' he asked.

I had to steady my voice before I could say it. 'Russell Winslow.'

I could hear plainly his sharp intake of breath. The words came out in a violent little explosion. 'You saw Winslow?' He started to say something else, then checked, and I had the feeling that the question he asked wasn't the one he had originally intended. 'What did he tell you?'

'He said that she was killed in an air raid – a few hours before they were to have been married.' I kept my voice calm and toneless. 'Adrian Mallory – her father – was killed at the same time.'

'What else?'

'We – just talked, that's all. About – Dorcas.'

'He's married, isn't he?'

'Yes. He has two children.'

'What else did you talk about?'

I shook my head although he couldn't see me.

'Nothing,' I said.

'Did you tell him your name?'

'No – there was no point after – ' I realised suddenly which name he meant. I shook my head again. 'No – '

We sat in silence for a few minutes. Several cars passed in succession and I could see that some of the restrained violence had gone from his face. He looked thoughtful and rather uncertain.

I said quietly, 'You knew, didn't you?'

He turned partly to face me. His voice had softened as he said, 'Yes, I knew.'

'Why didn't you tell me?'

He didn't answer and I asked him again 'Why didn't you tell me?'

His varying moods bewildered me. But underlying a new

harshness in his voice I could still detect the softer note. 'I didn't think it would help you to know that the girl you imagined yourself to be had been dead for more than fifteen years.'

I shivered uncontrollably. 'But when I asked you, you said that you didn't know either Adrian or – '

'Adrian Mallory was my stepbrother and Dorcas was his adopted daughter. I denied it because I thought it would be easier for you to get over this obsession if you didn't know that such persons had actually existed. What made you go off like that to Alderford?'

'I saw the Darlton Hotel – I recognised it. I saw the names in the register. I *had* to go.'

'If you'd waited I would have told you.'

'Yes . . . ' I trailed off miserably into silence. I couldn't tell him that when I had seen those names in that book I had had no thought in my head but to find Russ.

Charles said, 'Are you satisfied now, Lisa? Or do you still have this wild idea about being – '

I broke in, unaccountably embarrassed to be talking about this with him, as though discussing some very intimate subject with a stranger. 'I – I know I'm not Dorcas Mallory,' I said. 'I know I can't be . . . I'm sorry, Charles. I don't know why . . . I don't understand how I . . . '

I'd never heard so much kindness in his voice before. It filled me with compunction to realise that I must have been a great source of worry to him lately.

'You mustn't worry about it. I suppose it can all be very simply explained away. You'd heard me talking about this girl. Her rather tragic death preyed on your sympathies at a time when you were under the strain of Joanna's impending wedding – the combination of the preparations for one wedding got confused in your mind with the tragedy which prevented the other from taking place – '

'Yes,' I said hurriedly. 'Yes . . . ' I didn't want him to go on talking about it. The kindly consideration in his voice disconcerted me. I was relieved when he started the car.

'Well, then – ' he said, and I could detect the same relief in him, too.

I felt so cold and wretched that all I wanted was the comfort of that warm bed in the blue-ceilinged room.

Dorcas Mallory was dead. She had never had a place in

my life. Nor would she have one now.

I had my own life. I was Lisa Landry, this man was my husband of twenty years' standing, Joanna was my daughter. And this was my home that we were approaching now, with the lights glowing welcomingly through the gloom. I would be grateful for these possessions and this life, with no more senseless hankering for an existence I had never really known. In time, once the power of that delusion had finally died away, I would find, if not happiness, at least the strength to accept what I was and where I belonged. I would live a fuller life than before. I would take full charge of the house instead of leaving everything on Miss Rose's hands. I would make friends and entertain more. I would be to Joanna the understanding mother that I felt I had never been in the past, and establish the relationship between Charles and myself on a firmer basis.

But most of all, I thought, as I climbed stiff and shivering from the car, most of all I would be grateful for the warmth and comfort of this house which was home.

6

But the mood didn't last.

I caught a bad chill as a result of the journey and was in bed for several days, aching in every limb, with Miss Rose in efficient charge. I couldn't have asked for a better nurse in that way. She was untiring in her attention, but I would gladly have exchanged almost all her impersonal efficiency for a few moments of personal sympathy. Even the cool touch of her hand on my burning forehead brought me no comfort, for none was intended; she was merely gauging the progress of the fever.

Long before I was up and about again I knew how useless had been my determination to follow where reason led. It had been easy that night, after a day of such tension and shock, to make those firm resolutions. But the mind is not so easily controlled.

Nor did it help that this time I wanted desperately, with an almost pitiful eagerness, to be Lisa Landry.

I tried to remember her life before that fateful August morning – any little detail, no matter how small. When I was well enough to sit up in bed I had Miss Rose bring all the photographs and snapshots she could find and I pored over them, striving to recollect some circumstance of how or when they were taken. Perhaps if I had had someone to help me, someone who could have urged my mind gently down the road of memory . . . But there was only Charles, and I had that same strange reluctance to confide in him. In any case I didn't see very much of him, although I was aware that he was around the house; and when he came to see me he showed no more than a casual concern for my condition.

Miss Rose might have helped me, had she been more human, but I couldn't confide in her either. I was aware that she thought some of my actions very strange but I didn't enlighten her in any way.

Joanna came to see me. They had only just returned from their honeymoon and it was the first time I had seen her since I had known she was my daughter. It was only my second day up and I still felt weak and shaken, but I was glad of her company.

At first.

This was my child, born of my body in the agony of birth. How could I not remember that moment, or the first time she was put into my arms? How could any woman forget the wonder of motherhood? Why didn't I love her now with a deep and protective love? How could she be as strange to me as everyone else – no more than a nice, quiet girl for whom I could have felt affection had I known her better?

Joanna could perhaps have helped me more than anyone, but I couldn't burden her with the hurt of knowing that her mother had no recollection of her apart from those brief hours of her wedding day. She was quite radiant with happiness. I could never have marred it for her.

Charles came while she was still there and, watching them together, I could tell that a stronger bond existed between them than the one which bound her to me. I wanted to feel sad about it; instead I was aware of frustration and I was glad when she went. She only deepened my despondency.

When I was well enough I took to my long, solitary walks again – too fretful even to attempt putting into practice those fine resolutions I had made. I couldn't have interested myself in anything or anyone except myself.

Because I was heartbroken for Russ. I had thought that the loss of him would be easier to bear now that I knew he lived outside my imagination, and in a way it was. But I was still desolate without him.

No matter how hard I tried – and for the sake of my sanity, God knows I tried – my mind and my heart were Dorcas Mallory. Only my body was Lisa Landry.

Yet all of me *had* to be Lisa Landry. I couldn't possibly be a girl I knew had lain mouldering in a grave all these years. There was a madness in the thought from which my mind swerved in revulsion.

And still my reason asked me how, if I was Lisa Landry, I could remember nothing of her life but every last detail of the twenty years of Dorcas Mallory's existence. Details that no one could have known about but Dorcas Mallory herself.

How could I know these things?

If I was Lisa Landry – and I *was* Lisa Landry – how could my mind be Dorcas Mallory's? How could a dead girl's hopes and sadness be transferred to me after all these years? What kind of unnatural creature was I to suffer the sorrows of this girl I had never even known?

I lost weight at an alarming rate and I couldn't sleep. Or it may be more truthful to say that I didn't dare to sleep because my waking thoughts were bad enough, but my unconscious mind travelled a road which horrified me.

I walked some days until I was exhausted, and still I was afraid to sleep. The weather had changed again and the autumn days were warm and sunny, but the weather meant nothing to me. I forsook the big cream car because my body craved endlessly to be on the move. I had to go on and on until sometimes there was barely strength left in me to take another step, and still the fear in my mind drove me pitilessly on.

I walked until darkness compelled me to return to the house – a house that I hated now with cold, deadly intensity. There were eyes everywhere in that house, watching me. Not just Charles and Miss Rose, or the rest of the staff who all eyed me strangely — but calculating derisive eyes which seemed to know everything that was in my mind. Whichever room I was in they were there, peering at me from the dark blue ceiling in the bedroom, slyly peeping from a cushion in a chair, prying from the midst of a bowl of chrysanthemums.

At last I suggested to Charles that I should see a doctor.

'I haven't been sleeping very well lately,' I excused myself.

'You've been off your sleeping tablets, that's why,' he said. 'You don't really need a doctor.'

'But I'd like to see one,' I insisted, with unwonted stubbornness.

'If you feel like that about it, I'll run up to town in a few days.'

'There's a doctor in the village — I could go to him.'

He said, 'No!' sharply. Adding, 'I don't care for you to go to him. Wait until next week.'

It was a few days later, when I was returning home through the village in the dusk, that I thought of the church. And once I had thought of it I couldn't imagine why it hadn't occurred to me earlier. The only life I could remember had not been a deeply religious one but Dorcas Mallory had always gone regularly to church. And though, to my knowledge, I had never been inside this one, I felt irresistibly drawn towards it.

I opened the gate and walked up the path, conscious for the first time of a measure of peace in my mind. There was a light inside and the door was partly open. As I reached it, it was flung wide and the vicar stood on the steps.

I had seen him on various occasions around the village. He was a middle-aged man, bald-headed and pink-cheeked, with eyes which held a kindly, if shrewd, benevolence. And I knew suddenly that I could talk to him, that he would understand my need, that he would take my problems and share them.

He peered at me through the dusk. I thought he seemed surprised to see me there. He hesitated, his hand still on the electric switch by the door.

'Did you wish to come into the church, Mrs. Landry?' he asked.

All at once I was filled with confusion.

'No,' I said, and then, 'Well – yes – although it was really you I wanted to see.'

He stood aside. 'Will you come in?'

I shook my head. 'No. I – perhaps I'll find it easier to talk to you here.'

I stood there, at a loss how to begin, and after a moment he said, 'You look tired, Mrs. Landry. Are you sure you won't come in and sit down. The church is open to everyone, you know.'

I gave a little nervous laugh. 'You'll think it very dreadful of me, but I've never thought of coming here before.'

'No, indeed, why should I?' He spoke politely but there was an undercurrent of that faint surprise which I had sensed earlier.

I hesitated uncertainly, conscious of my tiredness, of that momentary peace which was slipping away from me.

'I – I don't know how to start to tell you,' I faltered. 'I must talk to someone but – I don't know how to start . . . '

He said gently, 'I am entirely at your disposal, my dear lady, but would you not find it easier to talk to your own priest?'

I stared at him uncomprehendingly. 'My own priest . . . ?'

'The good Father McClelland, of course.'

'Father McClelland . . . ?' I repeated it after him stupidly and then I burst out, 'But I'm not a Catholic!'

'Not a very devout one, I fear,' he said, and I could see that he was smiling gently, 'but a Catholic – yes.'

'But I'm not – I'm not!' I said it fiercely, in vehement denial. 'I don't know anything about the Catholic religion – how could I be a Catholic and know nothing about their beliefs, their . . . '

He was looking at me with grave concern. He took my trembling hand in his and the touch steadied me.

'You're not well, Mrs. Landry. Let me get my car out and I'll drive you home.'

'No,' I said. 'No . . . ' I gathered myself together with an effort. 'You're very kind – thank you. I'll be all right.'

As I stumbled down the path I heard him saying, 'If I can be of any help to you, Mrs. Landry, I beg you not to hesitate to call on me . . . '

Charles was already having dinner when I went into the dining-room and slipped into my chair. Lately, he had taken to starting the meal without me, as I seldom returned to the house until night was approaching and he had grown tired of my unpunctuality. It didn't make much difference as I only made a pretence of eating these days and my plates were carried away almost untouched.

'The vicar at St. John's has told me that I am a Catholic,' I said. 'It isn't true, is it?'

He glanced up momentarily from his food. 'Yes – why not?'

'But I can't be,' I protested. 'I don't know anything about the Catholic faith.'

'Perhaps you don't go to church often enough.'

'Do you mean that I have attended a Catholic church?'

'Yes. Not very regularly. You've never been very keen to go often – only when Father McClelland hauls you over the coals for poor attendance.'

I shook my head in bewilderment. 'But how could I . . . ? Surely the service – everything would be different – strange . . .'

He shrugged his shoulders, bored with the subject. 'Anyway, you're Catholic – so am I, for that matter. And Joanna, too.'

I took the car the following day and drove over to the Church of St. Joseph's, but I didn't go in. I saw a priest whom I took to be Father McClelland but I didn't approach him. He looked a pleasant, peaceful man but I couldn't have talked to him. Not only the man, but his religion, was alien to me. I watched him wistfully as he stood chatting for a few moments to a woman who was passing, but I knew that if I had gone into the church I should have felt like an interloper. I started the car and drove slowly away, conscious of a sense of irreparable loss.

I reminded Charles several times about seeing a doctor in town but he always had some good excuse for not taking me, and I was too listless to make the effort on my own. The state of my mind, the lack of sleep, and my non-existent appetite combined to rob me of any initiative. I lived on cigarettes during the day, and cigarettes and whisky at night.

I looked dreadful.

My eyes were sunken and haggard and dark-ringed, my cheekbones stood out almost gauntly, and my hair was dull and limp. I no longer bothered about going to the hairdresser. Occasionally I gave myself a shampoo, but I didn't care about my appearance or my clothes. Any garments would do – the first I came across. Sometimes I remembered to dab some lipstick on my mouth, more often I forgot.

Miss Rose remonstrated several times with me, her mouth pursed in shocked disapproval. When I took no notice she got into the habit of coming into my room each morning and laying out a suitable outfit for me.

Joanna was also outspoken, but there was a perplexed dismay in her protests.

'You look ghastly, Lisa. If you're ill, why don't you see a doctor?'

'Your father is going to run me to town one day . . . It's only that I'm not sleeping well,' I excused myself.

'But you're letting yourself go completely,' she protested, with a bewildered candour. 'Just look at your clothes . . . You used to be so particular about your appearance.'

There was a genuine distress in her eyes and after that, when I knew she was coming, I made an effort. But she started running down quite often, and it *was* an effort to bother about how I dressed, and no matter how much trouble I took I could see that she was far from satisfied with my condition; so instead of waiting in the house for her, I began to make a habit of being absent when she was expected. That didn't stop her from worrying about me, as I knew from how frequently she rang up when she had arrived back at their flat in Chelsea, but it was easier on the phone to pretend that everything was all right.

I had a feeling that Charles guessed at least a part of it. He made no comment whatever on my dress or appearance although I was aware that he wasn't blind to either. He didn't leave the house much, or at least if he did during the day I wasn't there to see. But he was there every evening when I returned, and rarely went out afterwards. While I wandered fretfully about, smoking constantly and drinking almost as heavily, he would remain quiet, never protesting at my behaviour.

And after a while I began to realise that he was watching and waiting. It took me a long time to sense, behind his calm immobility, that this was so; to know that while his eyes were fixed on the television or on a book, or while playing an idle game of billiards with himself, always he was conscious of where I was and what I was doing.

I don't know how I knew this. For he never betrayed himself by an inadvertent glance, a hint of restlessness, the least expression that shouldn't have been there.

But watching and waiting – for what?

I was only vaguely disquieted at first, and inclined to dismiss it from my mind. But after a few nights of this quiet surveillance I found that the idea of it irritated me. And once it began preying on my mind it wasn't long before I became so agitated that I couldn't bear to be in the same room with him.

Why did he watch me, and what did he wait for? Wasn't it enough that the house had eyes everywhere spying on me?

I was petulantly annoyed and then furiously angry – and then confused and terrified.

I started going straight to bed when I came in, without even a pretence of eating dinner, and lying there in the dark so that the eyes in the blue ceiling couldn't see me. Miss Rose, or sometimes Charles, would bring a bowl of soup and I would manage to get it down rather than argue about it; but once I was alone again I would switch out the light and lie smoking in the darkened room until Charles came to bed.

I was too frightened to analyse my thoughts. My only defence against them was to let my mind linger on Russ – on every remembered intonation of his voice, each fleeting expression on his face, the kindness and humour of his eyes, the peace and security of his arm.

And presently the tears would come – welling up helplessly in my eyes, running down my cheeks and neck until the pillows were wet with them.

I would cry until my body was too weak for further effort and a sleepless exhaustion claimed me.

I was going mad. And I knew it.

It was one of those exceptionally mild days in November when the sun has still a surprising warmth, and only the bareness of the trees and a slight haziness obscuring the distant hills proclaims that it isn't still September.

The path through the wood was thickly strewn with

leaves that rustled and crackled underfoot after the long spell of dry weather. The sunlight made intricate patterns of the bare branches on the leafy carpet.

I had been walking since soon after breakfast but I wasn't aware of any tiredness. I knew that in another hour or so the sun would be sinking to its early setting. The warmth was already going and the shadows lengthening as I followed the path out of the wood. It would be dark before I reached home but I wasn't concerned about that. There was more friendliness in the darkness of the countryside than I would find within the prying walls of the house. I wasn't in any hurry to get back to my lonely vigil in the blue-ceilinged room. I wasn't in any hurry to go anywhere.

A few brown hens were pecking around the back door of a small farmhouse, and through a low window I could see the warm glow of a fire. A fat, healthy-looking sow came grunting over the top of her pen at me, soliciting shamelessly for food, and I stopped and spoke absently to her.

I heard the child scream as I stood there. There was something about the sound that disturbed my apathy. It wasn't a loud scream, more thin and high, and if I hadn't stopped to look at the sow I might not have heard it. As it was I hesitated, and saw a woman hurrying out of the house.

I decided that there was no reason for me to hang around, the child wasn't alone, the woman would take care of it.

I had gone some little way when I heard the woman running and calling behind me.

She looked pale and anxious. 'Will you get the doctor? It's Jimmy – my little boy – he's fallen out of the loft. He's unconscious – he looks real bad . . . I saw you go past – I haven't anyone else to send and I can't leave him. My husband is over to the market at Hardleigh and won't be back for a couple of hours yet – '

I broke in, 'Where does the doctor live?'

'Oh, in Chadwell St. John. It's Dr. Broderick – he's the nearest – '

'But that's four or five miles away. Does anyone round here have a telephone?'

'There's a public one at the crossroads, about a mile from here. If you follow the cart-track down to the main road . . . Please ask him to hurry – Jimmy looks real bad . . . '

I was breathless from running down the uneven cart-track before I reached the road, but I kept on running. The woman had called it the main road, but it wasn't a very busy one. I'd gone about a quarter of a mile along it before I heard a car behind me, and I stood deliberately in its path, just in case the driver decided to ignore my signal.

It wasn't a very new-looking vehicle. I was hoping it had good brakes because it was uncomfortably close before any attempt was made to use them.

'That's a damned silly thing to do,' the driver remarked as he wound his window down. It was a calm, matter-of-fact statement, uttered quite dispassionately, as though the foibles and idiosyncrasies of other people had long since ceased to surprise him. I didn't notice anything else about him at that time except that he had a cleft chin, and I don't like cleft chins.

I managed to gasp out, 'Will you give me a lift – to the telephone box. It's very urgent – '

He said, 'Get in,' and had the door open before I had run round to the other side. I flopped into the seat, gulping air into my lungs, too breathless to do more than utter a brief, 'Thank you.'

He drove quickly and carefully, with a sure precision which I felt would characterise all his actions. As I got my breath back I had time to observe him more closely, and to note the firm mouth and jaw. There was a little white scar on the cheek nearest to me, reaching almost into the corner of his mouth. He was hatless and his hair was thick and brown, just a medium colour, neither dark nor light. His whole demeanour denoted a quiet, purposeful man, even to the strong, square hands which handled the wheel so capably. He looked to be about forty but I'm not very good at guessing ages even if sufficiently interested, which I wasn't. It was some attribute in his voice that had arrested my attention in the first place – a quietness that told of absolute confidence.

I hadn't fully recovered my breath before he drew up opposite the phone box at the crossroads and leaned across me to open the door.

I said 'Thank you.' In the act of getting out of the car I suddenly remembered. I turned back to him in some embarrassment. 'I'm so sorry – could you lend me fourpence? I – I haven't any money on me, I'm afraid, and this call is very urgent. There's been an accident and –'

He cut in, his voice curt, the words clipped off short. 'Is anyone hurt?'

'Yes – a little boy. He needs a doctor –'

He said coldly, slowly, 'What the devil are you playing at, Mrs. Landry? Who *is* the child?'

'I don't know. His name is Jimmy, I think – I ' I began.

'Foster?'

'I don't know,' I said again. I made a vague motion in the direction from which we had come. 'A little farm back there – the child fell out of a loft. His mother asked me to ring –'

'Get in,' he said. There was cold contempt in the words. I obeyed blindly. There was something in his tone which compelled implicit obedience.

I did protest feebly as he reversed the car on the crossroads, 'He needs a doctor...'

'I'm Broderick, as you very well know, Mrs. Landry,' he said bitingly.

I subsided into silence. There was something in his voice that discouraged all attempts at explanation. He didn't speak again until we were approaching the entrance to the farm.

'This is the Foster's place. Is this where the child is?'

I said, 'Yes,' and he turned the car and bumped us unceremoniously up the rutted track.

When we reached the house he got out without a word or glance in my direction. The woman came to the entrance of the outbuilding.

'He's in here, doctor,' she called. 'I didn't like to move him with not knowing –'

'Good girl,' I heard him say before he disappeared from sight.

After a few minutes I got out of the car and wandered over to the building. The sun had nearly gone now and the interior of the small barn was barely discernible. I hesitated, uncertain whether there was anything further I could do to help.

Dr. Broderick said, without turning his head, 'Get out of the doorway. You're blocking the light.'

The words were spoken automatically, impersonally, his mind totally absorbed with the figure of the child I could dimly see on the floor; but I moved quickly to obey him.

As my eyes accustomed themselves to the gloom I watched the practised movement of his hands, the certainty and the gentleness of them. The same gentleness was in his voice as he addressed the child's mother, reassuring more by its tone than the actual words. I had never heard such a soothing quality in a voice before; it fascinated me and held me against my will. So much so that I felt no resentment at the change in it when presently he spoke to me. He was abrupt, peremptory even. I didn't ever remember having met him before, but I knew I must have. And I knew he didn't like me.

'You can drive, can't you, Mrs. Landry? Think you can manage my car? Then get back to the phone box and ring up for an ambulance.'

Mrs. Foster broke in with a little stifled exclamation of dismay. He spoke to her as he had spoken to me, without once taking his attention from the child. But the tone of his voice was different.

'You mustn't worry, Mrs. Foster. It's only a precautionary measure. Jimmy's got a broken leg as you know, and maybe concussion; but it's wisest to have an X-ray and make sure there's nothing more than that, internally. You still there, Mrs. Landry?'

I said humbly, 'I don't know where to ring for an ambulance.'

He grunted and scribbled a number hastily on a piece of paper. As I went out I hoped I would be able to make it out. I could, but only just.

It was almost dark by the time I got back. Through the open door of the outbuilding I could see the glow of a hurricane lamp and an occasional elongated shadow as someone moved across its beam; but I didn't go in. I waited in the car until the ambulance arrived and then I slipped quietly away down the path towards the stream.

It was completely dark by then and it would have been easier to have gone home by the long journey down the cart-track and the main road, but some perverse instinct made me choose the shorter, more difficult route.

Dr. Broderick would have been sure to have overtaken me on the main road, and if he didn't like me I had no wish to put him in the position of having to offer me a lift.

It was childish reasoning and by the time I got back to the house I had almost forgotten him and the whole episode. Nearly a week went by before I was in that locality again and I'm afraid I had never given another thought to little Jimmy Foster; but once I was in the vicinity, I remembered and I had the impulse to see how the child was faring.

I had gone about a hundred yards up the cart-track when I saw the car coming down it towards me. There wasn't anywhere I could turn off so I stood and waited, drawing to one side so that he could pass me.

I looked up as the car drew abreast and said, 'Good morning'.

He answered me immediately, although I had a distinct feeling that if I had not spoken first, he would have said nothing. He was practically past me before he stopped the car and leaned across to unwind the nearest window. I thought I could detect a faint surprise in him, a puzzlement which sounded in his voice.

'Are you going to see Jimmy?'

I had no idea why, but there was a shyness troubling me. I was so astonished by the strangeness of this that for a moment I couldn't speak; and as I struggled for words I could see the momentary friendship he had offered being summarily withdrawn. He was already moving away from the window as though he regretted the impulse that had driven him to stop; as though he had anticipated a rebuff from me.

'I was wondering how he's getting on,' I said at last. 'Is he at home?'

The withdrawal was partially arrested. There was a forced cheerfulness in his voice which I didn't think had anything to do with Jimmy's condition.

'Oh, he's doing nicely. Been home a few days now. No broken skull as I was afraid there might have been. But go to see him for yourself. Mrs. Foster will be glad of the opportunity to thank you for what you did.'

I shook my head shyly. 'No – no, I won't bother, now you've told me about him.'

I could see now what I hadn't noticed the other day – that his eyes, which had seemed blue, held tints of green and brown, a contradictory combination of critical coolness and friendly warmth which confused me.

I said suddenly, 'I honestly didn't know who you were, the other day.'

I was as surprised as he was by the words because I had no intention of saying them. It was as if something had forced them out. But I was glad I had said them.

He smiled – a sudden, spontaneous smile and the scar on his cheek pulled one side of his mouth up a little farther than the other in an infectious, lopsided grin.

'I thought you were acting damned peculiar,' he remarked candidly, and I smiled back at him, strangely warmed by his friendliness.

'Where did you disappear to the other night?' he asked. 'I would have given you a lift home.'

'I'm used to walking,' I said.

'But it was dark. I expected to find you waiting in the car when I came out.'

For some curious reason the fact that he had given me a second thought pleased me immeasurably.

'It didn't matter,' I murmured awkwardly. 'You were busy . . .'

'Well, let me give you a lift now, if you won't go up to see Mrs. Foster.'

'I'm not really going anywhere,' I said.

'Nonsense! We're all going somewhere, even if we're not sure where. Come on, get in.'

I got in because, strangely enough, I wanted to.

He offered me his cigarette case. I knew that he noticed my heavily nicotine-stained fingers as I took one and, unexpectedly, I was ashamed of my appearance. I could see a ladder running down the side of my nylons. I didn't think it had been there when I put them on earlier, but in any case I probably wouldn't have bothered to change. The varnish was chipped from my nails and my hair needed shampooing and I couldn't remember putting on lipstick before I set out.

There was nothing much wrong with my tweed suit and woollen sweater, but that was thanks to Miss Rose and not to my fastidiousness.

I crossed my legs to hide the run in my stockings and I concealed my hands as best I could. And I knew I didn't deceive Dr. Broderick.

He made no attempt to start the car after he had held a

light to our cigarettes. He just sat smoking in a companionable silence and after a minute I found myself relaxing, too, and the tension going from me. I knew that unobtrusively he was observing me and I was not embarrassed by this, nor did I resent it.

He could be brusque to the point of rudeness, yet he was the most restful person I had ever encountered. I wondered why I had never liked cleft chins. On the right people they could be most attractive, I found.

It was pleasantly warm in the interior of that rather shabby car. There was none of the luxurious comforts or gadgets of the cream American car but it was stolid and comfortable in a friendly sort of way.

'Now,' he said finally, as he threw the cigarette butt out of the window, 'I'm going off to see an old lady over at Chadwell Heights. You know it? It's about five miles from here. If you're not going anywhere in particular, what about coming with me?'

I knew suddenly that I wanted to go. Those last ten minutes in the car with him had been the most peaceful I had known for several weeks. I was reluctant to end it.

'If – if I wouldn't be in the way?'

'Why should you be? There's some very pretty scenery at the Heights – although I suppose you know the place well enough? Anyway, you can come in and have a look at the old lady. She's a bit of a tartar – probably try to marry you off to me, but you mustn't mind what she says.'

I said, 'Oh, aren't you – ' and stopped, colouring in confusion.

'Aren't I what?' he asked. 'Married? No, not now.'

I murmured something about being sorry and he raised one eyebrow higher than the other.

'You're sorry? For what, pray? Why should *you* apologise?'

'I meant – for prying into your affairs,' I explained awkwardly.

'Oh, good Lord,' Dr. Broderick said, 'it's no secret. I should think it's very common knowledge – I'm sure all my patients know, at any rate, that I divorced my wife a number of years ago. And don't, for Heaven's sake, say you're sorry about it – '

'I wasn't going to,' I interrupted, with the beginnings of indignation.

'Well, you looked as though you were,' he said calmly.

I ventured, prompted by his own complete frankness, 'You don't sound as though it's something you regretted very much?'

He gave me a sharp, enigmatic glance from the corner of his eyes. Before he answered he turned the ignition key and pressed the starter. The car sprang into life with a loud splutter.

Then, 'That's where you're wrong,' he said. 'As a matter of fact, at one time it was a very big trouble to me. Still could be, too, if I let myself dwell on it; but it all happened many years ago. No sense in making yourself miserable over something you can't alter. I'm not sure now that I would alter anything, even if I could. Probably it was all for the best. Only just at the time you can never see it like that.'

'What went wrong?' I asked the question tentatively, although I was quite certain that he wouldn't resent my curiosity. Rather I had a feeling that he was, perhaps, deliberately inviting it.

He said airily, 'What went wrong? Oh, Lord, what didn't go wrong? To start with, we were too much in love. So much so that we just hadn't the sense to see that what we should have done was to go to bed together a few times and get it out of our systems. But no, we had to have everything all pure and idyllic and "till death us do part". So we got married and we were too young, and too poor, and too intolerant – and too everything that mattered to make a go of it. In the end it was neither pure nor idyllic – and we hadn't the time to wait "till death us do part". We took matters into our own hands and hastened the parting – or perhaps it would be more correct to say that my wife did. She ran off with a very rich and very elderly – and I'm sure very tolerant – American.' He gave me a quick glance again. 'I feel confident, Mrs. Landry, that you are about to say you're sorry again. Well, don't!'

'I wasn't – really,' I protested, not very truthfully.

'Of course you were! Well, are you coming with me or not?'

'I'd like to,' I said, and it was true.

He flipped the car into gear and released the handbrake. As we started moving I automatically got my cigarette case out of my pocket and opened it. Before I had a chance to offer it to him he reached over and took the case from me, snapping it shut decisively.

'You don't need another cigarette. You've just had one,' he said, and there was a note in his voice which brooked no argument. As he slipped the case back into my pocket he added, 'It's nothing but a damned silly habit. You can control it, if you want to.'

For a moment I tried to feel indignant but I couldn't manage it. Because he was right. I didn't really need another one yet. I put the lighter meekly away, too.

As he turned the car into the main road Dr. Broderick went on, 'On a morning like this, you know, I always feel that a G.P.'s life is a pretty wonderful one – especially with a country practice like mine. It's only when I'm called out in the middle of a cold winter night that I realise how bloody grim it can be.'

'Do you enjoy your work?'

'Who's talking about work? I'm thinking about all those poor devils cooped up during the day in some stinking office, and here am I, driving around these lovely country lanes on a fresh, sunny morning, with a very pretty woman by my side.'

To my astonishment, I heard myself say quite facetiously, 'You pay a very nice compliment, Dr. Broderick.'

'Yes, don't I?' he grinned. He went on, more seriously, 'You're a very surprising person, Mrs. Landry.'

'Am I?' I was slightly startled by the sudden change in his mood. 'In what way?'

'Oh – ' He gave a vague motion with his hand. 'You're not at all what I thought you would be.'

I didn't speak and after a moment he continued, 'After all these years during which we've never exchanged anything but the coldest civilities whenever our paths have crossed, I find it very hard to believe that you're the cold, disdainful woman I've so heartily detested and despised.'

His frankness shook me. I stammered, 'Detested and despised – '

'Oh, most thoroughly,' he assured me with a certain grimness. 'You were the very essence of everything I disliked most – your cold snobbery, your self-sufficiency, your disdainful aloofness. You weren't a human being, Mrs. Landry – you were a hard, uncaring, unfeeling machine. But you're not like that at all – and you make me wonder if you ever were. I rather pride myself on being able to sum people up pretty accurately but either you've changed drastically or I never made a bigger mistake over anyone in my life.'

I said in weak anger, 'You've no right to talk to me like this.'

'Oh, rubbish!' he said. 'What do you want to do – get out and walk because I've told you a few unpleasant home truths? Don't be so childish, my good girl. In any case, I can be a damned sight more unpleasant than that if I want to make the effort. I wasn't really trying then.' He changed gear preparatory to descending a steep hill before he said, 'I could hardly credit my own eyes last week when I saw the stately, superior Mrs. Landry breathless from running for help for a grubby little boy she didn't even know.'

'The child was hurt,' I said defensively.

'I know, but I hardly expected the haughty Mrs. Landry to put herself out on that account. Rather I would have expected her to ring graciously for a servant to deal with the matter.'

I said witheringly, 'In the middle of nowhere – in an isolated spot like the Foster's farm? You overrate the degree of luxury and efficiency in which you imagine I exist, Dr. Broderick.'

'Now, that's more like it – that scathing contempt, that icy scorn, that elevation of yourself to a superior level – '

'No!' I said suddenly. 'No – I'm not really like that – am I?'

He lifted his shoulders in a little questioning movement.

'I don't know, my dear girl – I don't know. And frankly speaking, from a personal point of view, I don't care. We don't live in the same world, Mrs. Landry, and it doesn't matter a damn to me what you are or what you do. Speaking from a professional point of view, I'll admit to you that I was trying to see if I could make you angry.'

'You were?' I said. 'Why?'

We were on a stretch of straight road, climbing up towards the Heights, and he risked taking his eyes from the road for a second to look fully at me. I couldn't read anything from his face. Apart from a certain gravity there was nothing in it but the impersonal scrutiny that belonged to his vocation. He let another car overtake him before he spoke.

'Still speaking from a professional point of view,' he said, 'I would strongly advise you to pay a visit to your doctor in the very near future.'

I didn't answer him until we had reached the row of cottages that nestled in a hollow underneath the final ascent to the Heights. He drew the car to a stop on the green in front of the last one in the row and was in the act of getting out when I said quietly, 'You're a doctor.'

He reached over into the back and lifted out his bag.

'But not yours, Mrs. Landry. I attend only to the lower members of your household.'

He said it quite without rancour, and I was positive none was intended.

'But you could be mine,' I insisted.

He inclined his head. 'I could, yes. But I would advise you to see your own man, one who knows and understands you.' He shut the door and leaned down through the window to ask, 'Are you coming in, Mrs. Landry?'

'No.' I shook my head. 'No – I'd rather not.'

'As you wish. I may be a little while in here. You've time to climb up to the Heights if you feel like it. The view is well worth the scramble if you haven't seen it before.'

I waited until he had disappeared into the cottage before I got out and started up the path that wound its way up behind the row of houses. I had been there before and I wasn't particularly interested in the view. It was the old restlessness that drove me on once I found myself alone, away from the calming influence of his presence.

I was panting by the time I got to the top and sank on to a small outcrop of rock. I got my cigarette case out with a certain amount of defiance and watched the blue smoke drift lazily away on the still air.

The view was a magnificent one even in the distant haze of the November morning. The sun caught and sparkled on the river as it wound its leisurely way far below. Bare of leaves, the wooded hillside had a stark beauty, and the fields still held practically the fresh greenness of midsummer.

I was sitting there, lost to time, when I heard the footsteps behind me and turned to see Dr. Broderick clambering over the uneven ground. I jumped up in quick remorse.

'Oh, I'm sorry – I've kept you waiting,' I said hurriedly, but he waved me back on to my rock.

'There's no hurry,' he said. 'I guessed you'd be up here. I often come up myself when I'm out this way.'

He sank on to the rock next to me. I noticed that he was not in the least exerted by the rather stiff climb. His breath came evenly.

And, strangely, I felt a return of that calmness. I sat there quietly with him, waiting. I had the feeling that he was waiting, too – serenely patient.

But it was a long time before I spoke. He hadn't invited my confidence – rather he seemed to have gone out of his way, a little earlier, to reject it. He might not like me but I felt that he would listen, and that he would have an understanding I could never expect from Charles.

And so I said at last, 'I think I'm losing my reason, Dr. Broderick.'

He gave me no more than a casual glance.

'And what makes you think that?' he asked calmly. 'As a rule, a person who is becoming mentally unhinged is the very last to suspect anything is wrong.'

'But I can't remember who I am,' I said, wretchedly. 'I know that I must be Lisa Landry, and that Charles is my husband and Joanna my daughter – but I don't know them. I don't know anyone with whom I come in contact – the servants, our neighbours – I didn't know *you* the other day – '

'Just a minute, Mrs. Landry,' he broke in gently. 'Loss of memory is a very common occurrence. There are many factors that can contribute to its cause. You mustn't worry that you're losing your reason because you're suffering from a temporary amnesia – '

'But it's more than that. Don't you see? I *have* a memory – but it isn't the right one.'

'What do you mean by that?'

I asked him then the question I had wanted to ask the vicar, that man of God. The question I had been too afraid to ask myself in the darkness of the unsleeping night.

I asked it unflinchingly, out of the stillness which had descended suddenly upon us.

'Do you believe, Dr. Broderick, that the soul of a girl

who has been dead nearly sixteen years could inhabit and take possession of a complete stranger?'

7

THERE was a bird singing in a tree near at hand. I couldn't see it but the high, sweet notes of its song held a plaintive, appealing sadness. The faint whirring of some distant machinery reached us clearly, a dull monotonous sound. When Dr. Broderick moved his foot suddenly I jumped nervously.

He had sat quietly, not looking at me, his face quite inscrutable so that I had no means of knowing what he was thinking. When he spoke at last he sounded oddly helpless in his hesitation.

'My dear girl – I don't profess to know anything about the spiritual body – only the physical one. A clergyman would be better equipped than I am to answer such a question. But tell me why you ask it?'

I took a deep breath and faced him fully.

'Because that's what I think has happened to me. If it hasn't – then I know I am mad.' I gave a little mirthless laugh. 'Take your choice, Dr. Broderick, which would you rather be if you were me – possessed or insane?'

'What makes you think you are either?'

'There's nothing else I can think – when the only life I know is that of a girl who has been dead more than fifteen years.'

I took the cigarette he offered, drawing at it raggedly. I gave him a quick, nervous glance but he wasn't looking at me. He was gazing out across the wooded stretch beneath us. I knew that he was waiting for me to go on but wouldn't hurry me, that his calmness didn't mean that he was disinterested.

I started to tell him about Dorcas Mallory. I began with abrupt, sometimes not quite coherent sentences, but presently beneath the soothing influence of his quiet attention I went on more fluently.

I told him about her adoption when she as a child – no more than three years old – so that there was no memory of a previous life before that with the Mallorys. There was only a vague recollection, too, of the new mother who had died not much more than a year later. But the memory of the life with Adrian Mallory was clear. I told him of her childhood in the house, High Towers – a lonely childhood, perhaps, but a happy one, with dear old Henrietta and the kindly Mrs. Bakewell. I told him of small, uninteresting incidents that only Dorcas Mallory could have known; those trivial, every day occurrences that meant nothing to anyone other than the person they happened to. I evoked memories of old Henrietta who probably hadn't been as old as she seemed at that time to the young Dorcas – of her warm motherliness and her fragrance of lavender; of Adrian Mallory, his shyness and his gentle kindness, and as I talked about him I think I realised for the first time that I would never see him again – that perhaps I had never known him, for how could I have done so? I know that I talked of him with a sadness that went deep inside me.

I recalled Dorcas Mallory's schooldays – rather lonely schooldays with not many close friends because the reserve that was in Adrian Mallory was in Dorcas, too. But she had not particularly felt the loneliness and the holidays had been happy ones – spent mostly at home, at first because of her father's reluctance to travel and then because the war made travelling impracticable.

When I told him about Russ I found it difficult to speak impersonally. There was so much that I couldn't put into words, not even to someone as understanding as Dr. Broderick. How could I possibly describe to anyone the love between Russell Winslow and Dorcas Mallory? My voice broke when I finally told him of the wedding that never took place, of the journey to London of Dorcas and Adrian Mallory, of the happiness of that girl on the eve of her marriage.

I sat silent at last, my head bent, watching the slight breeze lazily stirring a curled brown leaf at my feet. It rustled faintly as it moved, and then a sharper breath of wind caught it and hurried it away.

Dr. Broderick said gently, 'What then?'

I looked up, somehow startled that he had been unable to

follow the wistful trend of my mind. 'What then?' I repeated, and then, keeping my voice as steady and expressionless as I could, 'Dorcas and her father were killed in an air raid. There was no wedding. They both died that night.'

'This girl you have been telling me about – she is the one . . . ?' He paused uncertainly. I think his logical mind found it difficult to put my fantastic supposition into words. I waited to see if he would continue.

When he didn't, I said, 'I woke up on the day of Joanna's wedding thinking that it was *my* wedding day. I didn't know where I was, or why, but the events I have been telling you about – that evening in London – were so clear to me that I thought it was still April, 1944. I took up Dorcas Mallory's life exactly at the point where she died.' He stirred slightly as though he would have interrupted but I went on, 'I can't tell you a single thing about Lisa Landry's life prior to that morning in August, but I can tell you all about Dorcas Mallory. I can tell you of these things that no one – not even Charles – could have told me. I am Lisa Landry – but my mind is Dorcas Mallory.'

He said, 'Charles – your husband?'

'Yes.'

'Why do you say – that even Charles could not have told you? How could he know anything at all – '

'Charles and Adrian Mallory were stepbrothers,' I said. 'I – Dorcas never saw him until a few weeks before – before she died. He spent most of his time in Canada.'

'Did *you* know this girl?'

'No.'

'But you probably heard your husband talk about her?'

'He never really knew her.' I said it defensively, but against what I wasn't quite sure. 'I told you – Dorcas never met him until a few weeks before she was killed. And then she barely knew him – they only met a very few times. Charles couldn't possibly know all the things I have told you about her.'

'He could know a good deal of it,' he said gently. 'And some of the things . . . Are you quite sure that you *know* these things, or could you have imagined them?'

'No!' I said it with a sense of outrage. 'No one could possibly *imagine* everything I know about Dorcas Mallory

– every detail of her life – every incident, day by day. And Russ ...'

'The man Dorcas was to marry?'

'Yes – I knew him immediately I saw him. How could I have recognised a man *I* have never met?' I asked it almost triumphantly.

'You've met this man? Recently? Since – August, was it?'

'I saw the names in the register at the Darlton Hotel – where Dorcas and her father stayed that last night. Until then I thought that they couldn't have existed outside my imagination. But when I saw the names there I went back to Alderford to find my fa – to find Adrian Mallory and Russ. I saw Russ. I knew him, although no one could have ever described him to me. Charles never met him. But I *knew* him – I would have known him anywhere. And when we talked – there were things we talked about that only he and Dorcas could have known. No one else. Charles could *not* have told me.' I said it with passionate intensity.

'Did you recall these incidents or did this man mention them first?'

'Both.'

'Did you tell him that you thought you were this girl?'

'No.'

'Why not, when you made the journey expressly for that purpose?'

'I didn't know then that Dorcas Mallory was dead. Or that ...'

'Or that – what?'

'That Russ was married,' I finished tonelessly.

'If he had not been married, would you have told him?'

'I don't know. I don't think so. No, how could I possibly tell him? The girl he knew and loved was dead – I think it would trouble him greatly to think that – that ...'

'Her spirit haunted you?'

'Well – yes.'

He gave me quick glance.

'Why should it do so, do you suppose?'

'I don't know. Unless it was because she was killed on the eve of her wedding. And she was so terribly happy at the prospect of that wedding that her – spirit – couldn't bear the termination of all her hopes and dreams.'

'But in that case, why wait until now? The girl was killed

more than fifteen years ago. Surely if her spirit had been so unhappy about her tragic death it would have done something about it before – '

I broke in with a sudden bitterness. 'I believe you think it's all a great joke, don't you? That I *want* to believe that girl is haunting me? You make me sound like some glib charlatan who's trying to stuff you up with a lot of phoney talk about the hereafter and restless, wandering souls in purgatory – '

'On the contrary, my dear girl,' he said calmly, and I couldn't doubt him, 'I would be the last one to make a mockery of an afterlife, or what happens to our souls once our bodies have died. I'm not a deeply religious man but I don't gibe at what I don't fully understand. I told you at the beginning that the vicar would be better qualified than I am – '

'Do you think I'm insane?' I asked it bluntly.

'I think you've been living in a damnable private little hell of your own during these last few months,' he said quietly. I didn't realise until afterwards how neatly he had evaded a direct answer.

He was silent for several minutes, then he said, speaking more to himself than to me, I think, 'You know, Mrs. Landry, the human mind is a very curious thing. At a time of stress it has been known to completely reject any memory that was unacceptable to it.'

'You mean I don't remember because I don't want to remember?'

'Partly that, perhaps. Although that doesn't seem to be the full answer in your case.' He asked suddenly 'How old are you, Mrs. Landry?'

'Forty,' I said, reluctantly.

'And your daughter is – what? Eighteen? And she's young, pretty – and in love.'

I waited, with the beginning of an antagonism in me.

After a minute he turned and looked fully at me. 'What are you searching for, Mrs. Landry? What is there lacking in your life?'

I said, 'I don't know what you mean.'

'I think you do.' He said it thoughtfully, almost as though it were a question. 'What sort of childhood did you have? No, of course, you don't remember your own childhood, do you? Then your marriage? Would you call your married life a satisfactory one?'

'I don't know,' I said miserably. 'I can't remember anything at all about my own life prior to Joanna's wedding.'

'Well, since then? Apart from this trouble with your memory, would you say that you and your husband lead a normal, happy life?'

For some strange reason I felt the colour flooding slowly into my face.

I said, mumbling slightly, 'No.'

'Is it because of this loss of memory of yours, do you think? Or do you have the impression that any trouble there may be between you goes back before last August?'

I moved restlessly. 'What connection can there possibly be between my – relationship with Charles and – and this other . . . ?'

He gave the slightest shrug of his shoulders. 'Who knows, Mrs. Landry?'

I asked uncertainly, 'What are you trying to say?'

He told me slowly, as though weighing each word carefully before he uttered it. 'I think perhaps that for many years you have been searching for something, and your search has finally culminated in this desire to be this girl, to be deeply in love and loved in return. To be young again.' When I would have interrupted he stopped me with an abrupt wave of his hand. 'You have seen your daughter – she had the youth and happiness that were slipping elusively away from you. You may even have had an unconscious jealousy – '

'If it was as simple as that, how could I know so much about Dorcas Mallory?' I asked passionately. 'How could I immediately recognise Russ, know exactly where the house was, how the town looked?'

'You could have been there. Your husband would be next of kin to his stepbrother. He would probably be the one who had to see to everything after Adrian Mallory died – there would be the will and the property. He may have had to spend some time in the town to deal with everything – it's very likely that you were with him. That you even attended the funeral of this girl.'

I cried out in horror. 'No – *no!*' I scrambled to my feet, my mind darkening with revulsion.

Dr. Broderick caught my hand and drew me steadily back to my seat on the rock. Reluctantly, under the reassuring pressure of his fingers, I sat down again; and after a minute he released my hand.

'There's no need for you to be so upset,' he said.

I said, as quietly as I could, 'I don't think I have been to the town before. If I had – if I had attended the funeral, I would have been certain to have met Russ. When I saw him a few weeks ago I was a complete stranger to him.'

I hadn't realised how revealing my last words would be to him. But I couldn't mistake the quick gleam of compassion in his eyes. It was gone almost at once but I could sense a kindness in him, and kindness was something I needed more than anything else just then.

'You're in love with him, aren't you?' he asked.

I tried to control my trembling lip as I mumbled, 'You must think me an utter fool.'

'No,' he said, and he said it again, thoughtfully, as though he had made a discovery he couldn't quite credit. 'No.' He added, 'But it's a long time ago, Mrs. Landry.'

'Not to me,' I said. 'When I woke up on Joanna's wedding day, I thought that it was *my* wedding day. It's as recent as that. I thought it was April, 1944 and that I had woken in my hotel bedroom in London. Everything was unfamiliar to me – the bedroom, the house, the servants – even my own face.' I added, with a touch of bitterness I couldn't quite suppress, 'Have you any idea what it is like, Dr. Broderick, to look in a mirror and see a stranger? And to go on seeing that stranger, day after day?'

'You knew how this girl looked – although you had never seen her to your knowledge?'

'I *know* that Dorcas Mallory never met me,' I said. 'Even if the Lisa Landry part of me could have forgotten a meeting, the Dorcas Mallory part of me would know of it. But I knew her features as well as I knew every thought she had.'

'You could be mistaken. You could only be imagining the girl's appearance...'

'No. I couldn't be mistaken, even if Russ hadn't confirmed it all for me.'

'You'd really like to be this other girl, wouldn't you?'

'Yes.'

'Even though she's dead?'

'She was happy while she was alive. That's the important thing,' I said. 'And she was a nicer person than I am, Dr. Broderick. What you said to me earlier this morning – it was probably all quite true. It's all exactly what I thought when I first saw my own face and didn't recognise it – all the coldness and the disdain and hardness...'

'It's easy, perhaps, to be nice when one's happy,' he remarked.

'But I don't really feel cold or hard – or disdainful. I must have been all of those things, and more; but that isn't how I feel, not inside me. Under other circumstances...'

'Under other circumstances I should think you could be quite a nice person yourself, Lisa Landry.' He glanced at his watch for the first time. 'I'd rather like to meet your husband and have a talk with him about all this.'

I shook my head doubtfully, and he went on, 'I want to know a little more about your background – things that you can't remember for yourself. Nothing for you to worry about. Just your general health, whether you've ever had anything like this loss of memory on a previous occasion. That is, of course, if you want me to carry on with the case? I'm not quite clear whether you were consulting me as a physician or because I seem to have a good broad shoulder to cry on?'

I was still wondering about that myself, long after he drove me back to Chadwell St. John and dropped me off in the middle of the village.

It was only midday, an unusual time for me to be anywhere near home; but I walked straight back to the house. I was conscious of a strange sense of comfort in me, a lightening of a burden that had become almost unbearable. I could even enjoy walking through the lovely, twisting country lanes, with the warmth of the sun on the back of my head and neck.

The mood was still with me as I went into the house and for once its walls didn't seem to close around me. Charles wasn't at home but I allowed a surprised Miss Rose to persuade me to eat some lunch. Afterwards I took my coffee out on to the sunny terrace. In the act of lighting my second cigarette after the meal I flung it resolutely from me and watched it roll out of sight down the steps of the terrace.

'It's nothing but a damned silly habit. You can control it if you want to,' I said out loud.

I spent the entire afternoon washing my hair, manicuring my nails, trimming my eyebrows; aware, suddenly, of a feminine pleasure in the tasks. I kept my cigarettes to a minimum, and the bottle of whisky that awaited my nightly vigil I emptied scornfully down the hand-basin.

As I did so I realised how implicitly I had put my faith in Dr. Broderick.

Shortly after darkness fell I heard Charles return home but I didn't see him until dinner time. I was in my bath when he came upstairs to change and while I dressed I could hear him splashing gustily under the shower in his own bathroom.

I put on one of the new dresses I had ordered in London – a straight fitting heavy silk in an unusual shade of green. I was amazed to notice how emaciated I had become. I went over to the dressing-table and looked in astonishment at my sunken cheeks and dark-ringed eyes. The thin gold ring that I had tried so futilely to pull off on that fateful August day now slipped easily up and down my finger.

I was already in the grey-carpeted room with the bright chairs when Charles came down. I thought he looked surprised to see me – he probably was – and even more so when I refused the Martini he held out towards me.

I was honest enough to admit to myself that I would have liked the drink, that I was even beginning to need it, badly.

'It's only a damned silly habit, too,' I told myself. 'You can control it.'

I didn't feel quite as confident as I should have done, though. I thought it quite probable that it was easier for Dr. Broderick to say it than it was for me to do it.

It wasn't until the meal was practically over that I broached the subject of Dr. Broderick. We didn't talk much – hardly at all. I thought Charles inclined to be morose and moody. Perhaps he had been like that for some time now, but I had been too preoccupied with myself to notice.

He couldn't, after all, be having a very happy family life, himself. At one time, everything must have been very different between us. Could there be a regret in him, a yearning – did he really care as little as he seemed to, or was it merely a façade to hide a deeper hurt?

Was it even possible that some day – when I was cured of this obsession to be someone else – there could be an understanding between us – a comradeship, if nothing more? When I became truly Lisa Landry again, and Russ no longer had the power to torment me with longing, would I welcome a closer unity with this man who was my husband?

Charles spoke suddenly, breaking across my doubtful surmisings. 'What have you been doing to your hair lately?'

Automatically I put my hand up to touch it. It felt soft and smooth from the recent shampoo.

'It's newly washed,' I said.

Charles said, with a marked dryness, 'Yes, I can see that. It's quite noticeable these days when you take the trouble to have a shampoo.' He spooned sugar thickly into his coffee, looking at me thoughtfully while he stirred it. 'I meant the colour. It's lighter than it used to be. You used to have colour rinses when you went regularly to the hairdresser. What was it – henna, or something? Anyway, I liked it better that way.'

I walked across to the mirror and had a look at myself. I hadn't noticed before, probably because my hair hadn't been too clean, but it was definitely lighter in tone. There was practically no hint of chestnut about it now, only a russet gold – a warm golden brown which was not unattractive. But, looking at myself critically, I had to admit that the softer style in which I had set it didn't really suit me – it was too youthful, more appropriate on a young girl than a woman of forty.

'Start having the rinses again. I liked it better when it was a darker shade,' Charles said. I couldn't agree with him but it wasn't worth disputing. The colour of my hair wasn't important but perhaps Charles's interest in me could be, in the future.

As I went back to my chair I said casually, 'I saw Dr. Broderick today.'

Charles looked up sharply. 'Broderick? You mean from the village?'

I nodded. 'Yes. He – '

'You went to see him? After I had expressly told you that I didn't wish you to consult a local man?' There was a harshness in his tone that disconcerted me.

'I met him quite by accident,' I said defensively. 'I wouldn't have gone to him deliberately but when – '

'And what did you tell Dr. Broderick?'

I found a strange apprehension growing in me. I crumbled the remnants of a dinner roll uselessly between my fingers, irritated and yet disturbed by an unreasonable nervousness.

I said in a low voice, not looking at him, 'I told him about my loss of memory – about not knowing who I am or – '

'More to the point, what did Broderick say to you?'

'Not very much. He – he'd like to see you, Charles – he wants to know more about my background – about things, I suppose, that I can't remember. He suggested calling in tomorrow to see you, if it would be convenient for you.' I added in a conciliatory tone, 'He seemed anxious to help me – very understanding...'

I looked up appealingly as I spoke, eager for his co-operation and approval. I was dismayed and bewildered to see the signs of gathering fury in him. His face was already dark with displeasure, his eyes cold with suppressed anger.

'I told you distinctly not to see a local doctor,' he said, with barely controlled violence. 'I'll have no gossiping G.P. meddling in my affairs. Pushing his snivelling, prying nose – '

'Dr. Broderick isn't like that,' I protested, and he cut in, almost snarling at me.

'They're all alike in these country practices – tittle-tattling from one cottage to the next. I've met your precious Broderick – he's no different from the rest. Apart from that my dear Lisa, it's very evident that your memory is sadly at fault or you would remember that when I give an order I expect it to be carried out.'

I said, 'I'm sorry you're displeased, Charles. Honestly, it was quite accidental, the way I met him. And now that I have – '

'Now that you have, that's the end of it. I don't want to hear any more about your precious Broderick and I absolutely forbid you to consult him again. Do I make myself clear?'

I shivered a little. It was only my imagination, of course,

that found menace in his words. The dark mottling was leaving his face but I could sense, as I had sensed once before, the intense violence that still smouldered in him. But my newfound confidence had roused a rebelliousness in me that was not to be so easily intimidated.

I tried to speak quietly, to remain unflustered.

'Charles, I must have help. I can't go on like this. Dr. Broderick said he would phone in the morning to find out when it would be most convenient – '

'I'll save him the trouble,' Charles said grimly. 'I'll phone him tonight and tell him you don't need his services.'

I could feel a sudden hatred welling up in me. I got up and walked out of the room on legs that trembled. I hated him passionately in that moment for his egotistical inhumanity.

I was swept by a bitter sense of injustice, but presently when I had calmed down a little I determined that no matter what Charles said, I should not obey him. I knew deep inside me that Dr. Broderick could help me, that nothing Charles could say or do was going to prevent my seeking that help. I vowed it solemnly to myself.

But I was wrong. I hadn't known how wrong I could be.

I smoked a cigarette until I felt calm enough to confront him with my decision, and then I went downstairs. I was prepared for his displeasure, his anger, his violence – for anything, I thought.

But I wasn't really prepared for anything at all.

The lounge door was slightly ajar and I could hear the faint murmur of Charles's voice even before I reached it. I frowned a little as I pushed the door farther open to see who the visitor was, unwilling to have to postpone my showdown with Charles. But there was no visitor. Charles was on the telephone at the other end of the room, his back towards me, his fingers beating an irritable little tattoo on the table by his side.

He didn't see me and I wouldn't have stayed to listen to his conversation if I hadn't immediately realised that he was talking to Dr. Broderick. About me.

He wasn't speaking loudly but the words reached me distinctly, punctuated only by brief interruptions from the other end.

' – realised she intended consulting you or I would have

prevented it. Nothing personal, you understand, but I have already had my wife under the best medical attention that the country can offer. Mrs. Landry doesn't remember, of course – no, nothing they can do . . . Her mother suffered from the same kind of hallucinations – died in a mental home, hopelessly insane . . . Yes, a great trouble to me – oh, some long-sounding, fancy name . . . Yes, that's probably it – sounds like it. You realise this is quite confidential – yes, of course. No, I don't think there's any point in my telling you which specialist . . . Nothing further you can do, Broderick. Yes, I understand – very good of you but it won't be necessary. If you'll let me have your bill – oh, well, please yourself, of course. By the way, as I said, Mrs. Landry has no recollection of having been examined previously – if she should attempt to get in touch with you again I can rely on you not . . . Yes, felt sure I could. Sorry you've been troubled about this, Broderick. Yes – '

I was still standing there frozen to the spot when he put the receiver down and turned round and saw me.

I don't know what I expected from him. Compassion, kindness, regret, a sympathetic understanding . . .

I was really too confused and shocked to expect anything. Certainly I hadn't anticipated anger in him, but it was there. He was still controlling it, as he had done previously, but the effort made his voice unsteady.

'What the devil do you mean by listening to a private conversation of mine? How long have you been there?'

I shook my head in stunned bewilderment. 'It's true, isn't it?' I asked helplessly.

Charles gave a sharp bark of angry laughter. 'How much did you hear?'

'About my mother – about the specialists I've been to . . . ' I faltered into silence. My eye caught the brandy bottle in the well-equipped cabinet. I had to have a drink – no matter what Dr. Broderick said about damned silly habits. I had to have a drink.

I managed to force my legs to take me across the room and I poured the brandy with a shaking hand. Some of it splashed down the front of the green dress but what went down the inside of my throat helped to keep the gibbering horror at bay.

The glass made a sharp tinkling crash as I put it down on the cabinet.

'It's true, isn't it?' I said again.

If I had hoped he would prevaricate a little, offer me even the slightest loophole of doubt, I was doomed to disappointment. He was brutally frank, with a malignancy, I thought, born of the intense anger in him.

'Yes, every word of it,' he said. 'Your mother was a raving lunatic – crazy as hell let loose. And you'll end up the same way. Provided, of course,' he added viciously, as my hand strayed in hopeless horror towards the brandy bottle, 'that you don't drink yourself to death in the meantime.'

I hadn't really intended to go against his wishes but I couldn't sit in the house and wait for raving madness to overtake me.

For a few days I did. Despite all my own suspicions of the past weeks, their confirmation shattered me. My only comfort was the brandy bottle and I hoped that the gibe Charles had flung at me would come true.

I certainly did all I could to bring it about. And in the end the brandy did help me, but in a roundabout way.

For those first few days I hardly stirred out of my bed. I smoked and drank incessantly, but although most of the time I was far from sober, I was also far from being drunk. I never once lost sight of why I was drinking – that terrifying fact seemed to leer at me from the bottom of every glass I drained.

The only person I spoke to was Miss Rose, and that was only to refuse curtly the food she tried to press on me or to demand another bottle of brandy, which she would reluctantly produce.

I think she knew of the gruesome skeleton in my cupboard, or at least she had some inkling of it. Perhaps Charles had warned her that she was dealing with a potential maniac. I neither knew nor cared so long as she kept me supplied with my only two necessities.

Charles I didn't speak to at all – nor he to me. He dressed and undressed in his dressing-room, using the bedroom only for sleeping.

I knew he hated me. The vicious hatred had been there

in his voice when he had spat the truth at me with such indecent cruelty. It *could* only have been hatred that prompted him.

But I didn't waste much time thinking about his feelings. I had enough problems of my own – and Joanna was one of them. I refused to speak to her on the phone or even to see her when she came to the house; but I was greatly perturbed to realise the possible danger to her of a mental illness that was hereditary. She was my daughter, however much I failed to recognise her as such; even had she been a stranger, it would have horrified me to know that I had been instrumental, however innocently, in inflicting this sickness upon her.

If this was the reason why Charles hated me, then I couldn't blame him because I could hate myself.

She was hard to dissuade from her purpose of seeing me. One morning I heard her arguing with Miss Rose actually outside the bedroom door; but I knew Miss Rose would never let her pass, to see me in my present state.

The brandy gave out on the fourth day – or it could have been the fifth; I was far from sure.

Miss Rose told me firmly. I thought there was a satisfaction in her voice. 'You've drunk it all, Mrs. Landry. There isn't a drop left in the house.'

'Well, bring a bottle of whisky up, then,' I said petulantly.

'You've finished that, too. There's an order in for delivery tomorrow, but until then ... '

'Ring them up and tell them to bring the stuff today.'

'I hardly like to interfere, Mrs. Landry. As you know, Mr. Landry always sees to the liquor order personally – '

'Oh, for Heaven's sake . . . ' I pushed the bedclothes peevishly away. 'I'll go down into the village myself and get some.'

'Really, Mrs. Landry – do you think you should . . . ?' Her grey, expressionless face for once registered a vague consternation. Poor woman, she probably didn't know which was best – or worst: to have me wandering up and down the countryside all day long, or stewing in drink in my own bed.

I took the car, because walking no longer appealed to me. After the constant warmth of my bedroom I shivered until the heater warmed the car, but the cold cleared my head a little. I was quite capable of driving the car. I only scraped the wings twice as I manoeuvred out of the garage and once as I misjudged the gateway, but otherwise it was quite an uneventful drive.

I tried the Royal Oak first. The outer door was closed but I didn't let that deter me. I went in and banged loudly until the landlord came, but he wouldn't sell me anything. He told me firmly, repeatedly and finally, and I believe, with disgust, that it was out of hours, and when I couldn't move him I slammed out in a blaze of temper.

It was only about two hundred yards down the main street to the off-licence shop and I drew up in front of it with a squeal of brakes that would have done justice to Charles's driving. The small grocery department was busy and I waited impatiently to be served, shivering slightly again in the unheated shop.

When my turn came the proprietor was as adamant, if more apologetic, than mine host of the Royal Oak had been. The sight of that tantalising array of bottles on the shelves infuriated me beyond reason. I argued heatedly with him for a few minutes until I sensed that my abuse was only stiffening his resistance. He looked uncomfortably hot and distressed, far more conscious than I was of the wide-eyed, interested customers behind me who were eagerly listening to every word. I terminated the argument suddenly by leaning round one end of the counter, extracting a bottle of whisky from the shelf and slamming a five-pound note down on the counter with the other hand.

The little group of people parted to let me though. As I went out I caught a few odd murmurings from their midst. The word 'drunk' seemed to occur oftener than any other.

The proprietor followed me out, the five-pound note clutched in his hand. I got into the car but I couldn't shut the door because he held it firmly ajar.

'Really, Mrs. Landry – I must demand – '

'You've been paid for the thing,' I said irritably.

'That's not the point. The law says – '

'It's ridiculous!' I exclaimed. 'To have the stuff there and not to be able to sell it because the clock may say five minutes to the hour instead of five past.'

'I don't make the laws, Mrs. Landry. And I insist that you – '

'Oh, go boil an egg!' I said furiously. 'All this fuss . . . Are you going to let go of that door?'

'Not until you give me back my bottle of whisky.'

'It's not your whisky! I paid you for it – and paid you more than it's worth!'

He threw the money on to the seat of the car.

'There's your money, Mrs. Landry. I refuse to accept payment for it and I'll be very much obliged to you if you'll hand my property back to me . . . '

I don't know where the argument would have gone from there. Certainly I was wild enough to have driven off with him still clinging to the door. But at that point Dr. Broderick pushed his way through the little crowd that had gathered.

I think he thought there had been an accident, or someone had fainted – clearly he hadn't expected to be confronted with a rather crude dispute over a bottle of whisky.

I sat sullenly while my opponent indignantly explained the situation to him.

When he had finished, Dr. Broderick said calmly, 'Give me the whisky, Mrs. Landry,' and held out his hand.

I started to say angrily, 'I shall do no such thing,' and then suddenly, beneath the compelling force of those eyes, I meekly handed the bottle to him.

I heard him saying quietly as he passed it on to the rightful owner, 'Mrs. Landry has not been very well lately. She has been taking whisky under my orders.'

No one was deceived, of course, but he'd done his best, and the man said, 'If she'd said it was medicinal . . . ' half proffering the ill-fated bottle in my direction; but by that time I wouldn't have touched his damned whisky. I sat there with my head haughtily averted, although a little uneasy feeling in the pit of my stomach warned me that I would undoubtedly regret this arrogance by the middle of a dry evening.

Dr. Broderick said, 'Move over,' as he bent to get into the driving seat.

'I'm perfectly capable of driving,' I said icily, resisting the pressure as he pushed himself behind the wheel.

'I don't doubt you are,' he said, very plesantly, 'but

I've always had a fancy to see how it felt to manipulate one of these monsters. This is as good an occasion as any. Give me elbow room, Mrs. Landry – I've no wish to put us through the first shop window I see.'

I moved over, but he didn't drive far before he pulled up in front of a rather shabby, red brick house situated off one corner of the green.

It was badly in need of painting and the gate leading up the path to the front entrance was broken, but strangely enough you didn't get the feeling that the shabbiness was due either to neglect or indifference. There was a solid, comforting warmth about the building that rather gave you the impression that you had dropped in unexpectedly on a close friend and found her unconcernedly wearing an old, much used, but well liked dress.

When Dr. Broderick led me inside I saw that the interior was the same and I looked about me with unashamed interest.

The central hall was square, with doors opening from either side and a rather fine oak staircase leading the way to the floor above. The red Turkey carpeting was well worn, almost threadbare, but it was warm and cheerful, as was the room he led me into on the right of the hall.

It was quite low-ceilinged – a pleasant and comfortable room, with a huge fire blazing in the grate, and deep leather chairs. It may all have been shabby and much used, but there was a well polished air of cleanliness about everything. The carpet in here was Turkey red, too, and the furnishings oak – ordinary and unimaginative, but there was an air of homeliness that appealed deeply to me. I liked it all, from the gleaming copperware that stood on the narrow shelf running round the room, to the large ginger cat curled up on the cretonne window seat.

'That's Solomon,' Dr. Broderick informed me, pushing me gently in the direction of a chair by the fire. 'You may not have noticed, but there is a preponderance of ginger kittens in every litter that's born in Chadwell St. John.'

He went back and called out into the hall, 'Mrs. Hale – are you there, Mrs. Hale?'

There was a low rumble from the depths of the house and presently Mrs. Hale appeared. From the deep resonance of her voice I had expected a big, well-made woman, but apart from her huge matronly bosom she was small, slight in build, with quick, birdlike movements and the keenly penetrating eye of a bird, too.

She eyed me with unabashed interest and I knew that no detail of my appearance escaped her attention. I was quite willing to believe that she could calculate to a nicety exactly how many drinks I had had that day.

She didn't exactly sniff at the end of her inspection, but no sniff could have been more eloquent than her expression. Dr. Broderick stood and watched her with a quiet amusement in his face. He was evidently accustomed to these critical examinations of hers.

'This is Mrs. Hale,' he said at last, 'who rules me with a rod of iron and without whom I should be for ever lost and damned. She guided my first faltering footsteps and still does so, even though she tramples a little on my toes in the doing. Do you know Mrs. Landry, Haley, my love?'

'I've seen her around the village,' Mrs. Hale said uncompromisingly, and I gathered that she hadn't formed a very good impression of me in so doing. 'You'll be wanting your tea, Mr. Hugh?'

'That's right,' said Dr. Broderick, 'only we'll have coffee instead.'

'Coffee? At this time of day?'

'Coffee at this time of day, if you please,' he said firmly. 'Strong and black – and plenty of it.'

She gave me a look that told me she well knew whom to blame for this heathenish innovation – and why. And her expression implied that she knew my type. She'd met it before.

When she'd gone out, Dr. Broderick pulled a chair up to the fire and sat down opposite me.

'You mustn't mind old Haley,' he said. 'In self-defence she had to build up this impression of grimness when I was a child and I don't think she dare relax it now. She still lives in hope that her reputation will come in handy if she ever has to deal with any offspring of mine. Not that she ever managed to hoodwink me into being afraid of her.'

The big ginger cat abandoned his place on the window seat and leapt on to his lap, purring ecstatically as Dr. Broderick affectionately rubbed behind his ears.

'Now,' he said, 'what was that lot all about?'

I knew what he meant, although I had been hoping that he wouldn't make any further reference to it.

'I wanted a drink,' I said, still a little sullenly.

Dr. Broderick said dryly, 'I gathered that. Surely it wasn't so urgent that you had to make a scene over it in public?'

I flushed slightly. 'It all seemed so silly,' I began.

'What? The fact that you couldn't buy a drink exactly when you wanted one – or the fact that you couldn't wait?'

'It's easy enough for you to criticise,' I burst out. 'What do *you* know about the reasons why some people try to find forgetfulness – '

'Oh, for Christ's sake,' he said impatiently, 'stop wallowing in so much drunken self-pity.'

I was too furious to think whether the remark was justified or not. I was still trying helplessly to splutter out a retort when Mrs. Hale came in with the coffee. She put the tray down on a small table between us with just sufficient vehemence to mark her silent disapproval.

Dr. Broderick waited until she had gone before he raised a quizzical eyebrow and said, 'The best service, I see. Mrs. Hale may not like you but she's certainly trying to impress you. Would you care to pour out?'

'Thank you, no. I don't want anything to drink,' I said stiffly. I got to my feet with as much dignity as I could muster. 'I think I'd better be going.'

He didn't even trouble to look up as he poured out the coffee with a steady hand.

'Sit down, you stupid woman,' he said casually, 'and drink that. And when you're sobered up – stay sober!'

'You – you – ignorant *doctor*!' I managed to stutter. I stood glaring at him, enraged by his calm amusement, determined to go; and after a minute I sat down weakly in my chair. He seemed completely indifferent to whether I stayed or went; and I didn't even know myself why I didn't go.

I took the proffered coffee meekly.

'You've got no right to be so offensive,' I protested half-heartedly.

'Of course I have! What are you trying to do to yourself, Mrs. Landry?'

'I don't know what you mean.'

'Don't be idiotic! You know what I mean, all right.' He

passed a battered packet of cigarettes to me and held a light, regarding me enigmatically through the smoke. He flicked the match into the fire before he went on. 'Have you ever seen an alcoholic, Mrs. Landry?'

'I don't – I suppose so, yes ...'

'I doubt it. I very much doubt it. I don't mean someone who's just the worse for a few drinks – or even someone completely but temporarily blotto. I mean an out and out alcoholic.' He drew deeply on his cigarette, watching the lazy spiral of smoke as it drifted towards the ceiling. 'It's not a pretty sight. It is, in fact, about the most pitiful, depraved condition to which the human body can sink. If you're thinking of it as a pleasanter fate than the two alternatives you mentioned the other day –'

'It doesn't make a third alternative,' I said quietly.

He gave me a quick glance. 'Oh?'

I said, in the same expressionless voice, 'I know that I'm going insane, Dr. Broderick.'

'You sound quite convinced. Might I ask what makes you so sure?'

'I happened to overhear my husband talking to you on the telephone the other night,' I said.

He looked at me for a long time without speaking, his face quite impassive. A log settled down deeper into the heart of the fire with a little flurry of sparks, and continued to crackle cheerfully. The glow of the flames was bright and warming in the gathering dusk.

'In that case,' he said at length, 'You'll know that your husband doesn't wish you to consult me professionally.'

I nodded. 'There wouldn't be any point in it, anyway, would there? I'm sorry I took up so much of your time – I didn't know that I had already seen another doctor ... a specialist ...'

'Do you mind telling me whom you went to? It would be a London man, I suppose?'

I said apologetically, 'I'm sorry – I don't know. I don't remember going, you see ...'

'No, I realise that. I just thought that perhaps your husband had mentioned his name to you. Could you find out, do you think?' He asked it with an off-handed air, his mind and hands obviously occupied with refilling my cup.

'I'm not sure,' I said. 'I should have to ask Charles ...

Why do you want to know?'

He gave the slightest of shrugs as he stirred sugar into his own cup.

'Oh – just idle curiosity,' he said. 'A professional interest – it isn't important.'

His casual air chilled me a little although I didn't know why it should. I sat looking into the fire, thinking how strange it was that this man who could so easily provoke me to anger could yet bring me the only peace I knew. Despite the anger, despite the sudden chill, I had known a warmth in this room that had nothing to do with the fire or the scalding coffee I had drunk. He could be brusque or rude, or infuriating – but he could still give me comfort and a measure of strength. I wasn't even sure whether I liked him very much, but somehow that seemed less important.

I didn't know why but he suddenly reminded me so forcibly of Russ that I felt a quick pang of longing return with the memory.

I couldn't imagine any woman in her right senses ever leaving a man like Hugh Broderick, and I wondered what type of girl it was he had married who could so easily have done so. There were no photographs of her about the room but I noticed a large framed portrait of an elderly couple.

'My mother and father,' Dr. Broderick said, when he saw me looking at it, but I had already guessed from the likeness between the elderly man and himself.

The rest of the photographs were of a young man in uniform, a rugger team, and a small boy in a sailor suit who was unmistakably the doctor himself at a tender age, and another of two boys in their teens, the younger once more being Dr. Broderick, I thought.

He confirmed it a moment later. 'That's my older brother, David,' he said, nodding to it, and also to the one of the young man in uniform. 'He was killed in Normandy.' He pointed to another photograph behind me that I hadn't seen. 'That's Sarah, his wife – or rather, his widow – and the two children. They're both much older than that now, of course. The girl's still at school and the boy started medical school this year.'

'He's going to be a doctor, like you?'

'Like me, like his father, like his grandfather. The medical profession is inclined to be an infectious disease in a family, you know. Even Valerie – the girl – has strong inclinations that way, but I don't know . . . I'm rather hoping it'll be a passing fancy and she'll grow out of it.'

'Don't you believe in careers for women?' I asked curiously.

'Oh, by all means . . . No, the reason's only a financial one . . . ' There was a slight diffidence beneath the lightness of his tone. 'Although I suppose if she's still keen in another two or three years, the means will be found somehow. She deserves the best – she's a good kid. They both are, for that matter.'

'You sound very fond of them.'

'They're my family,' he said lightly, and I thought I understood the reason for the shabbiness of the house and car, for the poverty that had helped to break up his marriage.

'Do they live with you?' I asked.

'No, Sarah has a small flat at Hampstead Heath. She works now, you see. She couldn't at first, of course, when the children were young, but they're both away from home most of the time and she finds it easier to be near her work. They'll be here for Christmas, though. Drop in and meet them – you'll like them. Sarah's a grand girl – one of the best.'

I murmured confusedly about not being sure of my plans for Christmas and he said easily: 'Well, please yourself. The invitation is an open one. We shan't be doing anything very exciting, but you might enjoy yourself. You never know.'

'Why are you so kind to me?' I asked.

He looked startled. 'Kind? Good God, I didn't know I was being particularly kind. I'd ask any stray animal in out of the cold.'

'Is that how you see me – as a stray animal?'

'I think you've been lost for a long time, Lisa Landry,' he said. 'It's time someone took you in and offered you a saucer of milk.'

'I thought you didn't like me? Last time we met you told me that you detested and despised me – that I was cold and snobbish, self-sufficient – an unfeeling machine . . . '

'I also told you that I was beginning to believe I'd never made a bigger mistake over anyone in my life.'

'Today you called me a stupid woman – you said I wallowed in self-pity ... '

'What a one you are for harping on your grievances. I hope you remember the advice I gave you as well as you remember the insults.'

'What advice?'

'There you are, you see. I knew you'd only dwell on the rude remarks. I told you, my dear girl, to sober up, and keep sober.'

'Oh – that,' I said lamely.

'Yes, that!' he said. 'And while you're about it, start eating a few square meals each day. Solid food is better than a bottle of whisky any day.'

'I haven't got any whisky,' I said. 'You made me give it back.'

'What does your husband say about this drinking of yours? Doesn't he give you a clip over the ear every time he sees you reaching for the bottle?' he asked grimly.

I said evasively, 'Charles is usually away from home most of the day.'

'What about your daughter?'

'I don't see Joanna if I can help it. Although I don't believe we have ever been very close, I think it would trouble her ... I don't want her to see me like this.'

'Not even if she could help you? She might have a steadying influence on you.'

'I don't want her to see me like this,' I persisted. 'She's young – impressionable ... I wouldn't want her ever to see what she might become herself, some day.'

He sat looking at me for a long time in silence. I thought he seemed undecided, almost confused, as though he found difficulty in marshalling his thoughts. But there was neither confusion nor indecision in his voice when he spoke at last. Only a quiet conviction that I couldn't attempt to doubt.

'I don't think you need worry about Joanna inheriting any mental irregularity from yourself, Mrs. Landry. I've seen your daughter – spoken to her on several occasions. She's a nice girl – as stable and sensible as they come. It would be difficult to find a more normal, level-headed girl, or to discover even a trace of insanity in her make-up.'

He got to his feet suddenly, pushing the ginger cat on to the floor to an accompaniment of protesting mews.

'And now I'm sorry, Mrs. Landry, but I'm afraid I shall have to go, as I've still one or two calls to make. I've had a bit of engine trouble with the car and was on my way to pick it up from the garage when I ran into your little – contretemps.' He was smiling as he said it, robbing the words of any implied reproach, and suddenly I smiled, too.

'You were very brave to associate yourself with me, before all those people,' I said. 'I haven't thanked you for doing it.'

'I didn't think you *felt* thankful towards me for it. In fact, you looked most ungrateful at the time.'

'I'm not now, at any rate. Nor for the coffee.' At the door I turned and held out my hand. 'May I come again if I promise that tea will be all that's required?'

'Yes, do,' he said. 'Any time you feel like it. Don't wait until Christmas.'

I couldn't see his face, which was thrown into shadow by the lighted hallway behind him, but the warmth and confidence his handshake gave me remained long after I reached home.

8

But much though I wanted to, I didn't go again.

A whole week went by during which I had to struggle against presuming on what could only have been his kindness to a 'stray animal'. It seemed an eternity of frustration, and a needless one at that, because I kept telling myself that his answer to my self invitation had been spontaneous and genuine. If he hadn't wanted me to go he could have been evasive or half-hearted, or even, being Dr. Broderick, downright rude.

And that wasn't the only battle I waged. I tried desperately hard to take myself in hand.

I started going out for long walks again and exercising the chestnut mare regularly each day in an effort to confine the drinking to the evenings only. But the shortening days drove me in earlier and made the evenings longer and drearier. Under Charles's cynical eye I forced down a little food at dinner time, and watched some of the shorter items on the television. But eventually I would find it impossible to sit still any longer, and after wandering aimlessly round the house for a while I usually ended up in the ornate cocktail bar, perched on a high red leather stool, drinking whisky with a morose disgust.

At least I managed to cut down the amount I consumed. A little. But there was no one to help me – to encourage, or bully, or enrage me into a stiffer resistance.

I hadn't known how thankful I could be when at the end of that week I answered the telephone and heard Hugh Broderick's voice.

I had just come in, tired and dispirited, cold and wet with the depressing drizzle that had set in as darkness fell; but suddenly the tiredness vanished.

I said, senselessly, 'Oh – it's you, Dr. Broderick . . .'

'I thought you were coming to see me,' he said. 'I've been expecting you to tea each day this last week.'

I said shyly, 'I wasn't sure you meant it. Whether you –'

'I always mean what I say. You should know that by now.'

'I wanted to come,' I said simply.

'What have you been doing with yourself?'

I gave a rather shaky laugh. 'Trying very hard to do a lot of things – and not achieving very much, I'm afraid.'

'My dear girl, what are you expecting – an overnight miracle? Anyway, what I want to know is, are you interested in good music? I've had two tickets given me for a concert in Hardleigh tomorrow night and I wondered if you'd care to use one of them? The pianist isn't a world famous celebrity but the concerto is the Rachmaninov Number Two, so it should be rather good, I'm thinking. How do you feel about it?'

I said, stammering with pleasure, 'Oh – I'd love it. Yes, I – I . . .'

'That's O.K., then,' he said calmly. 'Would you like me to pick you up or do you think your car is more reliable than mine?'

'I'll call for you,' I said hurriedly. I didn't intend Charles to know I was going out with Dr. Broderick. He had only forbidden me to see him professionally but somehow I couldn't imagine him approving of my associating with him at all.

I hung up and went upstairs to change my wet clothes with a pleasant glow of anticipation.

I didn't have more than three drinks the whole evening.

In the morning I had a good brisk canter on the chestnut mare but I spent the entire afternoon trying to erase the ravages of the past few weeks from my face.

I had never, to my knowledge, spent as much time over my appearance and toilet as I did for that evening. I would have liked to have worn one of the very smart cocktail dresses that were hanging in the wardrobes, but I didn't think it would be a dressy sort of evening so in the end I compromised with a very plain black suit with a blue mink stole for warmth. I left the black suit bare except for a diamond and pearl clip in the lapel, and the matching stud ear-rings; and for the very first time I used the perfume I had rejected so forcibly on that day in August.

When I pulled up outside the shabby house I was suddenly nervous – afraid that the evening would not be a success, that somehow I would manage to spoil it. I sat in the car for several minutes, anxious and undecided, before I finally tooted twice on the horn.

He came out almost immediately. I could see Mrs. Hale in the background of the lighted doorway and caught one or two of the words he called back to her over his shoulder as he came down the path; and then, with his casual greeting, my nervousness was all gone.

I didn't remember a lot of the evening very clearly, except as an oasis of peace in which for a time I was neither Dorcas Mallory who was dead nor Lisa Landry who was going crazy.

I was just a woman enjoying an evening out with a pleasant companion.

I know we didn't talk much during the drive, and certainly not during the concert. Hugh Broderick sat as enthralled as I was.

And yet I knew it wasn't the music alone that held me, that had power to give me temporary release from the chaos of my mind. That, as I had realised before, had more to do with the compelling strength of the man by my side.

When we came out of the concert hall the night was still

and cold, with a raw dampness in the air. I shivered and pulled the stole more closely around my shoulders and Dr. Broderick said, 'Let's go in here and have a cup of coffee. It will warm you for the ride back.'

We were opposite an Espresso coffee bar, bright with lights and gleaming chromium. The steamy heat met us as we went in and found two of the vacant high stools.

As he held a light to my cigarette he said, 'You look very smart tonight, Mrs. Landry – and very expensive.'

I flushed slightly – with pleasure, even though there was a gentle raillery in the compliment.

'I couldn't disgrace you,' I said lightly, 'when you were kind enough to ask me out. Thank you for the concert, Dr. Broderick – it was wonderful.'

'I don't get many opportunities like this. Something generally crops up to prevent it. I'm glad nothing did tonight, though; I would have hated to spoil your evening. I don't think you go out very much, do you?'

I shook my head. 'No.'

'Why not?' he asked bluntly. 'It would do you more good than sitting moping at home.'

'It isn't much fun on your own,' I said quietly. 'And somehow I don't seem to have any friends.'

'What about your husband? If I remember rightly, you used to be about together – occasionally, at least. I've seen you on the golf course – and at a club dance . . . '

'It's probably my fault,' I said. 'I can't have been very easy to live with.'

'What about parents? Or brothers and sisters?'

I looked at him oddly. 'My mother is dead – as you know. My father too, I believe, although I don't remember anything about either of them. And I don't think I have any brothers or sisters.'

'What about friends in your old home town – where was it?'

'Ottawa, I think. I'm not sure and I don't – '

'Ottawa, *Canada*?'

'Yes. My father was French Canadian, my mother English.'

He looked oddly disconcerted for a moment, but the expression was so fleeting that I wondered if I had imagined it.

'Were you married in Canada? Where, do you know?'

I said, a little helplessly, 'I'm not sure. Unless – yes, I remember seeing it on the marriage certificate. I think it was Montreal.'

'Were you living there at that time? You said Ottawa was your home town.'

'I don't know much about it, Dr. Broderick. I think I remember Charles telling me that I was living there at that time but – '

'With your parents? Were they alive then?'

'No... Charles said they were not.'

'Did your mother die in Montreal or Ottawa?'

'I don't know. Perhaps not in either place. Charles said – a mental home. It could have been anywhere.' I said it with difficulty. I would have liked to change the subject but Dr. Broderick seemed impervious to my discomfort.

'Do you know the date?'

'About a year before I was married. That would make it – 1938, I suppose. I can't tell you an exact date – I don't think Charles mentioned it.'

'Do you remember your name before you were married? Or your mother's or your father's name?'

'I don't *remember* them, of course. But I've seen my birth certificate. I was born Elise Constance Fournier, my parents were Elizabeth Mary and Dominique Fournier. I – Dr. Broderick, I – '

'All right.' He laughed suddenly. 'The inquisition's over.'

'What was it all about?'

'Oh, shall we say it was just an effort to see if recalling those dates and events of the past would help you to remember them? Have you never thought about going back there, to where you spent your childhood? It might help you to recapture some incident – one memory would lead to another.'

'No. It doesn't seem part of *my* life. It's as though all that happened to a completely different person. I feel it would only bewilder me all the more.'

'You may be right, at that. Well, drink your coffee, Mrs. Landry, and then we'd better be on our way. Does your husband know you're with me?'

'I didn't tell him. I wasn't sure whether he would be

angry. He – he didn't want me to see you again, you know.'

'That was only professionally, surely?'

'I suppose it was. Perhaps he wouldn't care . . . He never does concern himself where I go, or whether I'm alone.'

'Well, then,' he said lightly, as he slid down from his stool and put a steadying hand under my elbow to assist me from mine, 'so long as I don't prescribe any pills for you, it won't matter, will it?'

I don't think we talked about anything very much on the way home. The village was quiet and dark as we drove through, although it couldn't have been very late, but there was the welcoming glow of lights from the doctor's house as we pulled up at the gate.

'I shall expect you to tea some day soon,' Dr. Broderick said as he got out of the car. 'I'm generally home about that time but if I'm not, amuse yourself with my radiogram. There's a good collection of records – quite a few of the concertos. If there are some you haven't got yourself you might like to play them over. I'll leave word with Haley to keep the Welcome mat always handy.'

'I don't know why you're so kind to me,' I began, but he was already moving away. When he reached the gate he turned to call, 'Just don't break any records, that's all. They're my one extravagance.'

'I won't,' I promised, but I doubt whether he heard me. He was striding up the uneven path towards the lighted doorway, and I slipped the car into gear and drove away.

But I didn't stay away long. I let two days go by – and the hours dragged with an irritating slowness that I found difficult to tolerate – but on the third day I decided I'd waited quite long enough and if he hadn't meant me to take him at his word, then he shouldn't have asked me.

I'd intended to wear one of the new dresses and my pearls and a fur coat, but heavy showers of rain combined with a blustery wind to make a dismal, cheerless afternoon. I didn't want to take the car. I had a feeling that it wouldn't do Hugh Broderick any good to advertise my presence by leaving it at his gate. So I put on a pleated skirt and a woollen sweater and never even stopped to ponder that I could, of course, have postponed my visit until another, more favourable day.

On my way out I collected a huge bunch of chrysanthemums I had ordered to be sent in from the greenhouse. By the time I pushed open the broken, squeaking gate they were as bedraggled as I was.

Mrs. Hale answered my ring, her ample bosom looming large before her. I wasn't sure but I thought I detected a slight lessening of disapproval in her. Or it might have been merely because I *wanted* her to be less grimly disposed towards me.

I pushed the flowers towards her as I stepped into the hall.

'They're for you, Mrs. Hale,' I said, and for a moment I caught her off guard. 'But I'm afraid the wind and the rain have spoiled them.'

'Well – that's very good of you, I'm sure, Mrs. Landry,' she said. Her deep voice boomed through the hallway as she went on, 'Why, you must be wet through. Have you walked in all this rain? Give me your wet things and go straight in to the fire. Doctor's not back yet but I'm not expecting him to be very long. Now go along with you.'

She bustled me through into the room, scolding me as she deprived me of my wet garments. The fire looked warm and cheerful, patterning the room in flickering fingers of gold as the flames leaped high in the grate. I saw nothing of the shabbiness – only the glowing, welcoming comfort.

Mrs. Hale moved a chair nearer to the fire and plumped up a cushion. She had recovered a little of her grimness, although I was sure now that she wasn't quite so hostile towards me. It might have been because I was sober – or had Dr. Broderick said anything to her about me? Was she perhaps humouring a mad woman, I wondered wryly.

'There's plenty of magazines on the table there,' she told me as I sat down. 'Are you sure your feet are dry – those overshoes don't look very serviceable to me. You can't beat a good pair of Wellingtons on a day like this, I always think. Well, if you're sure . . . I'll just take your things into the kitchen to dry out, then. Tea won't be many minutes, unless you'd rather wait until Doctor gets back?'

I assured her that I preferred to wait and she went out, popping her head round the door a minute later to say, 'Oh, Doctor said to tell you where the radiogram is, but I expect you've got eyes in your head to see for yourself that it's over there. You'll find the records in the compartment at the side, and in that little cabinet. I hope you know how to work it, because I don't.'

I was in the middle of the Brahms No. 1 Piano Concerto when Dr. Broderick came in. It was quite dark by then, although I hadn't noticed, nor had I heard him come in. The flooding of the room with light was the first indication I had that he had returned and I sprang up from the depth of my chair in some confusion.

'Sorry – did I startle you?' he asked.

'No,' I said. 'No ... I hope you don't mind ... ?'

'Your being here? Of course not. Why should I, when I invited you? You should have put the lights on. I didn't know there was anyone in the room until I heard the music as I came in. Your car wasn't outside; did you walk?'

He sat down in the chair opposite me in a way that suggested he felt it good to relax. He seemed brusque, preoccupied; despite his assurance I was still wondering whether he had really expected me to take him up on his invitation. I thought he looked tired and depressed; somehow I had never expected him to look either one or the other, and it disturbed me a little.

I said, 'Would you like me to turn the music off?'

'What?' He looked up as though he had forgotten my presence. 'No,' he said, 'leave it on. You've had tea, I hope?'

'I waited for you. Mrs. Hale wanted to make it ...'

He made a little irritable movement. 'Then for Heaven's sake give her a yell to make it right away, will you? She doesn't always hear me come in.'

I went to the door and called and Mrs. Hale's voice boomed back at me from the rear of the house. She came in almost immediately with the teatray laden with fine, delicate china and a silver teapot, and plates of hot buttered scones and crumpets.

She cast an appraising eye over Dr. Broderick and said to me, 'See that Mr. Hugh has something to eat, won't you, Mrs. Landry? He didn't have much lunch and –'

'Oh, stop fussing, Haley,' he broke in shortly. He looked up, caught my eye, and gave a little, half-ashamed laugh. 'I'm in a filthy temper, Mrs. Landry. It's just been one of those days when nothing has gone right ...'

When Mrs. Hale had gone I said, 'I thought it was because I was here. I was afraid you were displeased...'

'Good Lord, no!' To my relief he looked and sounded genuinely astonished at the suggestion. I flushed with pleasure as he went on, 'As a matter of fact, d'you know, it felt rather nice to come in and find someone waiting for me. I'd forgotten...'

He didn't say what it was he had forgotten but I could guess.

I poured the tea without waiting to be asked, as he made no move to do so. He took the cup I held out and gave a wicked little grin.

'Best china again, you see.' He whistled softly. '*And* the silver teapot. My God, old Haley's laying it on thick for you. That family heirloom is the pride of her heart – she'll only bring it out for Christmas parties and christenings – '

Mrs. Hale came back as he spoke, carrying a large bowlful of the chrysanthemums. She put them down on a table and tweaked the flowers round into place before standing back to admire her handiwork.

'There were so many, Mrs. Landry, I thought I'd bring some of them for the doctor. Look real nice, don't they? I'm very fond of a chrysanthemum, myself.'

'I was telling Mrs. Landry, Haley, that the silver teapot only comes out for visiting royalty.' There was still that glint of amusement in his eye and Mrs. Hale turned and gave him a look that should have pinned him back in his chair.

'I don't intend anyone to think that you haven't got any nice things, Mr. Hugh,' she said severely. 'Just because I don't let you use them every day doesn't mean that they can't come out when you have a visitor. And there was no need for you to pass any comment in front of Mrs. Landry. What she'll think about your manners, I don't know.'

She swept out again with great dignity and I turned to meet the full force of Dr. Broderick's broad grin. I was delighted to see that his moody preoccupation had gone.

'You've been trying to get round old Haley with flowers, I see,' he commented.

'No – not really.' I didn't know why I should feel a slight confusion. 'I – we have so many... I thought they would please her.'

The record came to an end with a little click that drew our attention back to the music.

'That is one of my favourites,' I said.

'Borrow it, if you like,' he said, helping himself to another scone. 'Although I should have thought you would have had it in your own collection, if it's a favourite.'

'Perhaps it is there – I've never looked,' I confessed. 'I'm afraid I've not been very interested ... '

'Then it's time you started taking an interest in things,' he said calmly. 'The trouble with women like you is that you have too much time and you don't know what to do with it. You get so wrapped up in yourselves, you forget that there are other people in the world. You not only don't know how to live, you don't know how to love.'

'That's not true,' I said, with a slight resentment. 'I *do* love someone – other than myself, as you imply – very much.'

'You do? Who?' He looked at me sceptically over the rim of his teacup.

I said, very quietly, 'Russ.' And after a moment when he didn't say anything, 'That probably sounds very silly to you – that I should love a man whom I can't possibly know and can have met only once. But it's true, for all that.'

I looked at him in some defiance, expecting a derisive retort but he had a very thoughtful expression on his face as he replaced his cup and saucer on the tray.

'It's very real to you, isn't it? This other life, I mean?'

'Yes, it is. Particularly Russ. Sometimes I ... '

'Sometimes you – what?'

'Oh – nothing,' I finished lamely, as I realised suddenly, with a sense of shock, that for two whole days I had barely even thought of Russ. That for the last two nights, instead of crying myself to sleep over Russ I had been dry-eyed and calm, still soothed by that evening with Hugh Broderick.

I was so disturbed by the revelation that as soon as I decently could I mumbled some excuse and hurried away.

I was still in some confusion about it a week later when I saw him approaching me in the bar of the country club. In an effort to do as Dr. Broderick had suggested I had asked Charles to take me to the dance. After a slight hesitation he had agreed; although once there, I was clearly expected to spend the evening in the bar.

Charles had his one duty dance with me but apart from that we occupied the high stools around the bar. I tried not to drink much but it wasn't easy.

I saw Hugh Broderick before he saw me – through the big, glittering mirrors that reflected the entire room behind me – and the surprised pleasure I felt did nothing to lessen my confusion. He was in a dinner suit and he looked smarter than I had seen him look before. Some trick of the lighting brought the white scar on his left cheek into prominence even from a distance. I hadn't realised what an attractive smile he had until I saw him greet someone he knew.

He came over as soon as he spotted me and I turned on my seat as he drew near. I believe my whole face was alight with the pleasure I felt. I was suddenly glad that I had taken trouble with my appearance; that the white brocade dress suited me.

Charles turned as he heard us greet each other. I didn't think he looked very pleased but he was cordial enough.

'What'll you have to drink, Broderick?' he asked, as he shook hands.

'Nothing at all, thanks. I merely came to ask Mrs. Landry if she'll have this dance with me,' Dr. Broderick said. I saw his keen eye take in a row of drinks accumulated on the bar behind me and there was a little flicker of amusement on his face.

I slid down from the stool and went through on to the dance floor with him. For a moment I thought that Charles looked as though he would intervene, but he gave a faint shrug of his shoulders and turned back to the bar.

Dr. Broderick said, 'I didn't expect to see you here tonight, Mrs. Landry.'

'I'm acting on your advice,' I said lightly, ' – taking an interest in things.'

'And how is it working out?'

'Not very well,' I confessed.

'I haven't seen you dancing much.'

'Have you been here long?'

'Oh, thirty – forty minutes. Something like that. You haven't been on the floor during that time.'

'No one asked me,' I said. 'Until you came. I think I must have been so in the habit of draping myself over a bar that no one expects me to do anything else.'

'I saw you'd got quite a collection of drinks in front of you.'

'People *will* buy them,' I said, a little helplessly. 'Someone comes up and insists on buying drinks and then of course Charles has to order a round – and so it goes on.'

'Not easy, is it?' he asked, and there was unexpected sympathy in the question. 'I thought you might have dropped in for tea again, or to borrow some records.'

'I was afraid of making a nuisance of myself,' I said shyly.

'Nonsense, why should you? I don't have many visitors, except when Sarah and the kids are here. It's quite a pleasant change to have someone to talk to over a teatray.'

'I don't think you really mean that. You're only being kind.'

'I always say exactly what I mean, my dear girl. Any kindness is quite incidental.'

But I still shook my head disbelievingly.

The floor was crowded and it made dancing difficult, but we weren't doing too well together in any case. It was a waltz – slow and dreamy and my favourite dance, but it didn't suit his forceful briskness. I thought he would probably be much better with a lively quickstep. He held me firmly in the circle of his arms, with the confidence that characterised all his movements. I had never been so close to him before so I had not noticed how nice he smelled – a faint mixture of a clean antiseptic soap, cigarette smoke and after-shave lotion.

When the music ended and he let me go I was aware of a curious sense of loss, and it was still with me after he had taken me back to Charles, thanked me very formally, and walked away.

I felt lonely – not with the desperate loneliness of the past months, but wistfully so.

I had given up hope that he would ask me for another dance before he finally approached me once more. Charles didn't see him – he had his back to me, engaged in a mild argument with some acquaintance of his – and I slipped away unnoticed.

The band was playing a cha-cha, a dance I didn't know, and I would have drawn back if Dr. Broderick had let me. But he held my hand firmly and pulled me on to the floor despite my protests.

'It's simple,' he said. 'If I could learn it, you can.'

'I thought you didn't dance much,' I said.

'I don't – but Sarah's kids believe in keeping me up to

date on the odd occasions I go with them. You may not believe it, but I do a pretty good Rock and Roll.'

It was fun, too. I hadn't known that dancing could be so enjoyable, even though my mind could remember the happy times that Dorcas Mallory had spent with Russ on a dance floor. But this was sheer, delightful fun and I enjoyed every minute of it.

As we stood applauding for the music to start again Dr. Broderick said, 'See? I told you it was simple. You do it better than I do, already.'

'I like it,' I said. 'I like the rhythm, and the funny instruments that the orchestra play.' I added soberly, a little hesitantly, 'I like the feeling of being young – and carefree.'

'Of course you do. Why not? That's what you should be.' As the music started again he said, 'Has anyone told you that you're looking very beautiful tonight, Lisa Landry?'

I missed a step and almost stumbled, and for a moment his arm tightened protectively round me. The confusion was back again and I could feel the colour flooding my cheeks.

I tried to meet his eyes and answer him lightly, and couldn't, and he said, 'My dear girl, don't be so intense about everything.'

I could detect the faint note of amusement in his voice and I said, rather defiantly, 'I'm not used to compliments from you, Dr. Broderick.'

'I'm not used to handing them out,' he retorted, 'but I hope that doesn't prevent me from paying them graciously – even if you don't know how to receive them.'

'At least you're not unaccustomed to being rude,' I said tartly, and he threw back his head and laughed.

'I knew that would get you. You like to be angry, don't you?'

'No, I don't!'

'It's the only time you really come to life. The rest of the time you're quite prepared to sit back and accept whatever fate has to offer you, with an air of long-suffering martyrdom. When you're angry, that's a different thing entirely. You forget about being a martyr and turning the other cheek. You even dance twice as well when you're hopping mad.'

I was compelled to laugh, if grudgingly.

'I don't know why I tolerate such rudeness from you.'

'My dear girl, you don't tolerate it. It makes you so furious you could spit in my eye.'

'You deliberately try to provoke me,' I accused him.

'Sure I do,' he said cheerfully. 'If anger is the only emotion of which you are capable, then better to be angry all the time than nothing at all. Come out of your dream world, Lisa Landry. Learn to like people – to hate them, pity them, love them – not just to be angry with them. Learn to live with them – all of them, the good and the bad; not just with your own important self and a dream love that's fifteen years too late.'

I started to pull myself away from him and his hand tightened on mine so that I couldn't get free without making myself conspicuous.

'Let me go!' I said in a low, furious voice.

'I'll let you go when I've finished,' he said calmly, 'and I haven't finished yet.'

'I don't want to hear –'

'And I don't care whether you want to hear or not, I'm going to say it just the same.' His grip was inescapable, and his face held no more expression than if he had been commenting on the state of the dance floor. 'Get out and do some good in the world,' he said, 'and give a little pity instead of wanting to secure it all for yourself. You don't have the monopoly of it, you know. Look around you and see if that poor devil over there isn't a damned sight worse off than you are. Give a little something of yourself, Lisa Landry, even if it hurts – which it will. But give it all the same, even if it breakes your parsimonious little heart.'

This time I succeeded in wrenching myself free and I didn't care who was watching.

'All right,' he said, 'that's all. You can go now.'

'Not quite all, Dr. Broderick,' I said, with a fury that I only just managed to control. 'I wouldn't like you to go without giving you the satisfaction of knowing that your excellent advice hasn't fallen on barren ground . . . '

He grinned at me maddeningly. 'I know what you're going to say. You're going to tell me that you hate me like hell.'

'I hope . . . ' I said, 'I hope . . . ' I choked on my own anger. I finished it viciously, childishly. 'I hope I never see you again!'

I stormed back to the bar. I was still hating him passionately as I fell asleep. I had the first peaceful, dreamless night since August.

I sulked for exactly three days. On the third day as I was driving back through the village in the late afternoon I stopped the car outside the shabby old house. At the time it seemed no more than a sudden impulse but afterwards I realised that ever since I awoke I had intended calling there that day.

I didn't care about leaving the car standing at his gate. I didn't care about anything except how good it felt to be walking up the broken path and ringing the bell on the paint-blistered door, hearing the deep boom of Mrs. Hale's voice. There was a delicious odour of baking cakes mingling with the smell of lavender polish and the unmistakable pungency of a doctor's dispensary, and I sniffed the air in appreciation as Mrs. Hale closed the door behind me.

I went in in some trepidation, wondering how he would receive me; but he greeted me cheerfully, casually, as though we had parted the best of friends.

Mrs. Hale followed me in with an extra cup and he grinned when he saw her.

'No silver teapot today,' he said.

'I didn't know Mrs. Landry was coming when I made yours, but as it's just fresh in only a few minutes ago I didn't see any point in making another lot. But in any case I'm sure she'll not mind,' Mrs. Hale said firmly, and her tone defied me to say that I did. I assured her emphatically that I didn't and she hastened out to attend to her cakes.

'I wasn't sure you were at home,' I said. 'I didn't see your car outside.'

'You wouldn't. The bloody thing is in the garage again. 'Fraid I shall have to pack it in and get another one, although God knows where the money is coming from, I don't.' He said it with matter-of-fact cheerfulness. 'Can't do with a car that's constantly letting me down. It's apt to do so at the one critical moment when it shouldn't.'

'You could borrow mine, if it would help you,' I offered diffidently. 'Or I could drive you round.'

'I might take you up on that if this turns out to be a bigger job than I expect. Shall you mind being called out in the middle of the night to chauffeur me to a maternity case a few miles away?'

It was good to be back on a friendly footing again with him, to be sitting cosily before a spluttering log fire in that homely room; to be chatting easily with him and able to shut out the memory of all else.

And after that I got into the habit of dropping in. I didn't go every day, although I wanted to, but I went often; and when he wasn't at home I still enjoyed that quiet hour or so and the tea, served always now in the brown earthenware teapot – which particularly pleased me, as it suggested that at last Mrs. Hale had accepted me and no longer felt a need to display the best china and silverware.

During those December days I came to know him very well; to know that his quick intolerance was offset by a great depth of understanding and that his bluntness concealed a keen sensitivity. He could be brusque and rude but never malicious, and his impatience held no rancour. He said exactly what he thought but he also expected the same frankness in return.

He angered me many times and occasionally he hurt me, but he gave me the strength to fight, and finally he gave me the hope that perhaps there could be a future for me.

He never actually discussed my condition – perhaps because Charles had warned him off – and I didn't know why he encouraged me or devoted so much time to me.

On the days I didn't go to his house I was restless and moody, inclined to morbid foreboding, but I didn't drink much now; and on the days when I visited the house I hardly drank at all.

I still dreaded sleep and only found it possible with the sleeping tablets that Hugh gave me, because in my sleep some of the old nightmare horror would flood back over me and I would awake drenched with perspiration, fighting my way frantically up through dark waves of terror. But not every night was like that.

And as the weeks went by I thought of Russ less and less.

I didn't realise at first that I was doing so and when I did the sense of loss was sharp and poignant. I felt almost as if I had abandoned a part of myself. But after a while only a wistfulness remained. The agonised longing was gone and remembrance of him brought only a pensive tenderness.

I could tell that Charles was puzzled and surprised by the change in me. He had seen me gradually sinking into utter debasement and I couldn't blame him because he had lacked the power to help me. It wasn't his fault that there was nothing in him to which I could respond. Nor that I couldn't confide in him now.

Because there was nothing between us at all and I couldn't believe there ever had been.

It was curious that it took me so long to start thinking about ending this strange existence we shared and yet did not share.

Because if there *could* be a future for me that didn't hold complete madness, then I couldn't spend it in this aimless way.

I wanted a real home. I wanted the busy but calm security of a life like Hugh's. I wanted the human, if blunt, kindness of a Mrs. Hale instead of the cold efficiency of a Miss Rose. I wanted to know people and to like them, and to have friends so that there would be no more loneliness.

I didn't know then that there was really only one thing that I wanted and that everything else was merely part of it. I could not have been more blind.

I had been looking forward with tremendous eagerness to spending some part of Christmas with Hugh and his family. They weren't expected until the day before Christmas Eve, but Mrs. Hale was in a great bustle of cleaning, polishing, and baking for a whole week in advance. All the silver and copperware had to be brought down and polished, and I spent an entire afternoon helping her with the task. I think it was this that won me her final approval, but that wasn't the reason why I helped. I did it because it gave me pleasure to have a part in the Christmas preparations.

For the first time I felt the pleasant satisfaction of having money to spend when I went up to town to buy presents, and I really enjoyed a whole afternoon given up to that pursuit. I hadn't met Hugh's family and it was difficult knowing what to choose for them; and in the end I bought a soft white woollen stole for Sarah, a beautifully equipped make-up box for Valerie, and a musical tankard for Keith who, according to Hugh, had started a collection of such things.

For Hugh I bought the complete recording of the

Schumann Piano Concerto, which I knew he wanted, and a delicate little cameo brooch for Mrs. Hale to replace one that she had just broken.

I had told Hugh previously that I intended buying the turkey as my contribution to the festivities, and he had accepted the offer cheerfully. He had no false pride about things like that. I had also arranged with Mrs. Hale that I would provide the flowers for the decorations and I spent a most happy evening with Hugh, decorating the Christmas tree and the rooms with festoons of gay bright streamers.

The only other Christmases I could remember were those of Dorcas Mallory's – and although they had been happy occasions there had not been much festivity.

So I was like a child with my first Christmas.

The copper gleamed from our cleaning, the tree was a fairyland of gaily coloured lights and twinkling ornaments, the great bowls of chrysanthemums vied with the holly and the streamers, and I don't remember seeing anything more beautiful in my life.

I was tired when we had finished but it was a happy tiredness, and Hugh ran me home in his car, putting me down at the drive gates.

I had told him I wouldn't go down the following night, as Sarah and the children weren't expected until early evening and I didn't want to intrude. But I was so restless after dinner, so tensed with anticipation, that I couldn't remain in the house.

It was a cold, clear night and although there was no moon the stars were bright against the deep blackness of the sky. I called to Candy as I went out and told myself that my only intention was to exercise her but I'd really known where I was going even before I set off. The place drew me like a magnet. I couldn't keep away and I didn't even wish to.

I hadn't intended to go in and I didn't do so, but I walked down to the village and across the green, with Candy by my side, and I stood outside the house. The lighted windows were uncurtained as I had known they would be, and I was happy just to stand there by the garden fence and look in – apart and yet a part of it all. I could see clearly into the room and it looked cosy and festive and homely. Hugh was there, and a dark-haired woman – tall and slender, with a face more serene than beautiful. The boy was tall and dark like his mother but the girl reminded me irresistibly of Hugh.

I couldn't hear what they said but I could guess that Hugh was teasing the girl, that there was a warm affection in his regard for his brother's widow, a pride in him for the boy.

I felt a little of loneliness and envy, but mainly a happiness. This was the sort of life I wanted.

I was still cherishing that picture as I walked home, still felt warmed by it; and I think it was then that I finally decided to end the life I shared with Charles.

I didn't stop to think about it. I only knew that that was what I intended doing.

I sent Candy round to the kitchens and went into the house, and the close, confining heat hit me after the cold crispness of the night. Charles was in the cocktail bar off the hallway and I went in to him, throwing my fur coat over a chair as I passed.

He held the whisky bottle up inquiringly and I shook my head.

'On the water wagon?' he said, as he filled his own glass.
'No,' I said. 'But I don't want one now.'

I watched him as he splashed soda water into the glass and took a drink. And a sense of the utter uselessness of our existence swept over me. There was nothing here! Nothing! Surely Charles could no more wish for a continuance of such a life together than I did.

I hadn't prepared any speech. I hadn't even been sure that I would broach the subject right then. So I went into it badly.

'I should like to discuss a divorce with you, Charles,' I said.

I startled him even though it was only briefly. I couldn't quite read his expression, apart from a certain wariness that crept into his eyes. He put his glass down on the bar counter and played with it idly, turning it gently with his finger.

'I presume you mean ours?' he said at length.

I said a little impatiently, 'Well, of course?'

'And what, if I may ask, has given you the idea you would like a divorce?' He asked the question casually and yet I knew that he was watching me closely under his lowered lids.

I spread my hands in a little dissatisfied movement.

'It's all so – so meaningless, so useless,' I said. 'Our life together, I mean. We have nothing in common apart from the fact that we live under the same roof. We have no interest in each other. We're like two strangers and we're not even concerned to try to adapt ourselves to each other. You no more know what I am thinking or doing or hoping, than I know what goes on in *your* mind. I – '

'On the contrary, my dear Lisa,' he broke in, 'I am quite well aware of what you are thinking and doing – and even hoping, I believe.'

I was far from sure he was right but I conceded the point.

'Well, perhaps so. But you don't *care* – '

'Once again I must contradict you. I do care – very much – about what you think and what you do. It's quite important to me.'

I looked at him, puzzled, unsure of his attitude, but there was nothing to be learned from his expression. He seemed absorbed in the movements of the glass across the bar counter. After a few moments I realised that despite his preoccupation he was keenly alert.

'I don't think that's true,' I said. 'Even if it is, the reason you care isn't because of any – bond of affection between us. There's nothing left to keep us together. If there was ever anything – apart from Joanna . . . If it has been my fault, Charles, I am truly sorry but I can't believe that a divorce would hurt or distress you . . .'

'Supposing,' he said quietly, 'you get down to the reason why you would *like* a divorce?'

I gazed across at him rather helplessly. 'I've just been trying to explain to you,' I said.

'I mean the real reason.'

'There isn't one – other than what I've told you.'

He turned and met my eyes for the first time. I thought I could detect a glint of something that could have been anger in his.

'Do you expect me to believe that? When you've tolerated these conditions all these years?'

'I don't know anything about those last years. I only know about what it has been like these last few months . . .'

'Well, I can tell you. I can tell you, dear Lisa, what these years have been like.' He pronounced each word distinctly.

'I can give you a brief synopsis which will put you completely in the picture. Those years were joyless, purposeless, fruitless – and loveless.'

Beneath the savagery there was a pathos mingled with something else. If it hadn't seemed too preposterous I would have thought it was amusement.

'I'm sorry,' I said, and I said it sincerely, with a deep regret.

'You're sorry! *You're* sorry!' he repeated, and now I knew I hadn't been mistaken. That the impression I had received many times before was correct. He *was* laughing – inwardly and without mirth – and at himself. 'My dear Lisa, why in God's name should you be sorry? You can't know it – but the joke's on me.'

He picked up his glass and drained it, setting it down again on the bar with a slight thud.

'There'll be no divorce,' he said heavily.

'But why, Charles? Why go on like this?'

'Aren't you forgetting that as a good Catholic you don't believe in divorce?'

I said, in dismayed protest, 'But I don't know anything about being a Catholic! How can I adhere to the rules of a faith when – '

'You're still a Catholic and so am I. I shall not divorce you, Lisa, nor shall I allow you to divorce me.'

I looked at him in sudden anger.

'I *could* divorce you,' I said slowly. 'On your own admission, you have not always been faithful to me.'

He laughed, a short bark of unamused mirth.

'My dear Lisa, you'd have to prove that – and you may find it more difficult than you think. Do you imagine I am such a fool as to put myself in a position which would allow you to dictate the law to me?'

'You can't make me stay with you,' I said. 'You can't keep me here.'

He looked up sharply. 'I think you'll find that I can. You haven't a penny in the world, Lisa, other than what I give you. If you had to leave me do you really believe for one moment that I would give you any money?'

'I could work. Other people do.'

His lip curled scornfully. 'In what way do you think you could earn a living? What have you ever been trained for except to be beautiful and decorative? You couldn't live a single day on what you could earn with your so limited talent, and I should hope you'll have sense enough not to try.' His eyes narrowed suddenly as he added, 'Or are you perhaps not entirely dependent upon yourself and your own resources?'

'If you mean is there another man . . . No, there isn't,' I said truthfully.

He looked at me for a long time, his eyes searching my face keenly. I didn't know whether what he read there finally satisfied him. There was nothing in his face but an unrelenting hardness.

He reached across for the bottle and replenished his glass. 'We won't discuss this again, Lisa. You may not remember but I have told you this more than once in the past years – that under no circumstances would I ever let you go.'

I got up and went to the door as I realised the futility of argument. When I reached it he called after me, quite casually, 'We shall be leaving in the morning to spend Christmas in London.'

I stopped in sudden dismay, then anger at the nonchalant way in which he planned my life.

'I shall not be going,' I said coldly. 'I don't wish to spend Christmas in London.'

'I didn't ask you what you wished to do,' he said indifferently. 'You will be ready to leave with me at eleven o'clock.'

He had his back turned to me. So far as he was concerned the subject was closed.

I said angrily, 'I'm not going! Why should I?'

'Because I have said so. And also because I'm closing the house down completely and giving the servants a holiday.'

'I shan't go!' I said stubbornly. 'You can't make me.'

'You'll go,' he said, still indifferently, and there was no change in his tone as he went on, 'And if I have any trouble with you, Lisa – any more arguing or talk of divorce – I'll have you certified as mentally insane and put away.'

I gasped, shocked by the callousness of his words and the indifference with which he had said them. He didn't terrify me as he would once have done, a few weeks ago, but I was still frightened by his cruel obduracy.

'You couldn't do that,' I stammered.

'Couldn't I?' He laughed, and it wasn't a very pleasant sound. It sent a shiver of apprehension through me. 'Dear Lisa, have you any idea how comparatively easy it is in this country to get someone certified and locked away? I'd have no trouble at all, with your background of insanity, even if you hadn't helped considerably by your – what shall we call it? – rather peculiar behaviour of these past weeks. I wouldn't want to hurry you into such a place, when after all it is only a matter of time . . . But I assure you that I will do so, dear Lisa, if you don't behave yourself. And it's much more difficult to get out of those places than it is to get in, so guard your freedom while you have it.'

I said, still stammering, 'Why do you hate me so much? What have I ever done . . . Did you always hate me . . . ?'

'Hate you?' He turned around to face me with a violence that knocked over his glass and sent the whisky dripping over the edge of the bar and on to the floor. He sat like that for a long time, until the spilt whisky was only dripping occasionally into the little pool which had formed on the carpet. And then he said, in some wonderment, 'Yes, I did hate you. But the trouble was that I didn't hate you enough.'

9

The bitter disappointment of missing the Christmas I had so looked forward to was more than I could bear.

We saw Joanna and Michael briefly on Christmas Eve and I spent most of Christmas Day propping up one bar or another and drinking far too much and being much too miserable to care.

By late afternoon of Boxing Day I knew that no matter what Charles said or did, I was going back to Chadwell St. John. I didn't tell him. I just slipped away while he was out, and I made the journey back through sleeting rain in record time.

For the first time since I had known it the house was cold as I let myself in and for a moment the darkness and the emptiness of it deterred me. I had never seen it other than warm and well lighted. When I switched on the lights the emptiness was still there, and I hadn't really realised until then what a big house it really was.

The kitchen was almost strange territory to me but among all the gleaming equipment I managed to find the stop tap and turned the water on, and when the electric kettle had boiled I made myself a cup of tea and smoked a cigarette while it boiled again. There was no hot water in the taps and I had to make do with that kettleful for a brief and rather chilly sponge down in a cold bathroom.

I knew which dress I intended wearing. It was a full-skirted blue taffeta with rustling petticoats beneath, and I wore no jewellery except the pearl ear-rings. But I brushed my hair until it shone and let it fall in a softer, fuller style round my face. When I stood back at last for a final look in the mirror I was startled and held motionless, disturbed by what I saw reflected; and for an instant I clutched frantically at a memory. It was fleeting, a tantalising, half-formed fantasy of the mind. And then the excitement of the evening before me returned and I snatched up my bag and the presents and ran down the stairs.

Hugh answered the door himself. He flung it wide when he saw me standing there.

'Where the devil have you been all this time?' he demanded. 'I thought you'd completely deserted us.'

'Charles wanted to go to London,' I said. 'I couldn't let you know.'

It didn't matter now. I was happy, with that warm, enveloping glow that can be a little intoxicating. I slipped my coat off into Hugh's waiting hands. It wasn't warm in the hallway but I didn't feel the cold. I just stood there and smiled up at him – a child at her first party, excited and shy.

Hugh said slowly, still holding my coat, a faint note of incredulity in his voice, 'What have you been doing to yourself?'

'Nothing,' I said. 'Why?'

He got rid of the coat and helped me collect up the parcels.

'You look about sixteen,' he said abruptly as he threw open the living room door and stood back for me to go in.

It was a wonderful party. It was everything that I had

known it would be, and I was part of it, not just an outsider looking in.

Although I suppose you couldn't really call it a party. We didn't do anything very much but I was deeply, gloriously happy.

We had the cold remains of the turkey for dinner and Mrs. Hale came in and shared it with us, and when we had finished eating we all went into the kitchen and helped with the washing-up. There were too many of us and we got in each other's way but it was all fun and no one minded.

It was easy to see why Hugh was so fond of Sarah and the 'kids', and they were equally fond of him. Watching him with them I thought that it was a great pity he had never had children of his own.

I waited until dinner was over before handing out my presents. I was a little dubious about it, hoping it wouldn't make any of them uncomfortable to receive a present when they hadn't one to give in return, but I needn't have worried. They all had something for me. Sarah had bought a very pretty head-square of fine silk, and Valerie and Keith had combined to buy an ornate bottle of bathsalts.

I asked Sarah, 'How did you know about me?' and she laughed.

'Oh, Hugh wrote to me a few weeks ago that you would be here,' she said.

'He didn't know,' I protested.

'Of course he did!' she said, with all of Hugh's forthrightness.

Mrs. Hale's present was a box of handkerchiefs, and Hugh's present I came to last of all. It was simple, inexpensive, and caught at my heart.

It was one of those round glass balls – a little country scene on which when the ball is moved the snow settles in gentle silence. I had once described to him one that I could remember seeing at High Towers, and how delighted the child Dorcas Mallory had always been with it. I was touched now with the same childlike wonder and fascination at that softly swirling snow.

I was aware of Hugh saying, 'I'm afraid it isn't very much.' There was no note of apology in his voice for the inexpensiveness of the gift, but I turned to him with shining eyes.

'It's beautiful,' I exclaimed.

'I thought you'd like it,' he said, quite casually, but I knew he was pleased at my delight.

I thought of the expensive diamond bracelet I had found on my plate on Christmas morning – a cold, impersonal gift from Charles that summed up our life together.

'It's beautiful, Hugh,' I said again, and I shook it gently and put it down on the table so that I could watch it once more.

Valerie wanted to go dancing but although when we took a vote on it I said I didn't mind, I was pleased when she lost by an overwhelming majority. I wanted to stay in this house.

We played the new Schumann Concerto through. We sat and talked. We played some kind of letter game which it seemed was all the rage. We danced a little, but not very successfully in the limited space available, to some of the latest records which Valerie and Keith had brought along with them. We watched the television for a while.

I don't remember what else we did, or whether we did anything else at all.

Sarah and I made the sandwiches and coffee for supper and wouldn't let Mrs. Hale help because Sarah said Haley had done nothing but cook for them the whole of the holiday. While we were busy in the kitchen Sarah gave me her address and asked me to visit her any evening or weekend when I was in London. I said I would, and meant it. I wondered how much Hugh had told her about me but I didn't mind if she knew it all. She was like Hugh in that she was the type of person to whom it would be very easy to talk. I was sorry when she told me they were leaving the following afternoon.

'I'm a working woman, you know,' she said with a smile. 'Hugh's been absolutely wonderful since David was killed but I can't let him take the full burden. I have to try to help.'

'He doesn't look upon you as a burden,' I said.

She spread butter rapidly and efficiently on the slices of bread.

'I'm sure he doesn't,' she said cheerfully. 'Nevertheless I am very guiltily aware that we are the reason why he has never been able to marry again.'

I said sharply, 'Is there someone . . . ?' before I pulled myself up.

'In particular?' she finished. 'Not that I know of. But there should be, for a man like Hugh. He's a potentially good husband absolutely going to waste. Sooner or later he's going to meet some girl . . . Do you think we shall have enough bread there or should I start into another loaf?'

We stayed chatting so long that Hugh came to see what we were doing.

'Do we have to starve for ever while you two gossip in here?' he demanded.

'I've been asking Lisa to spend New Year's Eve with us,' Sarah said. 'Do you think you'll manage to get up for it, Hugh?'

'I'll try. It's generally a busy time just after Christmas. People will eat too much – there's usually a spate of stomach troubles.'

'I should warn you, Lisa, that the flat will probably be teeming with bright young things. All Val's and Keith's friends just pop in as they wish.'

'It'll do Lisa good,' Hugh said. 'For that matter, she looks like a bright young thing herself this evening.'

'She does. You forgot to tell me, Hugh, how young and pretty she is.'

'Can't say I'd noticed until this evening,' Hugh said coolly. 'No need to blush, my dear girl. You should know by now that I always say what I think, and I've trained Sarah and the kids to do the same. If you look drab and middle-aged tomorrow, I shall be just as candid.'

'Hugh can be positively devastating when he's in the mood,' Sarah remarked. 'But you'll probably have found that out for yourself. I should hate to be a patient of his. Which reminds me, Hugh, I don't think Val is going to change her mind, you know. If anything I believe she's even keener than before about being a doctor. It's going to be pretty grim, isn't it?'

She was speaking lightly but there was an undercurrent of distress in her voice. I loved the way Hugh put an arm round her shoulders and gave her an affectionate, reassuring squeeze.

'We shall manage, old girl. We always have done. Now what about that supper?'

It was a happy evening and it flew on wings. I hadn't known that the hours could pass so swiftly. I wanted to cling eagerly to each minute and never let it go.

Hugh came out to the car with me when I left. Everything was still and cold and dark, the whole village seemed to be sleeping. Through the uncurtained windows I could see Sarah and Mrs. Hale tidying the room, plumping up cushions, emptying ashtrays. The tree was still aglow with its little coloured lights, the streamers were bright and gay, and the copperware reflected a dozen miniature rooms in each gleaming contour.

Hugh shut the car door softly as I settled myself in the driving seat. As I grew accustomed to the dark I could see the vague outline of him silhouetted against the starlit sky.

'Will you be all right?' he asked. 'I'm not so keen on you going back alone to that empty house. Sure you wouldn't like me to drive up with you – it won't take a minute to get the car out.'

'I'm not in the least nervous,' I said, and I wasn't. I was far too happy to be nervous of anything.

'Well, if you're certain,' he said, but still doubtfully.

'Positive!' I said with absolute conviction. 'There's just something I wanted to ask you, though, Hugh,' I went on. I tried to say it casually, to make light of it; but I couldn't quite keep a tremor out of my voice. 'Charles told me the other night ... I know it was only a threat and he wouldn't really mean it ... But just in case ... '

'What did he say?' he prompted me and I had never heard him so gentle.

I finished with a rush. 'He – he told me that if I didn't behave myself he would have me certified and put into a mental home. I know he didn't mean it – he was only trying to frighten me. But you wouldn't let him do it, would you, Hugh? You could stop him, couldn't you?'

'My God, and could I!' He said it with an intensity that the quietness of his voice could not hide.

'It's not as though I'm – violent – or anything like that, is it?' I persisted, and in the darkness I felt the warmth and strength of his hand over mine as it rested on the steering wheel.

'My darling girl, you're as sane as I am, and don't ever let that charming husband of yours convince you otherwise.'

'I wanted you to know – just in case.'

'Just let him try it!' he said grimly. 'Have you been worrying about this?'

'Only a little. I won't now that I've told you.'

'What made him threaten you?'

'Oh – nothing . . . I don't know,' I said evasively. I didn't know why I should feel shy about telling him that I had been asking Charles for a divorce. 'We were just – arguing.'

I knew he couldn't see my face but I had a strong feeling that he was trying to sense what was in my mind. I also had the feeling, enclosed from the rest of the world as we were in the surrounding darkness, that he would find it much easier to know what was in my mind than I did myself.

I said hurriedly, 'It's been a wonderful evening, Hugh.'

'I was afraid you were going to give us a complete miss,' he said quietly. 'I'm glad you made it.' He gave my hand a final reassuring pat. 'As I've told you, I shall probably be very busy tomorrow but if I don't see you I'll give you a ring later in the day. And don't worry – not about anything.'

'I won't,' I promised.

The drive back through the night, with the headlights making a bright tunnel beneath the canopy of trees, was all part of the enchantment of the evening.

I didn't hurry. I drove slowly, savouring every moment of my happiness. Returning to the empty house was only a brief interlude that would soon be over.

I switched off the engine and the lights and left the car by the front door. It was just too much trouble to take it round to the garage, and although it was cold there was no trace of frost. The lights streamed out welcomingly through the wide expanse of glass doors and even the warmth that greeted me as I went in was no longer a stifling airlessness, but pleasantly comforting. I was half-way across the hall before I realised that there should have been neither heat nor lights in the house, nor a door that opened only at the turn of a handle.

I stood still, suddenly startled but not unduly alarmed. I think I knew what to expect even before I retraced my steps and looked through the open door of the lounge.

Charles was sitting there in the centre of the room, quite motionless, his face still and cold in the glow of a table lamp, some trick of light accentuating the heavy eyebrows and making dark shadows of the deep lines on his cheeks. His face might have been carved in stone but for the strong throbbing of a pulse in his temple.

I stood wavering in the doorway on the outer fringe of that circle of light, unwilling to say or do anything that would break the wonder and happiness of that evening, yet unsure of what was in his mind.

His utter immobility made me uneasy, and I resented the intrusion of any emotion which might disturb my own mood. His voice was harsh when eventually he spoke, its roughness jarring on me.

'Where have you been?'

I hesitated, more from reluctance to discuss any part of the evening with him than from fear of his displeasure. I could see a vein pulsating in the back of his hand as it rested on the table – with the same heavy beat as the one in his temple.

'I'm tired, Charles,' I said quietly. 'I'll talk to you in the morning.'

I heard him calling after me as I turned and went up the stairs but I took no notice. I had already forgotten him by the time I reached the bedroom. I switched on the lights and drew the curtains and threw my fur coat on to the bed. I unwrapped the little glass ball carefully and put it on the dressing-table, and the snow eddied gently and peacefully around. I sat and watched it, childishly delighted, lost in the hush of that falling snow.

I hardly heard Charles come in. I was only dimly aware of his presence until I realised that he was standing by my side, watching the last few flakes settling softly. In the mirror I could see his dark brooding expression, the faint sneer on his mouth as he looked at the little ball.

I knew, from some inner knowledge, that the thin veneer of calmness had shattered, exposing the full force of his anger, I waited, as I knew I had waited before. I waited calmly, sustained and made remote by the happiness in me.

I looked up to find him staring at me and what there was in his face, I didn't know. It was impossible to tell. He just stood there staring at me and then he let the breath sigh slowly from him.

'My God,' he said softly, and then again, 'My God.'

And then the anger came back and this time there was

something else with it. I wasn't sure what it was – I couldn't believe that it could be what I *thought* it was. I was only sure of his anger, and there was no mistaking that.

His voice was brittle and he cut each word off short as though only in that way could he be sure of controlling it.

'Where have you been?'

I shook my head. I didn't want to talk to him while he was in this mood. If I could sense the anger I could avert it.

'You've been with some man, haven't you?'

I started to deny it and he cut me off savagely. 'Don't deny it. Do you think I can't see it in your face? Who is it?'

I said slowly, 'No, there isn't a man – not in the sense you mean ... '

He laughed. It was a harsh sound, with no mirth. 'In any sense, do you think I would believe you, if you denied it forever? Did you think I wouldn't know – did you really believe you could get away with it ... ?'

'There isn't anything for you to know,' I said steadily. 'I'm not trying to get away with anything – '

I broke off with a little gasp as he pulled me to my feet. The pulse in his temple was beating violently. His fingers numbed my shoulders where they gripped and he shook me slightly as he spoke to emphasise his words.

'Who've you been with? You'll tell me, you know, sooner or later ... '

'You're hurting me,' I protested. I tried to pull away but his grip tightened. I hated him for spoiling my lovely evening like this. Everything had been so peaceful and so beautiful. I gave an involuntary cry of pain as his fingers dug deeper into my flesh. 'Charles – please . . . You're quite wrong. There isn't anyone ... I've only spent the evening at Hugh Broderick's house – '

'*Broderick?*' The word came out like a small explosion. I could feel the hot breath on my face. 'You've been seeing him – going to him despite what I said – although I forbade you to go ... '

I struggled futilely to free myself. I could feel the anger rising in myself now.

'No, I haven't!' I said forcefully. 'I've never been to him as a patient. He's been a good friend to me – he's been kind to me in a way that you would never understand ... '

'*Kind* to you? You come tearing back here like this – you

can't wait to get back to him – and you tell me he's been *kind* to you. I could think up a better name than that for it, my dear Lisa, but it isn't one your fastidious little mind would like to hear.'

'You're wrong. It isn't anything like that.'

'Wrong, am I?' He laughed, and it wasn't a very pleasant sound. 'How long has this been going on? How many times have you been with him?'

'I haven't *been* with him as you so crudely suggest,' I said passionately. 'It was never like that. He was sympathetic – he helped me – and God knows I needed help. I could never make you understand what it has meant to me – how it has been with Hugh –'

'You expect me to believe that? You really think I'm such a gullible fool? You come in looking like this – all starry-eyed and dreamy – your whole face full of what you have been doing – and ask me to believe that you have been getting nothing but sympathy these last few hours?'

He gave the same grating laugh. His eye caught the little glass ball and he released me suddenly and picked it up. There was scorn in his eyes and in the curve of his mouth as he flicked it disdainfully.

'He bought you this?'

'Yes.' I said it defensively and put out my hand to take the ball from him. He looked at me, and then with quick savagery threw it from him. I gave a little cry of dismay as it hit the wall and rebounded to roll across the carpet by the side of the bed. But it hadn't broken. It came to rest in a frenzy of swirling snow.

I stood rubbing my arms where his fingers had dug into them. I hated him with a cold deadly hatred in that moment. I knew that if the little glass ball had broken I would have struck him. I couldn't look at him. I could hear the heavy sound of his breathing and it filled the room.

And then I heard him say, 'You're in love with him, aren't you?'

I stood watching those swirling snowflakes reflect the confusion of my own thoughts. I was scarcely aware of the pain as he caught my shoulders and swung me round to face him.

'Aren't you?' he said violently. '*Aren't* you?'

I looked at him almost unseeingly.

'Yes,' I said. 'Yes – I am,' and I was filled with the wonder of it and an amused incredulity at my own blindness. This, of course, was the explanation – and how could it have been any other? – of the peace and the happiness I had found in that shabby house. It wasn't the house – it was Hugh.

I was in love with him – passionately and completely in love with him.

I repeated it to myself over and over again, with an almost unbelievable sense of elation.

Rudely I was jerked back to awareness of Charles's face close to mine, mottled with anger.

'You slut!' he said, and the words came out through his clenched teeth. 'You damned filthy little slut!'

I was filled with fury at his cheapening of my feeling for Hugh. I was so angry I even found strength to fling off his hands.

I said stormily, 'You don't know what you're talking about! You've no right to – '

He cut in, his voice venomous. 'Don't tell me what rights I have or have not. Do you think I haven't lived with you long enough to know exactly what I am or am not entitled to expect from you? The cold, aloof Lisa! My God, when I think of all those years . . . Lisa the untouchable, the icy, frigid snow-maiden, the pure, chaste virgin . . . Damn you, you bitch, you never looked like this for me, did you? Broderick must be better in bed than I ever was, to send you home looking so – so replete, so fulfilled – so God-damned satiated!'

I realised suddenly that the astonishing suspicion I had had earlier when he first came into the room was true. The anger was nothing compared to the blind, unreasoning jealousy which filled him. It was there in the glaring bleakness of his eyes, in the twist of his lips, in the bitterness of his voice.

My own anger went, overwhelmed by a quick rush of remorse. If I had ever had pity for him before I couldn't remember it, but it was in me now. I put my hand on his arm in a gesture of compassion.

'I'm sorry,' I said gently.

I was totally unprepared for his violence, although the fury in his eyes should have warned me. He flung my hand off with a viciousness that sent me sprawling across my bed.

'You're sorry,' he mimicked. 'For what? For the hellish torture you know how to inflict on a man or because you've just realised what you've been missing all these years? You're *sorry*! It's too late to be sorry!' His eyes narrowed suddenly as he stood looking down at me. 'Or is it too late?' he said, and the softness in his voice alarmed me far more than his anger.

I knew a swift fear as I looked up at him standing over me, his bulk outlined against the soft lighting behind him. What I saw in his face made me feel suddenly sick. I struggled into an upright position, clutching at the heavy satin spread for support.

'Charles . . . ' I tried to keep my voice steady but failed hopelessly. There was a mockery in his smile which terrified me. 'Please . . . ' I begged. 'You're wrong . . . Wait – '

'I'm tired of waiting, my dear Lisa. You've kept me waiting at arm's length long enough. What are you afraid of? That I won't prove as adequate as your precious doctor? If you can't remember how efficient I am in bed, now is your opportunity to – '

The fear made my throat dry. I tried to speak clearly, and only succeeded in whimpering. 'You can't – you can't, Charles . . . '

I fought wildly as he pushed me back across the bed with a lazy indolence which I found infinitely more frightening than his violence. The whole ghastly, sordid struggle was so effortless on his part. He had one more moment of savagery, when he tore the blue dress from me. After that my half-crazed resistance hardly seemed to bother him.

His foot had caught the glass ball and set the snow madly whirling again. I could see it plainly, and that small globe of glass grew to immense proportions until the whole room was full of tortured, eddying flakes.

As I sank in shuddering horror into the darkness I knew that I had lived through this before. And I knew who it was that I had seen reflected back at me in the mirror earlier that evening.

I came back up out of the darkness slowly, reluctantly, to a dawn that was breaking feebly through the brocade curtains. In the dim light I could only vaguely discern the outline of the bedroom – the dark blue ceiling, the long, low dressing-table, the silken covered chairs and deep rose cushions, the wall of sliding doors behind which was a vast and expensive wardrobe, the expanse of off-white carpet with a little ball of glass lying on it, remote in its stillness. But I didn't need the light to tell me where I was.

With a startling clarity I knew exactly where I was and who I was.

I lay there motionless, and those years washed over me, bringing with them a bitterness almost beyond endurance. I hadn't known there could be so much bitterness in anyone.

The room gradually grew lighter but I was far away in another room, another time – nearly sixteen years ago. The April sun had poured through the window on to the girl who lay there, confused and perplexed by the strangeness of her surroundings. I could feel again the lost blankness of that girl – the hopeless bewilderment, the beginning of terror because there was nothing but a complete emptiness in her mind. The past was nothing to her – the only memory was of a confused feeling of having woken in that room, briefly on and off, and it seemed that it wasn't very long ago.

And there had been a face which hovered indeterminately in her mind during those brief periods of wakefulness, and the face had belonged to a man. It was no one whom she knew. From that moment there had never been anyone whom she knew, only the beginning of a lost loneliness which had never left her.

It was the memory of that first loneliness that brought the bitterness to me. It need never have been – it could have been different...

As long as I lived I would remember the helpless horror of that young girl, forced to accept a life that had no meaning for her, the violation of an innocence which only an instinct deep inside her could acknowledge. I could see her now, and feel again the loathing and terror with which she had had to submit to the claims of a husband of whom she had no recollection.

If there had been a little tenderness or understanding – a little time for adjustment. But there had been only an eager mouth and seeking hands which had repelled and shocked.

It hadn't helped to know that there was a child – a three-year-old daughter.

Nothing had helped really, except time, which had

brought a gradual acceptance, then resignation; and finally, much later when there was only cold frigidity left, a reprieve which no longer even mattered very much. For by then there was nothing left in Lisa Landry but an aloof indifference.

There had been no doctors, no specialists, who had said that she had insanity in her – and this brought the bitterness surging up in me, at the needless cruelty.

There had been doctors earlier, at the beginning, when there had still been warmth and hope in her, and they had said that some day the memory of her lost youth could come back just as easily as it had gone – though there was always the possibility that it might never return. It was nothing to worry about. Time, they said...

But time had gone on, and the years gone by.

And then the daughter's wedding had stirred memory, had served to achieve what time had failed to do. But fifteen years too late...

Fifteen years, I thought bleakly. Wasted in emptiness.

I would never forgive those barren years as long as I lived. There would always be this bitterness in me, and a hatred. I would never forget because I would never want to forget. If I was ever in danger of forgetting, all I would have to do would be to recall the repugnance and the pathetic, ignored pleas, the deceit, the lies, the loneliness . . . Oh God, I would never forget!

I got up and found a dressing-gown, kicking the torn dress out of my way. The other bed was empty.

I pulled the curtains back and let the pale sunlight into the room. There was a slight haze obscuring the distant hills but I wasn't concerned about the distant hills, or the haze, or the watery sun. All I cared about was leaving this house for ever and I couldn't do it soon enough. Even the sight of the little glass ball on the floor couldn't move me this morning. There were no nostalgic memories in me. There was only that hard bitterness.

I bent and picked up the ball automatically and as I put it down on the table Charles came in. He was carrying a tea-tray and I looked at him in amazement until I remembered that there were no servants in the house. He gave me a quick, questioning glance as he put the tray down and I looked back at him in a hard, stony silence. With a careless shrug he poured the tea, but when he offered me the cup I waved it away.

'I don't want it,' I said shortly.

'All right, all right,' he said. 'Please yourself.'

I got a cigarette from the box and lit it.

'Why did you do it?' I asked suddenly.

He was sitting on the edge of his bed, sipping the hot tea, and he looked casually over the rim of the cup at me.

'Oh, put it down to your irresistible charm, my dear,' he said lightly, 'but for Heaven's sake don't act all tragedy queen about it, as though I had raped you.'

'What would you call it?' I asked evenly. 'And that time all those years ago, when you told me you were my husband and gave me no choice but to submit – what would you call that?'

He put the cup down abruptly. His eyes were very watchful and wary as he looked at me.

'You know, do you?' It seemed more of a statement than a question.

'Yes, I know. Why did you do it?' I asked again.

I hadn't intended to question him but suddenly I wanted to know. Though I would never understand, never be able to forgive, at least I had the right to know.

'Just how much do you remember?' Charles asked cautiously, and I flicked the ash from my cigarette with a little movement which expressed my contempt.

'I remember it all. All except *how* you did it.'

'Well, it wasn't a case of *how* I did it,' he said. He seemed quite unperturbed after that one betraying start. 'As a matter of fact, dear Lisa, I didn't really do it. It was all done for me.'

I said scornfully, 'What do you think to gain by denying it now?'

'No, really,' he said. Except for the watchful wariness of his eyes he couldn't have been more at ease. He picked up the cup and looked at it thoughtfully for a moment before taking a drink. 'What's the last thing you remember of that night in London?' he asked.

I said slowly, 'After we left Russ at the station we walked back to the hotel. I know I was excited and very tired – it's all rather vague and I don't remember it very well . . . We – Father and I – we went back to the hotel – no, wait a minute!

We met you – you were waiting at the top of the street...'

'That's right,' he nodded. 'I knew which way you would come and I guessed you would walk. Taxis weren't very easy to come by at that time in London.'

'You were very persistent about talking to Father – I know he was impatient about it because you'd already talked to him during dinner. I don't know what you wanted but I think he refused – I wasn't taking very much notice of you...'

'No, you weren't, were you?' There was something in his voice, I wasn't sure whether it was grimness or resentment. 'You never did take much notice of me, did you, dear Lisa?'

'I didn't like you,' I said baldly.

For a moment he looked angrily disconcerted and then he laughed.

'Well, that's honest enough. I didn't realise that the dislike began as far back as that. Anyway, I'll tell you what I was asking your dear father for. I was asking for the loan of ten thousand pounds. Oh, don't look so surprised, my dear. You may not have realised it, judging by the modest way in which you lived, but your father – your *adopted* father – was an exceedingly wealthy man. Ten thousand pounds was a fleabite to him.' His voice had hardened as he went on. 'He could have lent it to me and never even have missed it.'

'And wouldn't he?'

'No, he wouldn't. Although I could practically have guaranteed to treble it at least.'

'He must have had good reasons for refusing.'

He gave me a sidelong glance that held faint amusement. 'Oh, doubtless. He didn't care for the way I intended to employ the money. And also, I think – and this is probably more to the point – like you, he neither liked nor trusted me. Anyway, we're getting a little away from the main issue. Although he'd refused me at dinner time I felt I'd have one more go before he went back north.'

'What did you want the money for?'

'Oh – ' He waved his hand airily, ' – there was a fortune to be made in those days on the black market. Only the trouble was you had to have some capital to start with and I had nothing. Adrian was a sanctimonius old fool but all the same, if he'd liked me, he would have put his blasted scruples on one side. But he never did – we never got on together. Anyway, I waited for you to return to your hotel, although I could guess what the answer would be. Do you remember what happened after that?'

'No – not really. It's very confused . . . I suppose we went back to the hotel – I can remember walking down the street. No – we walked only a little way – there was an air raid warning . . .'

'Yes, there was. Do you remember going into the shelter?'

'Yes,' I said. 'Yes – it was quite near the hotel. I think I was too tired to be frightened, although we weren't used to air raids in Alderford . . . I remember it was dark and smelt fusty . . . We weren't there very long, I don't think . . .'

'No, it was only a short raid. But do you remember a young girl of about your own age who sat next to your father?'

'I don't think so.'

'She was frightened, if you weren't. And cold. You lent her your coat.'

I struggled hard through memory. 'It's so vague –'

'When the All Clear went your father said he would see her home. You were practically on the hotel doorstep and he knew you'd be all right. I was there, in any case, to look after you. Do you remember anything after that?'

I put my hands up to my head. 'No,' I said. 'I don't think so . . .'

'You don't remember the solitary bomb which must have made a direct hit on your father and that girl as they walked down the street?' I shuddered violently. 'You were in front of me,' he went on. 'You'd just stepped out of the shelter and caught the edge of the blast. I was still behind the sandbags in the entrance and escaped it, but you were knocked unconscious. I got you back into the shelter and brought you round in a fashion. You were conscious but that was all – you could walk and you could talk but your mind was a complete blank even then. When I tried to take you back to your hotel the entrance to it was blazing and the street was full of fire engines, so I took you back to my flat. It wasn't far away but on the way you passed out again. I couldn't bring you round, so after a time I left you there and went back to see what had happened to your father. I didn't know until then where the bomb had actually landed; the clerk at the hotel told me when I inquired about Adrian.

He told me, dear Lisa, that Adrian Mallory – and his daughter – had been killed outright by the bomb. There wasn't enough of them ever found to make identification positive – only scraps of clothing, fragments of a watch, a portion of a ration book in a coat pocket –'

'My coat . . . ' I whispered. 'That girl . . . ' I put my hand to my mouth and closed my eyes.

'That girl,' said Charles, 'was buried – what there was of her – as Dorcas Mallory.'

'But you,' I said. 'You – you knew differently.'

'Certainly I did.' He said it lightly, cheerfully.

'Then why – why . . . ?' I faltered to a stop. I had thought that there was only bitterness left, but I was wrong. I felt cold and sick with the memory of how my father had died and that girl who could so easily have been me . . .

'Why didn't you explain that there had been a mistake?' I asked, brokenly. 'You could easily have put it right . . . '

'Oh, I had my reasons, my dear. Excellent ones. Two of them, as a matter of fact – and I'll give them in order of importance.' He smiled suddenly, a tight little smile that was almost a jeer. 'First of all, I saw it as a golden, heaven-sent opportunity to get the money – and not just the ten thousand, but a whole lot more than that. I was Adrian's only surviving relative. I guessed there would be nothing in his will for me – and how right I was – but with you safely out of the way I could claim the lot. The money was left to you, but you had no one – you were an adopted child with no one who could demand a halfpenny of the money from you. You'll never know, my dear Lisa,' he added, with a hardness which his casual air couldn't quite conceal, 'how much I had always resented you and your adoption. You were the only thing that stood between me and Adrian's money – and you weren't even his own flesh and blood. Although he didn't like me, apart from you he had no one else to leave his money to. He would have left it to me – and as he was a good deal older, I had stood a chance of inheriting it before I was too senile to enjoy it. But then, with your death so nicely arranged for me, it all turned out very simple in the end.'

'But how did you know I wouldn't remember – in a few days or weeks? At any time, memory could have come back ... You couldn't rely on my mind always being a blank...'

'No, I didn't rely too much on it at first. Later, as time went by, the possibility of your remembering seemed to get more and more remote. But at first I kept you pretty well isolated in the flat. I hadn't been in England long – no one really knew me. It was childishly easy to pass you off as my wife to whoever *did* chance to see you. And you were very obedient, you know.' He cast a sidelong glance at me and I shuddered. 'You knew it wasn't wise to anger me, didn't you?'

'But what if I *had* remembered?' I persisted, and he looked at me fully and directly, and told me with brutal frankness.

'In that case, my dear Lisa, I should have had no option but to get rid of you. It could have been arranged very simply during an air raid. You wouldn't have been the first person in those days whose fatal injuries were put down to bomb damage.'

I drew back in speechless horror. I could feel the uneven throbbing of my throat under my hand as I clutched at it involuntarily.

'Don't look so shocked,' he said. 'People have been killed for much less than you would have died for. Paltry sums, in some cases ... You read about them in the papers every day.'

'I would have given you the money ...' I whispered.

'It's easy to say that now,' he said, with an impatient wave of his hand, 'but do you think that at the time you'd have felt like being so generous – or that your lawyers would have allowed you to be? Anyway, you didn't remember and you knew nothing about the money, so the problem didn't arise. But I had a second reason for doing what I did. Aren't you curious about it?'

'No,' I whispered. 'No ...'

'I'll tell you whether you are or not.' He lit a cigarette and leaned back against the bedhead, blowing the smoke lazily from his nostrils. 'I told you a few days ago that the trouble with me was that I never hated you enough – and that was the truth. I hated and resented you for your adoption by my stepbrother, and I would have been a damned sight safer with you dead, instead of merely relying on a tricky memory that might let me down at any time. But I also happened to be in love with you.'

'You – you . . . ' I choked in disgusted disbelief.

'You find that hard to believe? It's not difficult, though. You were a very lovely girl, dear Lisa – you had a very sweet, dewy-eyed innocence that appealed to me. I wanted you, my dear – I wanted you from the first moment I set eyes on you. Nearly as much as I wanted the money. Not quite, but nearly. When I had the chance to have both, I didn't hesitate. I told you I didn't plan it – it just worked out that way for me. But I wasn't going to kick against a fate that had arranged everything so neatly for me.'

I looked at him with a sick loathing.

'All those years that you have wasted for me,' I said.

'Rubbish!' he said briskly. 'They weren't wasted. You always had a generous share of the money and no matter where you had been, your mind would have still been a blank.'

'If I had been in familiar surroundings – with people whom I knew and loved . . . The doctors said – I remember them saying – that that was the only thing to help me recover my memory. And even if I hadn't remembered – I would have been with Russ. All those years – ' I said brokenly, 'I would have been with Russ.'

'Yes,' he agreed thinly, 'it was always Russ, wasn't it? You never had eyes for anyone else, did you? I remember speaking to you at dinner on that last night before Adrian was killed – you never even heard me. You had a faraway look in your eyes. I was no more to you than a glass on the table or a printed menu card. Have you ever known what it is like – to both hate and love someone at the same time?' A vicious bitterness had been creeping into his voice but he managed to control it.

He drew deeply on the cigarette and watched the smoke spiralling lazily to the ceiling. 'I think there was a little revenge involved in it, too, for the way you so unconsciously slighted me. I thought you didn't even notice me – I would have been quite gratified to know that you spared time from your girlish love dreams to dislike me. But I didn't know that, although it wouldn't have made any difference if I had. So I took you and I moulded you. Yes, I moulded you, my dear Lisa, as surely as though I had taken a piece of clay in these hands and kneaded it into shape.'

He held out his hands, strong and possessive, and I shrank away with a shiver. 'You hadn't a thought, an emotion, a like or a dislike, that I didn't instil into you. I made you into another being entirely. I shaped your mind and directed your thoughts. I altered you outwardly as well as inwardly, but mostly what was inside you changed the outward appearance. It didn't need the different hair-styles or shaped eyebrows or the hair darkened with rinses – that was only necessary against the remote chance that anyone would ever recognise you. It was what was in you that changed you so much. And it gave me great pleasure and satisfaction to mould you completely – no one ever had better or more pliable material to work on. Oh, yes, I made you, my dear Lisa.' He laughed suddenly, without mirth. 'But the joke was on me. Because when I had made you, I didn't like you,' he added with cold contempt. 'There wasn't a single thing about you that I could love. Until last night – and you looked exactly as you used to look long ago – for Russ. But it still wasn't for me, was it?'

'No,' I said in a hard voice. 'No – it wasn't for you! It could never be for you!'

I could see the faint flicker of anger in his eyes and knew that I had touched him on an open wound; but I didn't care. I think I was realising fully for the first time that I was not married to him, that I was completely free. That I never had been married to him.

I said abruptly, 'You showed me some marriage lines...'

'Oh, everything was quite genuine. The birth certificate, the marriage certificate – they belonged to my wife, Lisa. The only thing I didn't show you was her death certificate. I destroyed that, to be on the safe side. She died a year before I came back to England.'

'And Joanna?' I said. 'Does she know about this?'

'Good God, no!' He said it explosively. 'She was too young to remember her own mother. When I came to England I took the flat in London but I didn't keep her there because of the air raids. She was in the country with some people who knew nothing of my background, although it wouldn't really have mattered if they had. When it seemed fairly certain that your mind was going to stay blank I bought a house and fetched her to live with us. By that time, everything was practically settled about Adrian's affairs – there hadn't been any trouble. The servants were all strangers, Joanna's nurse – no one knew us. Everything fell pat into place, just like a jig-saw puzzle.'

'You could have let me go,' I said. 'Years ago I asked you . . .'

'Oh, no, my dear, I couldn't. That was a risk I *couldn't* take – even though I no longer wanted you. There was always the fear, you see, that some day you might remember.'

'But I did – on Joanna's wedding day.'

'You only remembered a part of it. There was never any risk, so long as some part of your past remained blank. In fact, my dear, during these past months you've been building up a very satisfactory way in which I could dispose of you. You were making out a very strong case of insanity against yourself with your odd behaviour. Do you think people haven't noticed – acquaintances, the servants, Joanna? Coupled with your drinking, I was beginning to think that eventually I could have you certified nicely and quietly and put in some comfortable mental home. And once you were in there it wouldn't have mattered however much you remembered, or whoever you thought you were. You could have told them you were Napoleon or the Queen of Sheba – or Dorcas Mallory. They're used to hearing those sort of claims.'

I faltered, 'You're heartless – callous . . .'

'This is a highly competitive world, my dear Lisa. You have to be a little heartless and callous if you don't wish to go under. Anyway, you've rather put a little spoke in the wheel, haven't you, by remembering too soon.'

I said breathlessly, 'You can't have me certified, now. You'd never get away with it – Hugh wouldn't let you . . .'

'Hugh?' He raised his eyebrows inquiringly. 'Oh, your Dr. Broderick? No, he seems to have made that course rather an impossible one, doesn't he? That's a pity – you might have preferred it, in the end. I suppose you have told him everything?'

'Yes – everything. He knows all about me.'

'You can't possibly have told him that you really are Dorcas Mallory, my dear,' he pointed out urbanely, 'because you've only just discovered it for yourself. Even if he had decided to make inquiries at Alderford, he would find out no more than you did. Dorcas Mallory is safely buried – and very much dead.'

'But I can prove it now,' I said. 'I can go to Alderford. I can see Russ and tell him who I am – see my father's solicitors. Now that I can remember everything I can go – '

'You are going nowhere, my dear,' he said flatly, and he said it with so much conviction that I jerked my head, startled.

'What do you mean?'

'I mean, dear Lisa, that if I allowed you to go to Alderford you could cause altogether too much trouble for me. Funnily enough, you're even beginning to look like Dorcas Mallory again. I'm quite sure that your dear Russ would at least see a marked resemblance now. No, you'd manage to straighten it all out for yourself very nicely. But it wouldn't be very good for me, you know, would it? I should certainly have to forfeit the money – and I wouldn't like to have to predict what charge could be brought against me. I'm afraid I've never heard of a similar case to know what penalty, if any, it incurs. But the loss of the money is more than I'm prepared to accept. It's bad enough never to have had any – always to be poor; but to have known what it is like to have great wealth at your disposal, and then to lose it . . . You'll understand, my dear, what a great danger you have become to me by getting your memory back at this inopportune moment.'

'There's nothing you can do,' I said defiantly.

'You could be wrong there,' he said. 'However, I won't attempt to convince you otherwise.'

He leaned down and fumbled for a moment behind the table which stood between the two beds; when he straightened up he held the telephone in his hand.

I frowned in surprise. 'What are you doing with that?'

He walked towards the door, the wire trailing from the instrument.

'I've disconnected it, my dear. I wouldn't wish you to get in touch with your Dr. Broderick – not just yet.'

I said irritably, 'If you think taking that thing away can stop me from contacting him . . . I'm going down to see him as soon as ever I've dressed.'

'If you'll remember, dear Lisa, I told you that you weren't going anywhere,' he said levelly. There was no emotion in his voice. It was quite flat and calm, and it angered me intensely.

'You can't stop me,' I said.

He took the key out of the lock and inserted it on the outside of the door. I watched him in unbelieving anger.

'I don't know what you're hoping to gain by that,' I said contemptuously.

'I'm not really hoping to gain anything,' he said quietly. 'I'm just making sure I don't lose anything.'

He locked the door softly behind him.

10

THE day passed slowly, fretfully. I was consumed with impatience.

After nearly sixteen years it was intolerable to have to wait even another minute. I wanted to see Hugh and to tell him.

And I couldn't rid myself of the bitterness. It seemed as though it must always be there and I wasn't unduly concerned that it might be. I didn't particularly want to lose it, and being confined to that room didn't help any.

There was no other way out of it. It was a self-contained apartment, with the two bathrooms and the dressing-room all converging on the one main bedroom. The windows were too high even if I had been inclined to jump, which I wasn't.

Twice during the morning I heard the telephone shrilling faintly downstairs, and from the length of time it rang I guessed that Charles was not troubling to answer it. I didn't know whether he was in the house or not. I saw him once when he moved the car from where I had left it by the front entrance, but he only took it in the direction of the garage. Certainly he didn't trouble himself about providing me with any food.

I was resentful about that, although I didn't really want any. I bathed and dressed, ready to go out as soon as he released me. There was plenty of hot water. I supposed vaguely that it was connected with the central heating that Charles had got going last night.

I wondered when the servants were due back; I hoped it was soon. There was no alarm in me. Charles couldn't keep me confined here long. I didn't know what he hoped to gain by it, but it was all rather ridiculous. And infuriating.

In the middle of the morning I had a whisky, because I hadn't anything else to drink and I didn't fancy cold water. I drank it slowly and smoked a cigarette, staring moodily out across the wide stretch of rolling lawn and the swimming pool. It looked cold and uninviting, but I would have welcomed the opportunity to be out there. There was a stark bleakness about that wintry outlook that depressed me, but the interior of the room was no better.

I wandered around disconsolately, moving a cushion, hanging up a dressing-gown, straightening the toilet requisites on the dressing-table.

The little glass ball stood serene and peaceful on the table. The pleasure that its duplicate had brought me as a child seemed far away now that I could remember the whole span of my life. I recalled suddenly that I was no longer forty, but thirty-five – not quite thirty-six. Still young.

But not young enough, I thought bitterly. Nothing could ever give me back all those wasted years.

I sat and looked at myself in the mirror. The radiance of last night was dimmed now, and I looked my full age. It was no longer the young Dorcas Mallory who glanced fleetingly back at me, as she had done last night. But I could see the beginning of an older Dorcas, and not just in the lightening of the hair. The bitterness that was in me marred the resemblance and intensified the lines of my face but beneath it all I thought I could see what Dorcas Mallory would have looked like at this age, if there had been no Lisa Landry in her life.

Once the heavy shadows had gone from under the eyes and the cheeks had filled out...

I wasn't very much interested in how I was looking just then. By early afternoon my nerves were showing signs of fraying and I had another drink. Not a big one because the bottle was practically empty, but it steadied me a little.

There were plenty of books and magazines lying around

but I leafed irritably through them without seeing anything.

Charles came in about two o'clock. As he opened the door I could hear the telephone ringing again down in the hall before he shut and locked the door behind him.

I said angrily, 'How long is this going on?'

He had brought a bottle of whisky and some fresh cigarettes, and he put them down on the table.

'I thought you'd probably be getting rather low in supplies,' he remarked. 'Have a drink.'

He filled my glass which was standing there and put it down by my side. I gave him a venomous look as he did so. As he straightened up he was quite close to me and I noted with surprise a little nervous tic at the corner of his mouth. It was the only way in which he betrayed the fact that he was not entirely calm and at ease, and for some unknown reason the knowledge disturbed me. I had felt nothing but impatient anger and bitterness until then and I didn't enjoy the little spasm of doubt which suddenly shook me.

There was nothing he could do. Even if he kept me confined here, the servants would be back in another day or two at the latest. And I had Hugh's assurance that he would not allow Charles to carry out his threat.

I had complete and utter confidence in Hugh. I knew that after last night he would not let much time go by before he assured himself that I was all right. I knew that he was not the man to be put off easily with excuses. He would insist upon seeing for himself.

I could smile faintly to myself at the idea of anyone trying to prevent Hugh from doing anything he was determined to do.

I still didn't like that nervous tic.

'Your doctor friend seems quite impatient,' he remarked. 'This is the third time he's rung up.'

I didn't think it would be Hugh who was ringing but I didn't say so. I thought Hugh would probably be too busy to ring during the day. I watched Charles go out in silence. There was no point in questioning him; I knew I wouldn't get any satisfaction from him.

The long afternoon dragged on endlessly.

I drank more than I should have done, because for some silly reason I was getting jittery. It was only the frustration of being shut up in this room, of course; and my impatience, after all these years of waiting, to get everything straightened out. But there *had* been that nervous little tic . . . And I had never been aware of even a trace of nervousness about him.

It was damned silly to get agitated about a tic.

Still . . .

The whisky helped quite considerably. I knew I shouldn't drink so much and I wouldn't ever again, once this lot was all sorted out. But I still wasn't cured of the habit. I was doing quite nicely, of course, but when something like this cropped up . . . It is so easy to take refuge in whisky when you want to take refuge in whisky.

I despised myself for being so weak.

In the end I didn't know which way it was – whether the whisky caused the foreboding or the foreboding caused the whisky. But as dusk settled in, so did fear.

It was only the faintest flicker at first, and I dispelled it quickly by putting on the lights and assuring myself that it was too much alcohol on an empty stomach. When the telephone rang for the fourth time that afternoon, the fear was no longer a flicker to be casually explained away.

It was fear – plain and simple.

I wished I could answer the phone, or even that Charles would. There is something about the ring of an unanswered telephone that can be strangely disturbing.

I wouldn't have cared so much if I had had even the vaguest idea why I was so idiotically frightened. I had nothing to be afraid of – only boredom! And Hugh would be furious with me for drinking so much – and for smoking so many cigarettes. I couldn't count the ends stubbed out in the ashtray, but I could see exactly how much I had drunk out of the bottle.

I'd never realised before how isolated the house was. There was nothing nearer than the village in that direction; and the farm in the other direction, where the animals had been quartered during the Christmas holidays, was even farther away. It was strange how you never noticed these things when the house was full of servants.

There was such a stillness in the place. Charles must be around somewhere, but what was he doing all this time? There wasn't a movement in the whole building, not even a faint creaking or any of those other funny little sounds that a house will make when it is empty. I held my breath and listened, but there was nothing.

My nerves screamed as the key turned in the lock and Charles came in. I was so shaken I couldn't even feel angry. I sat and looked miserably at him as he eyed the bottle. I wasn't sure whether it was satisfaction I could see in his face and I wasn't caring because I'd just realised that he hadn't locked the door behind him.

If I'd stopped to think I would have let him get farther into the room and given myself a bigger start, but I just made a headlong dash for it. There wasn't even time to slam the door behind me. As I went down the stairs the telephone started to ring again but I knew before that that I wasn't going to make it. Charles was heavily built but he could have reached the front door easily as soon as I did, so I grabbed up the receiver instead. If Hugh was at the other end ...

I didn't have time to find that out or even to speak before Charles had snatched the receiver from me and slammed it down again.

I said childishly, 'Why don't you let me go?'

At that moment I was neither frightened nor angry. It had all become ridiculous, as if two children were playing a game of make believe which had got rather out of hand but they didn't know how to end it.

Charles said, 'Go back upstairs.' He was breathing heavily from his exertions.

'No, Charles,' I said. 'This has gone far enough. You can't keep me upstairs for ever.'

'Go back upstairs,' he said evenly.

I shrugged hopelessly and went. There was no point in trying to argue with him in this mood. Although I wasn't quite sure what mood he was in. I'd never seen him like this before.

As I went up the stairs I noticed that the time was just seven o'clock. That would probably have been Hugh on the phone. If only I could have spoken to him ...

Charles followed me into the bedroom and made sure he locked the door this time, putting the key in his pocket. I sat on the edge of the bed in dejection. I had my back to him and didn't see what he was doing until he came round to me and held out a glass of water.

'All right,' he said. 'Take these.'

There were six little white pills in the palm of his hand. I recognised them at once as my own sleeping tablets. Normally I took two and they would ensure several hours of deep sleep. I wasn't sure what six would do and I didn't feel disposed to find out.

'I won't take all those. I won't take any at all, for that matter,' I said.

He held the tablets out relentelessly before me.

'They'll not hurt you,' he said. 'I'm just making sure of where you are all night. They won't kill you, if that's what you're thinking – you'd need more than that. You'll sleep a bit heavier and a bit longer – that's all.'

'No,' I said.

'You'll take them,' Charles said flatly. 'You know I can make you. You'll find it easier to swallow them naturally, though. But I can make you, if you don't.'

I knew he could, too. Even if I hadn't been more than a little bit fuddled with the whisky.

I didn't like the way the nervous tic was more pronounced now. I think I would rather have faced up to his anger than speculate on the origin and cause of that tic.

I took the tablets slowly, with a sip of water with each one. There wasn't anything else to do, but I wasn't unduly worried. I thought it was quite likely that my system was so inured to them that their effect wouldn't be as drastic as on a normal person. I was pretty confident, without taking Charles's word for it, that they wouldn't kill me.

He took the glass from me when the last one was swallowed.

'Get undressed,' he said.

There was no sense in arguing, anyway. With six sleeping tablets inside me I couldn't think of a better place to be than bed. But I wouldn't get undressed in front of him. I took my nightdress and gown and went through into the bathroom, and I didn't hurry. When I was undressed I cleaned my teeth and removed the make-up from my face. Then I sat down and had a maudlin little weep because I was so full of self-pity at not being allowed to see Hugh and tell him my news.

Charles was sitting in a chair when I went back into the

bedroom and he hardly glanced at me as I slipped off the gown and got into bed. He just went on sitting there, not looking at me, with the tic jumping nervously at the corner of his mouth; and presently I could feel the tablets taking hold of me.

Curiously enough, I wasn't frightened any more. I was empty, drained – and then, gradually, very sleepy.

As the sleep gained on me, that tic grew to vast proportions until its heavy throbbing filled the room. After a while I realised drowsily that it was the thudding of my own heart I could hear. But the mists of sleep confused me and presently the two things fused into one again, and there was only the pounding, pulsating tic. It was bigger than me, bigger than the room...

And then suddenly it was gone, although I could still hear it. There was only a hazy, bottomless void where it had been. And through all the depths of sleep that claimed me, I knew fear.

A deathly, paralysing fear.

I tried to struggle up through stupefying inertia. Someone near at hand was making little gibbering moans and after a time, when I tried to force sound out of my own mouth, I realised that it was I who was making them.

I was frantic to find the tic again. I *had* to find it. As long as it was in sight it lost some of its menace. And then suddenly I saw it, quite close to me, and I tried to hold my breath so that I wouldn't make it disappear again. It was moving. It seemed to waver aimlessly before my clouded eyes.

At that moment the mists parted a little and quite clearly I saw Charles. He was so near to me that if I had had the strength to lift my hand I could have touched him. I hadn't seen or heard him move from his chair, but he was there.

He had an unlighted cigarette in his mouth and as I watched he struck a match and held it to the cigarette. I could see the bright red glow plainly and even after it was lighted he seemed to draw deeply at it. I became aware that someone was touching my hand and after a while I perceived, again in a vague sort of way, that he was putting something between my fingers. I tried to make a movement of repudiation but it was all too much effort, and unimportant, anyway.

The room which had been quite clear swam mistily into obscurity again. I tried to find Charles, and failed; and then quite distinctly I smelt whisky. I managed to focus my eyes long enough to see that there was a glassful by the bedside, and the bottle not more than eighteen inches away from me; there was a moment's confused surprise for Charles's consideration, before everything started to drift away.

As consciousness dissolved I became suddenly aware that the deep blue ceiling was gradually sinking lower and lower. It was doing what I had always known it would do some day – it was going to crush me. I watched it come nearer until there was nothing but that vast dimension of blueness. It stretched everywhere around and above me, enveloping and crushing and possessing me.

It was pain that dispersed it. A sharp, agonising pain in my right arm. But as a measure of consciousness returned, even more urgent than the pain which roused me was the frenzied need to find the tic again. The terror of having lost it was greater than the agony in my arm. I tried to see and couldn't but it didn't seem as though the fogginess of sleep alone prevented me. It was more than that. I couldn't breathe. I was suffocating and there was no air.

And then the searing agony of my arm overcame the effects of the sleeping tablets.

Through the swirling smoke I saw the fierce flames as they licked greedily at the bedclothes. The whole right-hand side of the bed was alive with flickering tongues of fire.

It was only those few moments of consciousness which the pain had granted me that enabled me to make the effort. I fell on to the floor, aware of nothing but the terrifying need to get away from that blazing bed. I was coughing and choking helplessly as I crawled to the door through the thick clouds of smoke.

I couldn't open it but I know I opened my mouth and tried to scream. I don't think any sound came out. Consciousness was going again now.

I couldn't see across the room. I found my way by instinct over that expanse of off-white carpet on my hands and knees. But even as I reached the bathroom door, the smoke and the tablets combined and there was only the tearing need for air in my laboured lungs – and then there was nothing!

It was two days before Hugh would let me talk about it. During that time I drifted quietly in and out of sleep, occasionally vaguely conscious of my surroundings and that sometimes Mrs. Hale was there, and sometimes Joanna, and I thought the other person seemed to be Sarah. Sometimes very distinctly I saw Hugh quite close to me and it was always immediately after that I drifted off to sleep again.

I was aware at times of a burning fire in my arm but that seemed to come from a long way off.

I wasn't sure where I was, except that I was in a bedroom, and that sometimes when I woke up a pale sun would be shining in and at other times there was the warm subdued glow of a lamp. But wherever I was, I was quite happy to be there. I felt safe and secure, in no hurry to be roused from this dreamlike existence.

But on the morning of the third day, after what seemed hours of lovely, dreamless sleep, I no longer floated into unconsciousness after being aware that Hugh was near me. That was the morning he let me talk to him, and when Mrs. Hale wanted to come in to straighten my bed he sent her out again until I had finished. I felt clear and level-headed, but I could still feel the bitterness in me. I knew by the way Hugh looked at me that it tinged my words but he didn't comment on it. He heard me out in complete silence. If I had expected some outburst of anger or indignation from him I was disappointed.

When I had finished he said quietly, 'Another day and this need never have happened.' I glanced at him questioningly and he went on, 'Well, I never did really believe in your insanity. You were suffering from a lot of things but I never quite felt that madness was amongst them. It was difficult to form a very clear opinion without knowing more than you could tell me, so I started making inquiries. I was curious to know the exact nature of your mother's mental disorder and whether there was a further background of insanity, so I set a man on to making inquiries in Canada. And when he cabled me that your mother – Elizabeth Mary Fournier – had died, not in a mental institution but in a train accident, I had him go deeper into the matter. He came up with a rather startling fact. And that was that Elise Constance Landry, née Fournier, had died in Montreal in 1943. I received the cable with that news the day after Boxing Day. I was busy but I tried to ring you twice during the day. To tell the truth, I was getting a little worried about you, my dear girl. You were either one or the other of two persons – and they were both dead! When no one answered the phone I thought it quite likely Landry had taken you off to London again, but I went up when evening surgery was over, just to make sure. I arrived in time to see you being brought out of a bathroom window. You and Joanna, both.'

'*Joanna?*' My eyes widened with astonishment.

'You won't remember anything about it, but Joanna saved your life. It seems she was pretty worried about you, too. By all accounts you and Landry should have spent the evening of Boxing Day with them. She wasn't particularly concerned when you didn't turn up – you'd been doing some rather peculiar things lately, I suppose – but when she tried to reach you at your hotel the following morning neither you nor Landry was there. Neither of you had checked out and your luggage was there, but you hadn't been back there to sleep the previous night. She kept ringing the house at intervals all day without any result, but she wasn't unduly worried about that until the last time she rang in the evening. And then although no one would answer, the receiver was lifted and she knew then that someone was in the house. So she got her car out and came down straight away – '

'I thought it was you,' I said, 'that time the phone rang – I hadn't time to speak before Charles made me put it down.'

'It was damned lucky for you that you managed to pick the receiver up, otherwise Joanna would never have made the journey. She couldn't see the fire from the roadway, with the bedroom facing the other direction – no one would have done until it was much too late. But she saw it as soon as she drove round to the front entrance. She put a frantic call through to the fire brigade at Hardleigh and then looked through the house to see if anyone was there. She'll be able to tell you better than I can, but I can give you a rough outline. It seems the bedroom was pretty far gone by that time and God alone knows how she managed to find you in the blazing inferno. Luckily for you, you'd crawled to the far side of the room away from the worst of the fire but by the time she found you the fire had spread across the doorway – possibly the current of air from the open door drew it. So she dragged you into a bathroom and put wet towels at the bottom of the door to keep the smoke out, and when the fire brigade arrived she was half out of the window yelling her head off to attract their attention.' He added, 'She's here now. She would like to see you.'

I shrank back against the pillows. 'No, I can't! Not yet! He – Charles – he tried to kill me, Hugh. He meant me to die . . . He deliberately set fire to that bed because he thought I was too helpless . . . It would have been so easy to explain away. Too many sleeping tablets, too much whisky – smoking in bed. Everyone knew that I took tablets and drank too much and smoked in bed . . . Miss Rose, the other servants, Joanna . . . No one would ever have dreamed of questioning that I was either too drunk or too doped – or both – to know that I'd set my own bed on fire.' I shivered violently. 'He meant me to die – in a dreadful way . . . '

'He's dead, you know.' He said it so calmly, so unemotionally that I couldn't believe I had heard correctly. I must have looked as stupefied as I felt.

I said, *'Dead – Charles?'*

Hugh nodded. 'He was killed in the fire, Joanna will be better able to tell you about it.'

'No!' I said. 'No – she's his daughter. . . . I can't see her yet.'

'You wouldn't be here now if it weren't for Joanna,' he said quietly. 'She saved your life. Even if her father tried to rob you of it, she more than made up for that by what she did. That's a nice girl, Lisa – don't try to blame her for something that wasn't her fault. She still thinks you're her mother, you know.'

'She'll have to know that I'm not. When it all comes out . . . '

'Need it all come out? You're free – why make a scandal or a nine days' wonder of it? What does it matter now whether you're Lisa Landry or Dorcas Mallory? Charles is dead – in the eyes of the law you're his widow. You'll get the money or a good share of it – '

'Oh, the money,' I said wearily. 'Money isn't important.'

Hugh said, in a dry voice, 'It's always the people who have it who say that. Of course it isn't important. But the lack of it is. Besides, you'll need the money if only so that when you're mad with me you can turn round and tell me that I married you for it.'

I looked up at him open-mouthed. 'Married . . . ?' I said, falteringly. I hadn't heard right, I was sure of that.

'Well, of course!' he said cheerfully. 'Don't look so surprised. My dear girl, you knew I was in love with you.'

'No – ' I stammered. 'No – I didn't . . . '

'You must have been the only one who didn't, then. Everyone else knew – Haley, Sarah – even the kids. How come you didn't know?'

I shook my head helplessly. 'How *could* I know? You never said . . . '

He raised his eyebrows in a look of surprise. 'I didn't? Are you sure?'

'Do you think I would have forgotten? You never gave a sign.' I added, half boldly, half shyly, 'You don't even kiss me now.'

'Good God, girl, don't you know it isn't ethical for a doctor to kiss his patients? What are you trying to do – get me struck off?'

'If you're marrying me for my money . . . ' I said shyly.

'All the money in the world couldn't change me from being a plain G.P., my darling girl,' he said, and although he said it lightly, I knew that he wasn't joking. 'That's my life and that's all I ever want to be. I won't deny that a little extra cash will come in handy, particularly if I've got an extravagant wife.'

'Had you me in mind when you told Sarah that you'd find a way to put Valerie through medical school?'

'As a matter of fact, no. I was thinking about lapsing an insurance policy and selling the best silverware. You *had* a husband than, remember?'

'You didn't tell me how Charles died,' I said quietly, and suddenly I knew that the bitterness was gone.

'He was in the bedroom when the floor gave way. He was badly burned but it was the fall that killed him.'

'But how could he have been in the bedroom?' I said incredulously.

'Well, I thought at first that he had gone looking for you, but after what you've told me that's very unlikely. It's probably that he kept a little distance away from the house until the fire was well under way. What we *do* know is that he turned up on the scene a few minutes after the fire brigade arrived, because he told a fireman that so far as he knew the house was empty – the servants were away and you had said you were returning to London. Then the fireman said Landry suddenly went white and exclaimed, "Oh, my God"! and dashed into the house before anyone could stop him. The place was full of smoke but this man was half-way up the stairs after him when the bedroom floor went. Landry was found in the burning debris in the room below.'

'But why – ' I whispered. 'Why would Charles go into the bedroom? He knew I was there – all along he knew that – and didn't care . . . He didn't want me to be rescued.'

'I think he went in after Joanna. Her car was parked by the front entrance when I got there. He couldn't have missed seeing it and must have guessed where she was. What he didn't know was that probably at the very moment he was running into the house, you and Joanna were being brought out of it through the bathroom window round the other side.' He paused, and looked at me searchingly for a moment. 'Let Joanna talk to you, will you? Poor kid, she's all cut up about it.'

'They were always very close,' I said. 'She must be terribly upset.'

'Then don't make it any worse for her. She doesn't need to know what her father really was.'

'I want to be Dorcas Mallory again,' I said. 'Try to understand, Hugh . . . '

'My dear girl, of course I understand. But what's in a name? What difference can it make? Anyway, you'll be Broderick before you know where you are, so what does it matter whether your name is Dorcas Mallory or Lisa Landry?'

'I hadn't thought of that,' I said happily. 'Of course it doesn't matter.'

'That's all right then,' he said, with a deceptive offhandedness which told me he had expected to have his own way all along. 'I'll send Joanna in.' As he reached the doorway he turned back to say casually. 'By the way, that was a proposal, so don't tell me afterwards that I haven't asked you.'

I heard him calling to Joanna as he went out.